THE HEAT OF BATTLE

Dolores pumped the lever on her Winchester, three aught-six rounds already gone, with one remaining in the rifle's chamber and another next on tap from its internal magazine. Of three shots fired so far, she'd definitely hit two *federales*, likely killing one who'd fallen from his mount and failed to rise, with one clean miss counting against her.

Shooting in the maelstrom of close-quarters combat was a hazard, bullets flying everywhere, some fired in panic with no serious attempt to aim. Her snowflake Appaloosa was not gun-shy under normal circumstances, but this chaos, with horses and their riders racing back and forth, exchanging shots or savage blows at arm's length, would have taxed the bravest man or animal.

She had already seen two of the *federales* try to flee, deserting under fire, and had dropped one of them herself, the other blasted from his saddle by some shooter she could not identify. Gun smoke had formed a patch of fog around the duelers, worsened by the rising dust from horses' hooves and bodies dropping to the arid ground. Her ears were ringing, as if she were trapped inside a giant bell with someone on the outside hammering its sound bow, till her head was ringing and the shouts of fear or fury rising all around her sounded muffled to her ears.

RALPH COMPTON

TERROR TRAIL

A RALPH COMPTON WESTERN BY

LYLE BRANDT

BERKLEY
New York

BERKLEY
An imprint of Penguin Random House LLC
penguinrandomhouse.com

Copyright © 2021 by The Estate of Ralph Compton
Penguin Random House supports copyright. Copyright fuels creativity, encourages
diverse voices, promotes free speech, and creates a vibrant culture. Thank you for buying
an authorized edition of this book and for complying with copyright laws by not
reproducing, scanning, or distributing any part of it in any form without permission.
You are supporting writers and allowing Penguin Random House to continue to
publish books for every reader.

BERKLEY and the BERKLEY & B colophon are registered trademarks of
Penguin Random House LLC.

ISBN: 9780593334010

First Edition: August 2021

Printed in the United States of America
1   3   5   7   9   10   8   6   4   2

Book design by George Towne

THE IMMORTAL COWBOY

This is respectfully dedicated to the "American Cowboy." His was the saga sparked by the turmoil that followed the Civil War, and the passing of more than a century has by no means diminished the flame.

———◆———

True, the old days and the old ways are but treasured memories, and the old trails have grown dim with the ravages of time, but the spirit of the cowboy lives on.

———◆———

In my travels—to Texas, Oklahoma, Kansas, Nebraska, Colorado, Wyoming, New Mexico, and Arizona—I always find something that reminds me of the Old West. While I am walking these plains and mountains for the first time, there is this feeling that a part of me is eternal, that I have known these old trails before. I believe it is the undying spirit of the frontier calling me, through the mind's eye, to step back into time. What is the appeal of the Old West of the American frontier?

———◆———

It has been epitomized by some as the dark and bloody period in American history. Its heroes—Crockett, Bowie, Hickok, Earp—have been reviled and criticized. Yet the Old West lives on, larger than life.

———◆———

It has become a symbol of freedom, when there was always another mountain to climb and another river to cross; when a dispute between two men was settled not with expensive lawyers, but with fists, knives, or guns. Barbaric? Maybe. But some things never change. When the cowboy rode into the pages of American history, he left behind a legacy that lives within the hearts of us all.

—*Ralph Compton*

CHAPTER ONE

Doña Ana County, New Mexico Territory

THE FIRST GUNSHOT—a rifle by its sound, no less than .30 caliber, fired at perhaps one hundred yards— woke Alejandro Aguirre from a fitful sleep precisely on the stroke of four a.m. He knew the time because an heirloom clock was chiming in the parlor of his ranch house, a familiar sound that rarely woke him even when his sleep was troubled as on most nights.

Lying wide awake and staring into darkness, Alejandro wondered if the shot had come from one of his vaqueros, taking out a stray coyote before it could raid the ranch's livestock, but that possibility evaporated with a sudden stuttering of gunfire, sounding as if someone had touched off a string of firecrackers.

Trouble! It could be nothing else.

Aguirre scrambled out of bed, the polished hardwood floor cool underneath his bare feet as he hastened to the window, drew back its curtains, and peered out—

side. Bright muzzle flashes winked at him like out-of-season fireflies, visible before the rattle of successive shots caught up, sound lagging for a split second behind the speed of light.

A seasoned rancher in this corner of the territory went to bed each night expecting danger, woke relieved at sunrise if the threat had passed him by, and then labored through his days prepared to do it all again. Aguirre knew what must be done now, only hoping that he would not be too late.

Returning to his large four-poster bed, he stepped into a pair of hand-tooled boots, not bothering with socks. Next, he retrieved the gun belt dangling from the nearest bedpost, buckling it around his waist, over the knee-length linen nightshirt that he wore. The pistol in its holster was a Colt New Service Model 1909, double-action revolver, chambered for the .45 Long Colt cartridge lately adopted by the U.S. Army.

Alejandro did not have to check the Colt. He always kept it fully loaded, ready to respond in an emergency. But with a raid in progress on his property, he also needed further firepower.

Rounding the bed, toward what had been his wife's side before typhus claimed her life, Aguirre reached a gun case mounted on the wall of knotty pine. Inside, their muzzles pointed toward the bedroom ceiling, were two Winchesters—a lever-action Model 1895 rifle, standing beside a Model 1897 twelve-gauge pump-action shotgun. He chose the rifle for its greater range, loaded with .30-06 Springfield cartridges that fired 220-grain projectiles at 2,500 feet per second, lethal well beyond three thousand yards in skillful hands.

And Alejandro rarely missed a man-sized target, never mind the time of day or night.

Aguirre cleared his bedroom as a brass bell started clanging on the covered porch outside. Its warning was superfluous, given the shooting still in progress, but his houseman, Manuelito Obregón, would stand his post—and join the fight himself, if necessary—until any danger had been quelled by force.

Passing the darkened dining room where he took three meals daily with his son and daughters, barring the rare trip away from home on business, Alejandro reached the front door of his *casa grande*, opened it, and stepped outside into the early-morning chill. New Mexico baked under a relentless desert sun by day, but after sunset, temperatures dropped twenty degrees or more, forcing vaqueros on the night shift into fleece-lined coats.

Aguirre scarcely felt that as he reached the broad porch of the home he'd built from scratch, expanding over three decades as he acquired more land, more stock, more money in a bank vault at the county seat, Las Cruces. He had built a reputation from the ground up, paying dearly for it, and was ready to defend it now at any cost.

"*¿Qué pasa?*" he asked Manuelito.

Barely glancing back at his employer, Obregón stated the obvious. "*Bandidos, jefe.*"

While he rang the warning bell with his right hand, the slender houseman clutched a double-barreled shotgun under his left arm, prepared to fire if any of the trespassers came into range. Aguirre knew it would be loaded with ball bearings, stainless steel, which Obregón preferred to leaden buckshot. Tucked beneath his belt, as if he'd risen fully dressed from bed, a Smith & Wesson Model 3 top-break revolver dragged the waistline of his baggy trousers down.

"How many?" Alejandro queried.

"*Cuarenta, más o menos, jefe.*"

Forty, maybe more, increased the danger to Aguirre's property beyond the petty skirmishes his night shift sometimes fought with drifters hoping for an easy score, perhaps escaping with a horse or two for sale across the borderline.

This was an act of war and must be treated with the rigor it deserved.

Descending from the covered porch, Aguirre moved across the yard with long, swift strides, calling his men on duty and their fellows scrambling from bunkhouses in a daze.

"To me, vaqueros! Rally here to me!"

M AKE HASTE," FRANCISCO Villa ordered his subordinate, "before they rally and we have a full-scale battle on our hands."

"*¡Sí, general!*" his aide replied. "Just as you say!"

In fact, Villa—called "Pancho" by his friends—was not a general. He held no military rank at all below the Rio Grande. Even the name by which most knew him was a lie.

He had been born Doroteo Arango, to rural peasant parents in San Juan del Río, Querétaro, Mexico, and raised in abject poverty around Durango until he had learned to steal and specialized in rustling livestock. As a bandit, he had used multiple pseudonyms over the past thirty-two years, eluding prison or a firing squad by guts and guile until he turned sixteen.

That year, his sister had been ravished, brutally defiled, by either the employees of a wealthy rancher or a squad of *federales* serving President Porfirio Díaz. While rumors varied on that point, they all agreed that Villa—called "Arango" in those days—had hunted down the rapists, slaying each in turn before escaping on a stolen horse into the wild Sierra Madre Occidental. There, he joined a gang led by Durango's infamous Ignacio Parra, then organized his own *pandilla* of young rowdies like himself, supplying stolen animals and other goods to wealthy backer Pablo Valenzuela, adopting the surname of his maternal grandfather, Jesús Villa.

In 1902, when the *federales* captured him at last, they spared his life but drafted him into the military service of Díaz. Villa waited a year, then murdered his commanding officer and fled to Coahuila on the victim's stallion, forming a new gang under the nickname of *la Cucaracha*—the cockroach—and raiding as he pleased throughout the state he had belatedly adopted as his own. Only in recent months had Villa turned his thoughts to politics, a brooding hatred for *el presidente*'s ruthless policies, and ways to profit from that loathing of his homeland's government.

The first answer that came to mind: horses.

Villa had known of the Aguirre ranch by reputation for some time, and finally decided it was ripe for picking. With his cadre of *bandidos*, he could steal its prized herd, spoken for under a pending contract with the U.S. Cavalry, whose troops had stolen so much land from Mexico during the war of 1846–48. Over the course of barely two years, the United States had claimed 530,000 square miles of Old Mexico, adding insult to injury with the pathetic "compensation" of five cents per acre.

Who in his right mind could blame Villa for punishing the gringo government and pocketing some pesos for himself in the process?

The problems: First, he had to steal the herd, roughly four thousand animals according to his spies. Next came the crossing in Mexico, only a few miles distant from the rancho he was raiding and across the Rio Grande, their escape facilitated by cutting the telegraph lines between Alejandro Aguirre's home and the county seat at Las Cruces. Finally, they must evade the prowling *federales* who might seek to intercept them and seize the stolen herd for President Díaz's cavalry or else return it to the States, to curry favor with the gringo government in Washington.

As far as finding buyers for the prime *caballos* he was liberating, Villa had no qualms on that score. They would not be branded yet, so anyone across the borderline could claim them as his own, as long as he had ready cash on hand.

Defensive gunfire was increasing from Aguirre's men, a problem Villa had anticipated in his planning for the raid. He risked losing some of his own *bandidos*, but each of them had assumed the risk when volunteering for this mission, and the families of any slain along the way would be recipients of fair payment.

There would be time enough to count his losses later, weighing them against his gains.

C LINT PARNELL HIT the ground running, first out of the small house that he'd earned upon ascending to the rank of foreman two years earlier. He was accustomed to disturbances at night on the Aguirre spread, but not to waking in the middle of a full-scale firefight ninety minutes prior to his alarm clock going off.

Still, he was wide awake and ready to participate, whatever might be happening. There was no point in guessing what had happened when the situation should be clear to him in seconds flat.

And if it called for killing, Parnell reckoned that he was equal to the task.

Leaving his house, he'd flung a pistol belt over his shoulder, then retrieved his Browning Automatic-5 from where it hung on pegs beside his bedroom door. The twelve-gauge shotgun measured fifty inches overall and weighed nine pounds with four rounds in its magazine and one more in the chamber. Relatively new, the weapon was designed by firearms innovator John Browning in 1898, patented two years later as the world's first semiautomatic shotgun. Parnell kept it loaded with buckshot, the double-aught size, each round packed with the equivalent of nine .33-caliber pistol slugs, and he had yet to miss a target within fifty yards.

The pistol hanging underneath his left arm was old-fashioned by comparison, a Colt Peacemaker, Single Action Army model, eleven inches long, tipping the scales at three pounds with its half-dozen .44-40 Winchester rounds. In a steady hand it was a killer out to thirty yards if there was killing to be done.

Tonight, from what he'd heard and seen so far, Parnell figured there was.

He did not try discerning faces in the dark, of men either afoot or galloping on horseback. Some would be Aguirre hands, working the night shift or roused from sleep by sounds of battle on the property. Others—only the mounted ones, he guessed—were raiders, shouting back and forth among themselves in Spanish, straw sombreros on their heads, wide brims and pointed crowns, strapped underneath their chins to keep from falling off and getting lost.

Parnell watched them for two, perhaps three seconds, then decided he could separate some of the enemy from men he worked with daily on the ranch.

And once they were identified by type, if not by name . . .

He brought the Browning to his shoulder, sighted quickly down its barrel, index finger on his right hand taking up the shotgun's trigger slack. His first target, a husky Mexican aboard a leopard mount, was circling the main Aguirre herd, firing a six-gun overhead to get them moving in the right direction, southward. Parnell took his shot, rode out the Browning's recoil as his target vaulted backward from the saddle, giving out a breathless squeal before he hit the ground.

Call that a kill, with buckshot pellets rupturing the bandit's heart and lungs. There'd be no saving him, even if Parnell had a doctor standing by and cared to waste his time.

However many pellets found their mark, the deed was done, the Browning's empty shell casing ejected while Clint sought another target in the darkness before dawn.

The battle wasn't even close to being won.

He thought about the family he served, the twin sisters especially, and hoped that they would keep out of harm's way. A vain thought, Clint supposed, but it was all the human feeling he could spare just now, with gun work still remaining to be done.

D OLORES AGUIRRE HAD never run from a fight in her life. She had been first into the world, nine minutes older than her twin, Sonya, and she had always felt it was her role to help defend the family, its property, against all threats from the outside. At times, that attitude displeased her father and her elder brother, Eduardo, but they had never managed to dissuade her from a fracas if she felt that honor was at stake.

Tonight, there was no question of it in her mind.

Instead of cowering inside the ranch house when gunfire had jolted her awake, Dolores rose at once, slipped on a robe she kept draped on a straight-backed chair beside her bed, and snatched a weapon from the top drawer of her nightstand. It was relatively small, a Colt 1877 double-action revolver, the "Lightning" model chambered for .38-caliber rounds, but she could score a bull's-eye nine times out of ten at thirty feet, firing one-handed from a classic dueler's stance.

So far, her target practice had been limited to rattlesnakes and empty bottles lined along a fence, but when she thought about facing a human enemy, Dolores felt no fear.

This morning, she expected to be challenged on that point.

Manuelito Obregón was still ringing the brass alarm bell of the porch, although it seemed that no one living could have missed that racket or the gunfire that threatened to drown it out. Scanning the yard in front of her, Dolores searched for targets, picking out her family's vaqueros whether mounted or afoot, distinguishing the raiders from employees of the ranch by torchlight. Moving toward the barn and seeking cover there, she had not traveled far before she saw her father standing in the open, looking almost humorous in boots and nightshirt, while his rifle tracked one of the trespassers.

Dolores waited for his muzzle flash, a body spilling from its saddle, but before that could occur, her *padre* staggered, reeling, dropping to one knee, and clutching at his shoulder. Fresh blood, black by moonlight, welled between his fingers as he toppled over backward, sprawling in the dirt.

"Papa!" she cried out, sprinting to reach him. She was almost at his side when a *bandido* galloped up and bent down from his saddle, leveling a six-gun at her father's supine form.

Dolores fired her Colt without a heartbeat's hesitation, barely taking time to aim from forty feet while on the run. Her bullet drilled the mounted gunman's left shoulder and pitched him from his saddle, and he twisted in midair as he went down.

A hit, but not a kill.

Cursing in Spanish, the *bandido* struggled to his hands and knees, retrieved his gun, and saw Dolores rushing at him like a raging harpy from mythology. He swung the pistol toward her, cocking it, but her Colt's double-action feature saved a crucial second from the confrontation. When the pistol bucked against her palm again, Dolores saw a dark vent open in the gunman's forehead, spurting as it overflowed with blood, masking his startled face.

That was a kill.

She knelt beside her father, cradling his head with her free arm, while the right still held her weapon poised and ready to defend the pair of them.

Trying to reach him through his pain, she told him, "Hang on, Papa! You are safe now."

Even as she voiced that lie, it seemed to scald her tongue. Instead of daring to repeat it, she cried out for help from someone, anyone, beginning with her siblings in the dark. "Eduardo! Sonya! Help me! *¡Dense prisa!*" And repeated it for emphasis in English: "Hurry up! For God's sake, hurry now!"

No answer reached her ears over the crash and rattle of gunfire, men shouting curses in two languages, horses squealing in panic as they raised dust, running to and fro. The absence of immediate response did not dismay Dolores. She was terrified, if only for her father's sake, forgetting any danger to herself as she applied herself to aiding him.

At last, when more shrill cries for help had gone unanswered, she decided to take action on her own. Gripping her Colt's warm barrel in her teeth, she slid both hands beneath her father's armpits and began to drag him yard by yard, duckwalking backward, toward the cover of their foreman's humble home.

EDUARDO AGUIRRE WAS late arriving in the farmyard, after grappling with his boots and trousers in a dream-daze, then belatedly arming himself. Outside at last, he stood aghast at the chaotic scene before him, horses racing all around while riders whom he did not recognize attempted to direct them southward in a rush.

Watching that grim tableau, Eduardo wished that he had grabbed a weapon other than his Model 1866 Winchester "Yellow Boy" rifle, so called after the hue of its receiver's bronze-brass alloy, also know as gunmetal. Granted, the weapon held fourteen .44-caliber rimfire rounds inside its magazine, but as he faced the swarm of shouting raiders now, Eduardo wished that he had something better. Something *more*.

A Gatling gun, perhaps, six barrels fed by a top-mounted magazine and powered by a smooth hand crank.

"*¡Ridículo!*" he muttered to himself before the whim had even finished taking form.

It *was* ridiculous, of course. The Gatling functioned only when it sat atop a wheeled support vehicle, and it burned through ammunition at prodigious rates. Worse yet, it would have slaughtered men and horses indiscriminately, many of the animals belonging to his family and promised to the U.S. Cavalry for sale next week, bringing top dollar into the Aguirre bank account at Las Cruces.

Better to make do with what he had in hand, as the vaqueros roused from sleep were doing now. Eduardo spared a passing thought for his father and sisters, wondering where they were in the midst of so much gunplay, but he had no time to seek them out.

He hears Dolores then, her shrill voice stuck somewhere between anger and fear, reverting to the first language the Aguirre siblings learned at home. "*¡Padre, no te mueras! ¡Quédate conmigo!*"

Translating the strident plea: Father, don't die! Stay with me!

Scanning for its source, Eduardo spots his sister backing toward the foreman's quarters, dragging something in her wake. A body, by the look of it, and from her words, he understands it is their father, even though he cannot recognize the man who gave them life.

Eduardo starts off in that direction, jogging for the first few yards, then escalating to a sprint. He was about to call his sister's name when something strikes him from behind, with all the force of a pickax. The bullet shatters on his shoulder blade, its fragments boring tunnels through his back and chest, ripping his lungs, his spine, slicing through the aorta where it joins his heart's left ventricle.

Already dead before he drops, Eduardo stumbles, falls, a puppet with its strings cut, impact with the soil raising a little cloud of dust.

Sonya Aguirre, slow to wake from an alluring dream at the first sounds of gunfire, threw aside her goose-down comforter and scrambled out of bed, grabbing a robe, belting its tie around her waist before she grabbed a Springfield Model 1903 rifle from its slot between her mattress and nightstand.

Shooting meant danger, and she did not plan to miss it for the world.

The Springfield was a military weapon, introduced in the United States after the "splendid little war" with Spain. A bolt-action man-stopper, it weighed nine pounds loaded with five .30-06 rounds in its magazine. The rifle's flip-up graduated sights were calibrated to a range of twenty-seven hundred yards, but in the early-morning darkness Sonya knew she would be lucky to achieve a solid hit within one quarter of that distance.

Still, one solid hit should be enough for any man.

Taking no chances, Sonya yanked the top drawer of her nightstand open and removed three five-round stripper clips, dropping them into the right-hand pocket of her robe. Instinct told her that if she needed more than twenty shots, this night—or morning, rather—would most likely be her last.

Sonya had never shot a man before, but knew it was an ever-present possibility while dwelling so close to the Mexican border, where rustlers and *bandidos* crossed the Rio Grande at will, with little interference from the county sheriff's office and less yet from the New Mexico Rangers, a tiny force of eleven mounted officers created five years earlier, tasked with patrolling 122,000 square miles occupied by some 327,000 settlers.

Those odds were virtually hopeless, leaving each man and woman to defend him- or herself against predators, human or otherwise.

Rustlers had preyed on the Aguirre family before, though few had profited from the act, and this morning's attack—for what else could it be—was alien to Sonya's personal experience.

She was prepared to do her part, however.

That, at least, was what she told herself as she stepped into moccasins and left her home behind, clearing the porch to find a battle underway.

Manuelito Obregón, still clanging the alarm bell, saw her clear the tall front door and cautioned Sonya, "You had best remain inside *la casa, señorita*."

"Is my sister still inside?" she answered back, and brushed on past the houseman, jogging down three wooden steps into the yard.

As soon as she arrived on level ground, Sonya hoisted her rifle, snugged its butt against her shoulder as she cranked its bolt action to chamber a live round. With horsemen racing here and there, some firing pistols, others ducking bullets, Sonya had to time her shot precisely and make sure she did not wound one of her family's vaqueros by mistake.

No sooner had she formed the thought than a stranger appeared in front of her. He was a burly *mexicano* whom she did not recognize as an employee, mounted on a prancing dun, aiming a shiny pistol toward the porch and Manuelito Obregón. From thirty feet, she barely had to aim the Springfield, squeezing off a tad too hastily in her excitement.

As the rifle bucked against her shoulder, Sonya heard the gunman shout a curse in Spanish, doubling over, clutching at the spot where she had drilled him through the fat on his left side. Yelping, he wheeled away and gouged his mount with spurs, already dwindling into dusty darkness before she could work the Springfield's bolt and try again.

She chased him with another wild shot, nonetheless, cursing the miss almost before she pulled the rifle's trigger.

It was then that Sonya heard her sister's voice, coming from her left, crying, "Papa! Hold on! We're almost there!"

Spinning in that direction, she beheld Dolores dragging a limp figure toward the foreman's quarters, struggling against its deadweight.

Papa!

Instantly forgetting about any danger to herself or to the herd, Sonya Aguirre ran to help.

RÁPIDO, HOMBRES!" PANCHO Villa shouted as he raced along beside the herd of captured horses, flanked and trailed by the vaqueros who had managed to escape from the Aguirre ranch unscathed, or at the very least able to travel with their wounds.

There had been no time yet for counting either stolen animals or the survivors of his border raid. He guessed, from prior experience, that five or six men had been left behind, all dead or dying from defensive gun-fire. More concerned about the horses, Villa estimated that his raiders had escaped with three fourths of the herd. Call it fifteen hundred animals that he could sell across the border, after skimming off a few, replenishing his own remuda for the hectic times ahead.

To Villa's left, along the eastern skyline over Texas, gray light had begun to infiltrate the desert sky. They would be at the Rio Grande soon, no reason to expect a *federale* welcome party waiting for them on the river's southern bank. No one from the Aguirre rancho could have spread the news so quickly, and their first impulse would be to reach out for the sheriff's office in Las Cruces, wasting further precious time.

If he had staged his raid across the territory's eastern border, Texas Rangers might have rushed across the border to pursue his company, but Pancho Villa was no fool. He understood the sorry state of law enforcement in New Mexico, and its governor's ambition for advancement to the hallowed halls of Washington, D.C. Governor William Mills was well past sixty years of age and dared not rile his party's leadership by sending his pathetic force of rangers into Mexico.

As for the U.S. Cavalry, if they chose to pursue the horses they had lost this night, they would be far too late.

Events were heating up in Mexico, and Villa sensed that he would be caught in the middle of it soon. Now, however, he could only think about this morning and the boost his reputation would receive from pulling off the greatest border raid in history.

He would be satisfied with that for now and think about tomorrow when it dawned.

CHAPTER TWO

Pale dawn crept over the Aguirre ranch like a sneak thief approaching a deserted market stall.

Not that the hacienda was abandoned; far from it. All hands still fit to walk, ride, work, or to defend themselves had plunged into a whirlwind of activity as soon as the intruders who had struck the spread were out of sight. Pursuit was futile in the early-morning darkness, and the prospect of an ambush on the trail made chasing after the attackers doubly dangerous.

Four members of the rancho's staff were dead, two others wounded and requiring a physician's care. Alejandro Aguirre was one of the wounded, drilled through the shoulder, in and out. His daughters had managed to stanch the bleeding, dress his injury, and wedge his arm into a sling, but they could not restrain him from prowling the grounds, confirming all they'd lost within the scope of half an hour, maybe less.

Aside from human deaths and injuries, the worst loss came to fourteen hundred eighty-seven first-class horses slated for sale to the U.S. Army at $300 apiece, for a total exceeding $446,000 all told.

But the loss Alejandro grieved the most, together with his two surviving offspring, was the murder of his son—the twins' brother—Eduardo, shot down in the farmyard by some unidentified gunman. His twenty-fourth birthday was two weeks off, but Eduardo would never see it now, would never marry, would never give his father grandsons to perpetuate the name Aguirre in New Mexico.

For that alone, vengeance was mandatory, but his shoulder wound meant Alejandro would not be a part of seeking it.

Repayment of a blood debt could not wait that long.

Off to the northwest, well beyond the larger of the rancho's two red barns, Aguirre saw a team of his vaqueros digging graves for those who'd fallen in the raid. Not the *bandidos*, who had been hauled off in wagons to the farthest limit of the hacienda's property and dumped into a gully as coyote food. For all Aguirre cared, their bones could bleach there. Sometime soon, before they finally were gnawed away, he might ride out at sunset to their final resting place and curse them all to everlasting hell.

But for the moment, he was more concerned with tracking down the man behind the sneak attack, likely well into Mexico by now. That villain, nameless at the moment, must be hunted down and slain, even if searchers could not locate all the rustlers who had joined him on the raid.

That was a debt Aguirre owed his murdered son.

A debt he owed himself and generations of his bloodline never to be born.

And if he could not pay that debt himself, he must see to it that a man he trusted saw it through.

Clint Parnell was approaching, likely bearing more bad news. Aguirre raised his one good arm to flag the foreman down.

* * *

NECESSITY MEANT RUSHING through the funerals with no priest in attendance, little in the way of normal mourning rituals except for women weeping at graveside. Two had lost husbands in the firefight, one had lost a lover, and the fourth, a son. There were no words of scripture that could comfort them, and Alejandro—speaking for the remnants of his family—made no great effort to achieve that goal.

The urgent need was to observe law and propriety unless those mainstays of society were proved inadequate.

First, because the stolen horses had been spoken for by Uncle Sam, although not yet paid for, the army's nearest representative must be informed of the attack and loss. Likewise, since all relationships with foreign nations were the purview of the U.S. State Department, only Washington could lodge a formal protest or attempt to bring the horses back from Mexico.

Under the law, that was. But if pursuit of justice through established channels failed . . .

Aguirre, flanked by his twin daughters, watched the gravediggers begin to cover his son's casket, but a portion of his fractured thoughts was miles away. The nearest army outpost, Fort Bayard, was barely staffed by fighting men—only enough to guard the fort's perimeters against outside attack—and would be useless in pursuit of the *bandidos* who had made off with his stock. Aguirre knew the man in charge, Lieutenant Colonel Isaac Stern, and recognized him as a weak man who preferred avoiding contact with armed adversaries.

If the State Department, in its wisdom, should decide upon retrieval of the stolen herd, a hunting party would be ordered up from some other outpost, possibly Fort Whipple, former capital of Arizona Territory until 1881. A three-week journey from Las Cruces at full gallop—which would guarantee none of Aguirre's horses were recovered.

There was an alternative, of course, and Alejandro had discussed it with his foreman, but preferred to trust his government.

Up to a point.

His secondary plan would be a last resort, with long odds against ultimate success.

But one way or another, Alejandro swore that he would be avenged.

Women were trailing past the graves now, strewing wildflowers and mumbling prayers. Turning away from them, Aguirre and his daughters moved back toward their home, its façade pockmarked by bullet holes inflicted overnight. Both girls, still shy of their twenty-first birthday, insisted that they should join Clint Parnell on his ride to Fort Bayard, starting soon.

Without members of the Aguirre family on hand to plead their case, why should Lieutenant Colonel Stern treat them seriously? Why even consider what their father had in mind?

Relenting finally, aware that one or both might ride away without his blessing, Alejandro urged them both to caution, needlessly reminding them that only they remained of their *familia*. That brought the sisters close to tears, but they were resolute and would not be dissuaded.

Finally, with Papa Alejandro tucked up in his bed to rest and under guard, the twins rushed off to change their clothes for traveling and arm themselves.

Few men who glimpsed their carbon-copy faces in that moment would have dared to intervene.

THE PREPARATIONS FOR departure took an hour following the funerals, despite the fact that only three survivors of the raid were traveling. Dolores and

Sonya Aguirre made up two thirds of the team, while Clint Parnell was riding as their chaperone, his post as foreman on the ranch filled temporarily by top vaquero José Esperón.

The raiders, thankfully, had not attempted to steal any private horses from the rancho's barns. Parnell sat astride his dapple gray gelding, the sisters mounted on a snowflake Appaloosa (for Dolores) and a varnish roan (for Sonya). Expecting to be gone two nights minimum, on a round trip of one hundred seventy miles, the trio carried guns and ammunition, ample food and water for the trail, and blankets that would swaddle them around a fire on frosty desert nights. Upon returning, either they would have a pledge of government assistance—for whatever that was worth—or else they'd pursue a secondary plan, drawn up in haste, which placed them all at greater risk.

Departing from the ranch, the sisters rode on either side of Clint Parnell, Dolores to his left, facilitating conversation on the trail. Some of the older women living on the hacienda whispered criticism of them, leaving their *padre* Alejandro on his own with no kin left to care for him, although he was unlikely to lie abed complaining of his injury.

If the twins were conscious of those few whispered objections, they revealed no sign of it and frankly did not care. Both knew the origins of Doña Ana County, founded back in 1852 and named for Ana Gomez Robledo, who'd died there at age seventy-six, after fleeing with relatives from the Pueblo Revolt of 1860, near the present site of Santa Fe. While neither twin would consciously have chosen Doña Ana as a role model in life, they understood her grim tenacity, having acquired it from their father as they grew from children into women.

The riders could have saved themselves a day, at least, by traveling directly to Las Cruces and the county sheriff's office, but all three agreed with Papa Alejandro that it would have wasted time, which they could not afford. Sheriff Patrick Lucero was a politician first and foremost, nothing like the man he had succeeded ten years earlier. *That* sheriff, Patrick Garrett, was best known for killing one Henry McCarty—alias William Bonney or "Billy the Kid"—at Fort Sumner in 1881, and while *he* might have led a posse to pursue and punish the Aguirre rancho raiders in his day, those times were gone.

Today, it was the U.S. Army or a private effort, which the three determined riders knew might see them killed across the border, dumped in shallow graves, or left to feed coyotes where they fell.

But none of them were backing down.

For the Aguirre sisters, lethal insults to their family demanded vengeance, as the theft of property cried out for recompense. Their brother's death, the wounding of their father, and the theft of animals whose sale would see them through another year in style required that Sonya and Dolores do their utmost to eradicate that slight against their clan.

To Clint Parnell, devoid of blood ties to the family he served, the task was simpler. He was paid, and well by present standards of the time and place, to safeguard the Aguirre property. The theft of nearly fifteen hundred horses on his watch hurt Clint more deeply than a slap across the face or swift kick to his groin. He knew honor was involved, and he would do whatever was required to make things right.

Or, failing that, to stain the desert of Old Mexico with outlaws' blood.

And if that effort meant his own death . . . well, so be it. He would be remembered, at least briefly, as a man who understood his duty and spared no expense to follow through with it.

No great believer in an afterlife himself, Parnell guessed that would have to be enough. He knew himself

too well to make believe that he would ever pass through
pearly gates or walk down streets of gold. And if there
was no heaven, then what did he have to fear from hell?

Clint had seen death aplenty in his thirty years, first
as a soldier chasing red men, later as a drover, finally
as vaquero and foreman on the Aguirre ranch. Last
night aside, he'd personally killed at least a dozen men,
though skirmishes with Navajo and Jicarilla renegades
made a precise accounting of the adversaries he had
put down impossible.

Clint never bragged about it, nor was he ashamed.
In each case where he'd pulled the trigger on an adversary, the decision had been his life or the other guy's,
and he had no regrets about surviving any life-or-death
encounter fate had sent his way.

This time around, as in the past, Parnell would do
whatever was required, and when the smoke cleared, if
he was aboveground, he would learn to live with it.

FORT BAYARD, LOCATED eighty-five miles northwest
of the Aguirre ranch in Grant County, would not
have been the trio's choice for army contact points, but
time was of the essence, forcing them to settle for a
poor bargain.

Founded in 1866, one year after the War Between the
States, Bayard had started as an outpost for the U.S. Cavalry defending local farms and settlements against at-
tacks by hostile Native tribes. The facility was named for
Brigadier General George Dashiell Bayard, a Union officer fatally wounded at the Battle of Fredericksburg in
1862. Most of its troops in those days had been African
Americans, dubbed "buffalo soldiers" by their opponents, who compared their curly hair and dark skins to
the bison that were even then being eradicated nation-
wide to clear the plains for railroad tracks. Despite their

recent service in suppressing the Confederacy, they were relegated to the Southwest's hinterlands under the leadership of white commanding officers who treated them with varying degrees of credit or, more often, racist disrespect.

In either case, Fort Bayard's tenure—as an active fort, at least—was not destined to last. Within two decades of its opening, after Apache chief Geronimo surrendered for the third and last time in September 1866, shipped off to die in Florida, the U.S. War Department slated Bayard for deactivation. What eventually saved it was tuberculosis, an increasing plague among both Native tribes and Anglos in the West. Military leaders transferred control of the ex-fort to the U.S. Army surgeon general in 1900, whereupon it had become—and still remained—Veterans Hospital, a treatment center for military veterans who had contracted the "white plague," also referred to as "consumption."

The Aguirre sisters and Clint Parnell did not relish visiting a nest of pestilence, but in their present circumstances it remained the nearest contact point from home to any formal military outpost. There would not be healthy troops enough on hand to mount an expedition into Mexico, assuming that unlikely prospect was approved from Washington, but with the hacienda's telegraph cables waiting to be repaired, it was the next best means of contact to authorities who could decide the matter.

The travelers had little hope of ultimate success, considering the Taft-Díaz agreement signed at Ciudad Juárez during October of last year. On the first day of that meeting, two Texas Rangers traveling with William Howard Taft as bodyguards had captured a would-be assassin whose expressed intent was the elimination of both presidents. Despite that rude surprise, the U.S. had agreed to give Porfirio Díaz a helping hand with his eighth presidential race, thereby protecting several billion dollars of American capital then invested south of the border. Another result of the summit was short-term agreement that the disputed Chamizal strip—six hundred acres of land connecting El Paso to Ciudad Juárez, caused by a shift in the Rio Grande's course—would be considered neutral territory with no flags of either nation on display until the matter was resolved in later talks, however long that took.

No one at the Aguirre ranch expected Washington to roil those muddy waters with a border crossing to pursue horse thieves, regardless of the personal and economic damage to their owners. Buyers for the U.S. Cavalry would simply find more horses elsewhere, but despite the futile nature of that mission, Papa Alejandro had decreed that they must try.

And even wounded, hobbling about his hacienda with attendants and a crutch, his word was law to the remainder of his family and those in his employ.

A T SUNDOWN, STILL some thirty miles short of their destination, Parnell and the twins agreed to camp out for the night. They were prepared for that, and for a second night of sleeping on the trail when they returned to Doña Ana County, and had not considered pushing on through darkness when potential risks from man and beast alike increased.

The sky was clear, no likelihood of rain during the night or anywhere along their route of travel for the next two days, so they had packed no tents, deciding to make do with blankets only and a fire to keep them warm. That was a risk, potentially attracting drifters bent on robbery or worse, but Parnell and the twins were all well armed, in no mood to be merciful with interlopers who approached their camp.

Aside from that, they had agreed to stand watch through the dark hours, in shifts. Parnell initially had volunteered to stay awake all night, but the Aguirre sisters quickly vetoed that, insisting that they do their share, regardless of their rank as his employers in their father's absence. For her part, Dolores settled things by taking the last shift, from one a.m. until sunrise, ostensibly allowing her companions to catch up on sleep before the break of dawn.

In fact, although she'd kept it to herself thus far, Dolores realized that sister Sonya had a crush of sorts on Clint, although she could not say how deep the feelings ran. It would be Sonya's job to break that news if liking should develop into something more, and she would have to hash that out with Papa Alejandro, if and when the time came. Her affection for the hacienda's foreman had not yet passed beyond the stage of watching him at times as he proceeded through the routine of his working days, growing distracted from her own appointed tasks.

Dolores had not mentioned it and would not, until such time as her twin saw fit to raise the subject of her own accord. Despite their naturally close relationship, it would be intrusive and impertinent.

The trio ate a frugal meal of beans, tortillas, and coffee, expecting to see it repeated at breakfast and once again on their homeward journey from Fort Bayard, when they would spend another night out on the trail. Once they had cleaned their metal plates with sand, conserving precious water in their various canteens, Dolores left her sister and Clint Parnell chatting by the fire and tucked into her bedroll. Sonya would rouse her when the time came for her turn on guard.

Until then, she could only wish away what all of them assumed would be two days of wasted time, before the journey to retrieve their vanished herd began.

CHAPTER THREE

Veterans Hospital, Grant County

BREAKFAST HAD BEEN hasty, barely tasted, following an uneventful desert night. Coyotes howling at the moon had wakened the two sleeping campers around midnight, but they posed no threat, and nothing larger than a beetle had trespassed within their homey ring of firelight, while the landscape's other predators—ranging in size from scorpions to rattlesnakes and Gila monsters—wisely shied away.

Dolores, on the graveyard shift, had started cooking well before first light, letting aromas still familiar from their supper rouse Sonya and Clint Parnell from their bedrolls set twenty feet apart, flanking the campfire. By full daylight they had stowed their gear and watered their animals, and were progressing toward their final destination.

Thirty miles might be traversed at a killing gallop, but the travelers restrained their horses to a combination walk and trot, conserving energy and sparing them from damaging overexertion as the morning's heat increased. Thus, it was nearly nine o'clock before they glimpsed Fort Bayard—now Veterans Hospital—standing athwart the old Apache Trail.

A sentry on its southward-facing elevated catwalk spotted them from half a mile distant and called a warning down to someone else, concealed from few behind the military base's stockade wall. As they approached within earshot, the lookout hailed them with a gruff command.

"Stop where you are and state your business!"

Clint, their chosen spokesman for the necessary introductions, called back with a summary of the attack on the Aguirre hacienda and their urgent need to see Lieutenant Colonel Stern. The sentry shouted back, "Hang on a minute," then ducked out of sight, presumably conferring with someone of higher rank.

More like three minutes passed before the stockade's double gate began to open, one blue-coated soldier manning either side, straining against their weight, while two more armed with rifles watched the visitors advance.

Once the trio were all inside the walls made out of upright logs, the gates swung shut again, preventing any change of heart and hasty exit from the compound. Under guard, the travelers dismounted, left their weapons stowed in saddle scabbards, and proceeded toward the base's central structure under guard.

Dolores trailed a step behind her sister and their foreman, not at all enthused about their entry to the hospital with its contagious patients. Even though one of their escorts had assured the trio that Lieutenant Colonel Stern's headquarters were completely separate from any active wards, she knew tuberculosis was an airborne pathogen, and could not fully shake the sense that she was walking into danger.

Even so, uneasy as she was, Dolores forged ahead.

The fort or hospital's command post was constructed out of logs, like the stockade. Considering the open desert that surrounded it, Dolores could not guess how far building materials had been transported overland to reach the site, or what that effort might have cost. Three wooden steps rose to the headquarters' covered porch, reminding her a bit of home until a young soldier wearing lieutenant's bars emerged to greet the visitors. He introduced himself as Cyrus Finch, shook hands with Clint Parnell, and nodded to the sisters without offering his hand to either one.

"This way to the lieutenant colonel, if you please," he said, a Boston accent audible.

The new arrivals followed Finch inside and through a foyer where the walls were lined with wooden filing cabinets, along a short hallway, to reach a door marked PRIVATE, where Finch knocked and waited for an answer from within.

"Enter!" a deeper male voice ordered, offering a vague hint of an Irish brogue softened by elocution lessons over time.

Finch ushered the three visitors inside, snapped off a quick salute to his commanding officer, and then closed the door behind him as he left.

FACING THE MAN they'd traveled overnight to see, Clint Parnell doffed his flat-brimmed hat while sizing up the office and its occupant. He judged the room was twelve to thirteen feet on any given side, well kept, but not without the dusty air that desert climates add to any manmade structure over time. Its only furniture, a spacious desk with three plain chairs in front of it, was overshadowed by a portrait of the current U.S. president, his image flanked by Old Glory immediately to the right, and to its left, the red-and-yellow banner of New Mexico.

Their host, Lieutenant Colonel Stern, stood ramrod straight behind his desk, so the solemn face of William Howard Taft loomed in the background and his famous double chins appeared to rest atop the base commander's head.

Stern moved around his desk to greet the unexpected visitors, repeating his aide's ritual of shaking hands with Clint Parnell, then bowing slightly to the twin Aguirre sisters. Clint made the introductions for his team, feeling the heat that radiated from the twins, unhappy with their relegation to the role of hangers-on, with Stern assuming that a man must be in charge.

The camp's commander was approximately six feet tall, an inch or so shorter than Clint, but made up for it with his uniform and grooming. The brass buttons on his jacket had been polished till they gleamed like freshly minted golden coins. His riding boots were spit shined to the gloss of mirrors, and he wore a pistol holstered on his left hip for a cross-hand draw favored by members of the U.S. Cavalry. His auburn hair was parted on the right and thinning at the temples, while Stern compensated with a handlebar mustache that framed thin lips the color of raw veal.

"Please, sit," Stern said, with a vague gesture to the three chairs facing toward his desk.

Clint took the left-hand seat, with Sonya to his right, Dolores just beyond. As he sat down, Parnell noted the base commander's polished desktop, decorated with a lamp, a fountain pen and inkwell, plus a broad red leather blotter. As for the anticipated paperwork, no trace was visible.

"My aide informs me that there's been some trouble at your ranch," Stern said as he relaxed into his tall-backed swivel chair. "A raid of some sort, I believe?"

Dolores spoke before Clint had the chance. "Yes, sir. It left our father wounded, killed our only brother, and the *bandidos* escaped with nearly fifteen hundred horses under contract to your cavalry for a delivery next month."

Stern raised a hand, its index finger stroking his luxuriant mustache. "Ma'am, if you'll pardon me," he said, "it's not *my* cavalry. We operate a hospital, as I presume you are aware."

Sonya Aguirre spoke up out of turn. "Yours is the nearest base that we could reach in time, sir," she replied.

Stern frowned across his desk. "In time for *what*, exactly?"

Clint's turn now. "To fetch the horses back," he said, "and meet the deadline for delivery."

Lieutenant Colonel Stern leaned back, forcing a squeak out of his chair, tenting his fingers underneath his chin as he replied.

"I see," he said. "But as to that, we have a problem that I should explain to you."

S EATED BEHIND HIS desk, Stern normally expected deference from the subordinates who stood before him during any given day. The presence of civilians— and two women in the group, both of them clearly Mexican in ancestry—put him off stride, feeling as if he'd been transported from his normal element into an atmosphere distinctly alien.

It did not help when one of the twin sisters challenged him directly.

"Problem?" she said, leaning slightly forward in her chair. "What kind of problem? Army horses have been stolen. People under your protection have been murdered."

Stern rocked forward, planting elbows on his desktop blotter.

"Ma'am, as I've informed you," he replied, "this is a hospital for ailing veterans. It has not been a normal army base for years now, and my men do not patrol the territory as you seem to think."

The second sister chimed in then. "But you're still *soldiers*, are you not? When army property is stolen—"

"Please don't let the uniforms confuse you, ma'am," Stern said, forgetting whether this one was Dolores or Sonya. "I am the ranking officer of this facility, but I command a staff of medics, orderlies, and nurses. We receive our orders and our paychecks from the surgeon general's office, not the U.S. Cavalry."

"Lieutenant Colonel," said the dusty man seated across from Stern, Clint Something, "all we want is help. It's no concern of ours who pays your salary, as long as you're in uniform."

"And I sincerely wish that I could help you," Stern replied, "but chasing horse thieves is not part of my assignment here. And as for tracking them across the Rio Grande into Mexico, well . . ."

"They've already made it there by now," one of the sisters said, a challenge in her tone.

"Exactly!" Stern agreed. "And so, you must see that my hands are tied. I have neither the troops nor jurisdiction to invade another sovereign nation."

"But you know someone who could," Clint Something answered.

"I know the mandatory channels that must be pursued," Stern granted, feeling cornered now. "But that takes time, and given the inherent delicacy of relations between Washington and Mexico . . ."

"But you could *try*," one of the twins said, talking over him.

Stern felt his shoulders start to slump and squared them with a will. "I can dispatch a telegram," he granted, "but I must advise you to expect a disappointment."

"Try that, please," the other sister said. "Before we have to handle this ourselves."

Frowning, Stern said, "And I must warn you in the strongest terms that any private effort to pursue these miscreants in Mexico would leave the individuals behind it open to arrest and prosecution."

"Let's take one step at a time," Clint Something said. "Now, how about that telegram?"

SENDING THE TELEGRAM and waiting for an answer from the nation's capital wasted the better part of three hours. The commander of Veterans Hospital offered them food while they were waiting, but all three of his unwelcome guests declined. That seemed to put him off, as if he'd been insulted, but Dolores frankly did not care.

Finally, a sharp knock sounded on the base commander's door. Stern shouted, "Enter!" and Lieutenant Finch obeyed immediately, crossing to Stern's desk, saluting him before he passed a flimsy piece of paper to the officer in charge.

Dolores recognized the telegram, watched Stern peruse it before handing it across his desk to Clint Parnell. "Alas, as I expected," the lieutenant colonel said. "Feel free to read it for yourself."

Dolores watched Clint scan the text, frowning, before he passed it to the twins. They huddled, reading it together, faces souring as it extinguished fleeting hope. The wire read:

WAR DEPT., WASHINGTON, TRANSMITTING TO
VETERANS HOSPITAL, NEW MEXICO.

Regret the incident reported but advise no action on your part. Repeat, no action, by direction of the Secretary. Refer-

enced contract voided without penalty for either side. Forbid
civilian vigilante trespass onto foreign soil. Matter referred
to State Department and Commander-in-Chief, who concur.
Stop.

"You're doing nothing, then," Dolores said, when
she had read the message twice.

"And you," Stern said, "I fear, must do likewise. Despite your feelings in this matter—"

"You know *nothing* of our feelings," Sonya snapped
at him, both sisters on their feet now, Clint Parnell rising a fraction of a second later. "As you *do* nothing to
protect us!"

"Ma'am, having read this message from the highest
of authorities—"

"We leave it with you," Sonya interrupted as she
dropped the telegram onto Stern's desk. "Why don't
you have it framed and hang it on your wall?"

Stern made no effort to detain them as they left his
office, which was wise, considering the trio's mood. Outside, they found their horses fed and watered while
they'd waited for the telegram, mounting in unison and
reining toward the stockade's gates. No one attempted to
prevent their leaving, and they put the fort turned hospital behind them, starting back the way they'd come.

D O YOU THINK that he will send a troop of soldiers
after us?" Dolores asked when they had ridden a
full mile beyond the hospital.

"I doubt it," Clint Parnell replied. "First thing, he
doesn't have a troop at his disposal. We already saw that
for ourselves. If the War Department goes that way, the
order will come out of Washington, most likely routed
through a fort still active in patrolling the frontier."

Dolores ran the short list in her head. That meant

Fort Union, north of Watrous in New Mexico, or maybe even Fort Bliss at El Paso, Texas. Mobilizing troops from either post, dispatching them against her family's rancho, would take a few days at the very least, likely more than a week.

"We need to hurry, then," she told Clint and her sister Sonya.

"But without killing our horses in the process," said Parnell. "We'll have to camp again tonight, no matter what."

Dolores thought about her snowflake Appaloosa, knew that Clint was right, but still chafed at the waste of precious time, when every passing hour took her brother's killers and the hacienda's stolen livestock deeper into Mexico.

Logic told her that the raiders had most likely emanated from Chihuahua, nearest to the southern border of New Mexico, but she would take nothing for granted. She intended to pursue them wherever they ran and tried to hide themselves, regardless of the cost. Aside from getting justice for Eduardo and her father, bringing back the herd—or most of it, at least—would mean preserving that year's income for the ranch and for her family.

Threats of arrest by Isaac Stern and his superiors in Washington meant less than nothing to Dolores. Her primary debt, for the life she enjoyed before last night—indeed, for life itself—was to her kin and to the local empire that her *padre* had carved from the desert with an outpouring of sweat and blood.

If distant strangers tried to interfere with that responsibility . . . well, they would have to wait in line.

CHAPTER FOUR

Ascensión, Chihuahua, Mexico

PANCHO VILLA LIT a thin cheroot, inhaled its bitter taste, and turned to his *primer teniente*, Javier Jurado, speaking through a cloud of acrid smoke. "What word from the border?"

"Nothing yet, jefe," Jurado answered. "They will first complain to someone from the military."

"Who will offer them no satisfaction," Villa said. "The gringos are afraid of war with Mexico just now."

Jurado nodded. Said, "As they should be, considering *los alemanes*."

That was true. Germany's emperor and king of Prussia, Kaiser Wilhelm II, had been pursuing diplomatic ties with Mexico, seeking not only the ore drawn from its mines, but also an alliance for the future if a war broke out involving Germany and the United States. Porfirio Díaz, while welcoming foreign investments in the nation he had ruled since 1884, still balked at signing an agreement that would agitate his nearest neighbor with an army large enough to challenge Mexico's and seize more of its borderlands if foolishly provoked.

In Villa's estimation, Washington would not risk war over the onetime theft of fifteen hundred horses, even if they had been earmarked for the U.S. Cavalry. Rather then squander men and resources, upsetting the fragile Díaz-Taft summit, they would locate *caballos* elsewhere, possibly dispatch a formal protest that would have small impact—maybe none at all— upon his operations in Chihuahua.

Ascensión felt safe for now, at least. One hundred twenty miles of high desert and the Sierra Madre Occidental lay in between the city and Chihuahua's capital at Ciudad Juárez. The land was unforgiving, temperatures topping one hundred nine degrees Fahrenheit on summer days, then plunging to minus nine degrees after nightfall. Díaz had *federales* in the area, of course, but for the most part they were lazy, little more than bandits in their own right, although graced with uniforms and modern guns.

"How long until Zapata reaches us?" Villa inquired.

Jurado shrugged. "He's on his way, jefe, but coming from Morelos, who can say?"

Morelos was the second smallest of Mexico's thirty-two states, after Tlaxcala, located some twelve hundred miles southeast of Chihuahua. A trip like that, crossing mountains and deserts, navigating woodlands while dodging *federales*, might consume two weeks or more. Villa disliked waiting, sitting still and serving as a target while news of his strike across the border spread like wildfire, but if he was going to divide the stolen horses with Emiliano Zapata's band of anti-Díaz activists, a face-to-face agreement was required.

Zapata, one year Villa's junior, was a man of rural roots who loathed Porfirio Díaz for favoring landowners with monopolies on land and water used for sugar cane production. Peasant villagers were suffering because of such corruption, and Zapata—known among his people as El Caudillo del Sur, "Attila of the South"—had earned a reputation for ambushing federal troops, divesting them of arms and ammunition to support his cause, and was increasingly admired for his audacity of opposition to the current president of Mexico and his regime of *el porfiriato*.

To survive, however, Zapata required more than weapons and courage. He also needed a steady supply of horses to replace those killed or captured during skirmishes with the authorities.

And that was where Villa came in.

If only he could stay alive and free to see their dealings through.

Doña Ana County, New Mexico Territory

Clint Parnell and the Aguirre sisters finished breaking camp after their second night of sleeping rough around a campfire, huddled with their guns, and taking turns on guard. Gray dawn enfolded them as they mounted and turned their animals toward home.

Parnell had spent the better part of yesterday, after they left Veterans Hospital, trying to talk the twins out of their plan to ride with him and a selected handful of vaqueros to retrieve their stolen horses and—with any luck—punish the raiders who had slain their brother among other members of the household.

Not that Sonya or Dolores had agreed with him, mind you. Far from it. Both were dead set on participating in the chase, and Clint would have to leave the final say to his wounded employer. Alejandro had a fair record for curbing his twin daughters if they chose a course of action he deemed rash, but they were still his youngest children—and the sole survivors of his family today.

Whether he could dissuade them, even order them to stay at home, remained an open question in Clint's mind.

There would be no escaping from the chase for Clint himself, of course. He was prepared to cede his post to José Esperón for the duration of the hunt, assuming that Parnell ever returned from Mexico. He'd spent most of the prior afternoon selecting ranch hands to ride with him when he crossed the Rio Grande, leaving it to volunteers and weeding out vaqueros who had wives and children on the hacienda.

Would that number be enough, considering the force that had attacked them two nights earlier? Parnell deemed that unlikely, but he had not settled on a source for reinforcements yet.

Around midmorning, Sonya eased her varnish roan beside Clint's dapple gray, lowered her voice a bit, and said, "I'm sorry that we argued, but you understand, *¿no?*"

"I do," he grudgingly admitted, "but it's still a bad idea. Two women on the trail, chasing a gang of killers . . ."

"Give it up, will you?" Dolores chided, riding within earshot on his other side. "You wouldn't argue with Eduardo if he chose to follow them."

Parnell felt brutal saying it, but could not help himself. "Eduardo *can't* join in, remember? Do you want to leave your father worrying about the pair of you? You're all that he has left."

"We will persuade him," Sonya said, with perfect confidence.

"And if you can't?"

"Then we come with you anyway. The choice is ours."

"Okay, then," Clint replied. "It's like I said last night. Whatever Alejandro says, I'll go along with it. That doesn't mean I have to like it, though."

Sonya reached out to let her fingertips graze Parnell's sleeve. "It's sweet of you to worry," she observed.

"Sweet doesn't enter into it," Clint answered. "I come back—assuming that I *do* come back—and tell your father that he's childless, you can bet I'll be the next one who gets his brains blown out."

"Never!" Sonya assured Parnell. "He loves you like a second son."

Clint nearly had to snort at that but kept it to a negative head shake. "I guess we'll find out soon enough," he said, and left it there, counting the empty hours still ahead of them, before his boss settled the argument for good and all. Whatever the decision, Clint reckoned the odds were fifty-fifty that he would be riding to his death in Mexico.

TWO ARMED OUTRIDERS met the homeward travelers as soon as they had crossed onto Aguirre property, then stayed behind to make sure no one had been trailing them. Another half hour elapsed before the ranch house and its other buildings rose out of the desert into view, the sisters and Parnell urging their horses to a faster pace as they neared home.

Forewarned of their arrival, Alejandro met them on the porch, standing erect without the cane that made him feel too much like an old man before his time. Granted, he was not young or at full strength, considering his wound, but he refused to let his workers view him as disabled or defeated.

Beside him, Manuelito Obregón anticipated Alejandro's order, saying, "I shall tend their horses, jefe."

"*Gracias, hermano*," Alejandro said, watching his daughters and their foreman close the gap, then finally dismount. As Manuelito led their animals away, Aguirre turned and beckoned with his good arm, saying, "Come inside with me."

He waited until they were in the dining room, with

Alejandro seated at the table's head, flanked by his daughters, Clint Parnell to Sonya's right. Reading their faces, he began, "You bring the news that I expected."

"No one from the army means to help us, sir," Clint said. "In fact, they warned us against taking any action on our own."

"Because the fat man, Taft, fears causing problems with Díaz," said Alejandro.

"You were right, sir," Clint confirmed.

"Then we must act in spite of them," the hacienda's owner said.

Aguirre saw his daughters' faces light up as they heard. He felt them yearning, like young whippets straining at their leashes, eager to be off and running on a rabbit's trail.

"You wish to join the hunt," he said before either could speak aloud.

"Papa, we must," Sonya replied. "Eduardo—"

"Lost his life to these *cobardes*," Alejandro cut her off. "Would you ride off and leave me without any living family?"

"Why do you doubt us, Papa?" asked Dolores.

Alejandro was about to answer tartly, when he realized he lacked the proper words. His daughters, although young, were women fully grown. Was *that* his only objection to their plan, based solely on their sex?

They had been trained, to all intents and purposes, the same way that he had prepared Eduardo to fulfill his role as son and heir of the Aguirre rancho, share and share alike among the three siblings. Both sisters were skilled riders and crack shots, as they had proved on hunting expeditions and, more recently, during the rustlers' raid. They stood as much chance of surviving on the southward journey, traveling with Clint Parnell and others he selected as companions, as their brother might have done, had he survived to face this day.

But still, Aguirre knew the risks were greater for a woman on the outlaw trail. If they were captured, by either the *federales* or *bandidos*, Alejandro knew full well what they were likely to endure in hostile hands. Men might be executed, sometimes tortured, but for women in captivity . . . it made him sick to think about the possibilities.

Finally, his shoulders slumped, Aguirre said, "I do not doubt you, either of you. But I fear for you. Can you not understand that? We have lost so much already. First, your mother, then—"

"And that is why we must recover what we can," Sonya cut in, placing her left hand over Alejandro's right, and giving it a squeeze. "If we do not participate, what good are we?"

He hesitated for another long moment, then faced his daughters each in turn, nodding resignedly. "*Bien*," he finally replied. "Do as you like, then. I shall pray for you each day and night until you finally return."

"You won't be sorry, Papa," said Dolores.

Forcing a grim smile, their father thought, *But I already am.*

D OLORES AND SONYA Aguirre stood together, hand in hand, beside their brother's grave. The soil that covered his remains still had a fresh-turned look about it, but they knew the desert sun would bake that out within a few more days.

"I didn't think he would agree to let us go," Dolores said.

"We gave him no choice," Sonya answered. "Now, at least, he can absolve himself of guilt whatever happens."

"You don't think we will succeed?"

"*Por supuesto que sí*," Sonya said. "Of course I do. But we must be prepared for . . . difficulties."

Dolores nearly laughed aloud at that gross understatement. "Difficulties, certainly," she granted.

Crossing into Mexico for starters, with their foreman and a small team of handpicked vaqueros, tracking ruthless killers and avoiding *federales* who were equally as bad. From there, they had to trace their missing horses, with the raiders who had stolen them, and, they hoped, before the herd was broken up for sale across two states or more. If *that* could be accomplished, then they merely had to take the murderous *bandidos* by surprise, eliminate enough of them to liberate the herd or what was left of it, and then successfully retreat across the border to New Mexico.

Where, if Lieutenant Colonel Stern made good upon his threat, they might all be arrested by the U.S. Army under charges pending from the State Department, for invading Mexico.

The only way to face that list and deal with it, Dolores knew, was taking one step at a time.

"Has Clint told you which hands he has selected?"

Sonya feigned bewilderment. "Told *me*. Why would he tell—"

Dolores stopped her sister with a knowing smile. "Because you seem to share a certain confidence. Do you deny that much, *hermana*?"

"Well . . ." Sonya was blushing as she said, "He mentioned certain names. Unmarried men, younger where possible."

"And will they be enough, do you suppose?"

"I wonder about that myself. I do have one idea that might assist us."

"What would that be?" asked Dolores.

Hesitating for another moment, Sonya finally replied, "We have some friends among the Mescaleros."

"And have you suggested that to Clint?" Dolores asked.

"Not yet. I hoped we might present it to him as a thought we shared."

"Surprise him with it, eh? Well, if we're going to . . ."

"There's no time like the present," Sonya finished for her twin.

Dolores nodded, and they spent a final moment with Eduardo, praying silently for his assistance by whatever means were feasible for one no longer present in the living world. Then, linking hands, they departed from his grave site and went off to drop their bomb of a surprise on Clint Parnell.

You MEAN THAT?" Clint asked both of them together. "Mescaleros?"

Neither of the sisters should have been surprised by his reaction. While their family had certain friends among the Mescalero Apaches, that nation's interaction with whites and Hispanics alike had been frequently hostile, bloodstained, and bitter.

Mescalero Apaches were, in fact, divided historically into at least ten separate bands, which might collaborate or battle one another as their needs and territory dictated. Scattered across America's Southwest and northern Mexico, they included the Chilpaines (from the mountains south and west of Pecos River); the Ch'laandé ("Antelope Band People," from New Mexico's Tularosa Basin); the Dzithinahndé ("Mountain Ridge Band," of northern Chihuahua and Coahuila); the Guhlkahéndé ("People of the Plains," centered on the Texas Panhandle); the Natahéndé ("Mescal People," between the Rio Grande and Pecos River); the Nit'ahéndé ("People at the Edge of the Earth," found mainly in New Mexico's Sierra Blanca); the Tahuundé ("Mountains Extending into the River People," found on both sides of the Pecos River in New

Mexico and Texas); the Tsebekinéndé ("Rock House People," centered on the Nuevo Casas Grandes in Chihuahua); the Tsehitcihéndé ("People of Hook Nose," found throughout the Guadalupe Mountains of northern Coahuila and Chihuahua); the Tuetinini ("No Water People," also from northern Coahuila and Chihuahua); and the Tuintsundé ("Big Water People," of south central Texas and northern Coahuila).

Parnell was familiar with all of the bands, to varying degrees, although his closest ties—perhaps as close as any white man could profess—lay with the Ch'laandé, whose hunting grounds were close to the Aguirre hacienda. After sporadic years of intermittent war between them, Alejandro had forged ties of friendship with the Antelope Band People, hiring some to work around his spread, allowing others to hunt game around the limits of his property to feed their families.

Would they respond if he invited them to join an expedition into Mexico?

Perhaps, if they were properly rewarded and their tribe were promised compensation for whichever warriors fell along the way.

The only way that he could know for sure was to approach their leaders and find out.

And once a Mescalero gave his word, there was no turning back.

Still, Clint had doubts. He asked the sisters, "Have you run this past your father?"

"Not yet," said Dolores. "We were hoping that you would come with us."

"But we're almost certain that he will agree," Sonya amended.

"*Almost* certain?" Parnell's look and tone were equally skeptical.

"He has an admiration for their people," said Dolores. "Even when they fought, he recognized their courage."

"And they are renowned for expert tracking," Sonya added.

Clint nearly shook his head, then stopped himself at the last instant. He could not dispute the points the twins had made in favor of allying with the Mescaleros, probably the Ch'laandé, to avoid more wasted time in searching for a contact with them. Still, he understood that crossing into Mexico with Native riders doubled any risk their plan had carried previously. Back before the Alamo, in 1835, Sonora's government had placed a bounty on Apache scalps, specifically one hundred pesos for a male aged fourteen years or more. Soon afterward, a fifty-peso bounty had been tacked on for the hair of women, half that for the scalps of children. Prices soared after the Mexican-American war, and some scalp hunters, like John Glanton's gang, enriched themselves by killing random Mexicans as well. One dead Apache warrior was worth more than most Mexican peasants earned in any given year, but while those heinous laws expanded throughout northern Mexico, remaining on the books for close to half a century, sheer risk eventually drove the scalpers out of business.

Yet still, a brooding legacy of bitterness remained among the people of both sides, and *federales* working for Díaz were not above annihilating tribal villages if they perceived a chance for what some of them deemed as "sport."

Another problem to be dealt with, Parnell thought.

But he told the anxious twins, "All right. Let's find out what your father says."

CHAPTER FIVE

I DO NOT LIKE the added risks involved," said Alejandro, when his foreman finished laying out the plan. Although Clint Parnell had proposed it, Alejandro recognized his daughters' influence at work and heard an echo of their voices in Clint's words.

Clint nodded. Grudgingly admitted, "I was thinking that myself, jefe, but—"

"Even so," the hacienda's owner interrupted, "I reluctantly agree."

Three pairs of eyes blinked back at him, Parnell starting to frown, apparently confused, while Sonya and Dolores broke out into smiles, confirming Alejandro's first impression of the notion's origin.

Before one of the twins could speak, their father pressed ahead. "Two things I must insist upon," he said. "First, Clint and I will ride alone to the Ch'laandé village."

"Jefe—"

Before Clint could protest, Alejandro cut him off.

"Their friendship is primarily with me," he said. "For them to honor this entreaty, it must seem to be my personal request."

He saw Clint's frown and caught the worried look exchanged between his daughters. Alejandro was expecting it when Sonya said, "But, Papa, what about your injury?"

"Never mind that," he replied. "It pains me but is healing. I must speak to Nantan personally, as one headman to another."

Nantan—"spokesman" in the native tongue of the Ch'laandé—was chieftain of the local tribe, a few years Alejandro's senior, battle-scarred and proud. It must be his decision whether to lend a few of his young men for the excursion onto hostile soil.

"And the second point, jefe?" Clint asked.

"We offer the Apaches the same terms we shall apply to our vaqueros. First, no men with wives or children. Second, all must freely volunteer. And finally, we will negotiate fair payment to the men who ride with us, as well as to the tribe itself. For those who fall along the way, if any, there must be indemnity."

"Makes sense," Clint said, although his tone said he was having doubts about the plan originally offered as his own.

"They will have guns and ponies of their own," Aguirre noted. "We shall supplement whatever food they bring along with them."

"And if they don't agree?" asked Clint.

"Then we part company and go ahead without them," Alejandro said. "Tomorrow morning is the latest that our party can afford to leave."

And as Aguirre knew too well, they were already lagging untold miles behind the raiders who had struck his hacienda three nights earlier. Each passing hour placed them that much farther out of reach unless some unknown circumstance delayed their flight. Nothing could be predicted or anticipated except trouble, once his people crossed the Rio Grande and began the chase that might lead them nowhere except to bloody, dusty death.

How long that search might last could not be guessed. In the worst-case scenario, they might be ambushed early on, by the *bandidos* they were tracking or by *federales*, neither showing any mercy to intruders from *el norte*. Another possibility: that they might chase a phantom trail for days or even weeks on end, defeated finally by the knowledge that their quest had failed and nothing lost could ever be restored, nothing put right.

But that would not forestall the effort being made.

Whatever consequence it brought about, they must at least attempt to balance out the scales or die in the attempt.

B EFORE THE TERMS of their enlistment in a private war had been explained, every vaquero on Aguirre's ranch had volunteered to join the hunt. They had lost friends during the raid and, worse, their self-respect, a debt of honor that they owed to their jefe for failing to protect his herd.

A moan of disappointment greeted Alejandro's order that no men with families would be considered for the hunting party. Their jefe would have no widows and no orphans left behind. Some of the married men tried pleading with their boss, ignoring the expressions of anxiety written across the faces of their wives, but all in vain. Aguirre thanked them all but stood firm on his original decision limiting the team to bachelors in fighting trim. That ultimately narrowed down the field of prospects to five men.

Their foreman, Clint Parnell, would serve as leader,

while his function at the hacienda was assumed by José Esperón for the duration. Other members of the posse would be Joaquín Cantú, Ignacio Fuentes, Arturo Lagüera, and Paco Yáñez, ranging in age from twenty-one to roughly thirty-five. Upon selection, they shook hands with fellow members of the hacienda's staff who had not made the cut, and then fell out to organize their mounts and trail gear for the task that lay ahead of them.

That would include whatever guns and ammunition each possessed, plus bedrolls and canteens, dusters and neckerchiefs, spare clothing for the trail, and any creature comforts—pipes, tobacco, and the like—that would not weigh them down unnecessarily. Provisions for the trip would be provided by Aguirre's kitchen staff, including smoked or salted meats, hardtack, tortillas, dried beans, hominy, with a few all-purpose cooking tools, the lot assigned to a packhorse known for its easy-going temperament.

While the selected riders gathered up their gear, loaded their guns, and sharpened their knives until they could have served as shaving razors, Alejandro and his foreman saddled up their mounts for a ninety-minute journey to the Mescalero village where Chief Nantan would decide whether to risk the lives of his best warriors on a quest that would not normally concern him.

White men fighting Mexican *bandidos* was no problem for the Ch'laandé tribe, unless Aguirre could induce them to enlist as mercenaries on his side. That role was alien to Mescaleros, although some had taken sides during the War Between the States, typically fighting on the side opposed to slavery.

And if they decided not to join the hunt . . . what then?

Clint would proceed with fewer men and strive to do the best he could against long odds.

That would inevitably make the job more dangerous,
less likely to succeed, but Clint was not a quitter and he
could not change his nature this late in the game.

Whatever happened in the Mescalero village, there
would be no turning back.

THEY CHOSE A buckboard for the journey, drawn by
a matched pair of overo geldings. Both men traveled fully armed with long guns and six-shooters, as
prepared as they could be for any danger met along the
way until they reached their destination.

Two scouts spotted them when they were still a mile
out from the nameless village, closing on the buckboard with their single-shot Sharps carbines cocked,
their index fingers flush against the trigger guards.
One of them seemed to recognize Aguirre, although
Clint possessed no memory of meeting either mounted
rifleman before. He noted that their ponies were unshod in standard Mescalero style and ridden bareback,
with reins made from handwoven rope.

The older of the riders raised his open left hand to
Aguirre, asking him in Spanish whether he had any
business with Chief Nantan. Alejandro answered in
the same language, briefly explaining that he had an
offer for the chief and elders of the tribe. After a hastily whispered conversation, the first Mescalero who
had spoken told Aguirre and his foreman to proceed,
escorted to the settlement by his companion.

The last mile struck Parnell as the longest of their
journey from the hacienda, though he understood that
was illusory, based on his heightening anxiety. As they
approached the cluster of some forty tipis—conical
tents stitched from animal skins with vents at their
peaks for emission of smoke—Clint noted men, women,
and children coming out to greet them. The adults

seemed wary, and most of the men were armed, while younger faces mirrored curiosity at the advent of unexpected visitors.

Chief Nantan stood before his lodge, the largest in the village, by the time their escort stopped and signaled Alejandro to rein in his team at a respectful distance from the headman's tipi. Parnell had not seen Nantan for three years, give or take, and now he saw the chief had put on weight since then, his hair shot through with streaks of gray that somehow made him look stronger, more resolute, than at the last occasion of their meeting.

Nantan raised an open hand as Alejandro pulled up short, addressing Parnell's boss in what Clint took to be the Mescalero's native tongue. Aguirre answered fluently in the same language, handed Clint the buckboard's reins, and climbed down from the driver's seat with barely any hint that he was freshly wounded.

Nantan saw it, all the same, switching to English as he said, "You have been injured, *nitis*." Parnell recognized the Mescalero word for friend before the chief continued, saying, "We were told of the attack upon your home. I grieve the passing of your son and loss of property."

"You have my gratitude. It's for that reason we have come."

"Oh, yes?"

"We need your help if you believe it to be possible."

Nantan considered that, not quite frowning, then half turned toward his lodge and said, "Come in. We talk."

Parnell stayed on the buckboard's high seat until Alejandro gestured for him to climb down and trail his elders to the tipi. Handing off the reins to their escort, Clint left his weapons where they were, following Nantan and his jefe through a flap into the tent.

A fire was burning in the middle of the lodge's floor, inside a ring of stones on desert sand, but clever ventilation drew the smoke away, upward, before it irritated eyes or throats. Two women waited in the tipi, one approximately Nantan's age, the other some years younger, until both were sent away with an instruction Clint could not translate. As if on cue, three other Mescalero men entered the lodge, circling the fire, until all five within had formed a ring and taken seats on blankets spread around the ring of stones.

When they were settled in, Nantan spoke first. "What is this help you seek, *nitis*?" he asked.

Aguirre kept the story short, since Nantan had already heard of the nocturnal raid. He spent more time explaining how the U.S. government had failed him, ruling out pursuit of the *bandidos* while insisting that Aguirre take no action of his own accord.

"You plan to disobey them," Nantan said, stating a fact, not questioning.

"I have no choice," said Alejandro. "Once *ladrones* learn that they can victimize my family and face no consequence, we shall be finished in the territory."

Clint picked up the Spanish word for thieves and waited for Nantan to ask his next question.

"How would you have my people help?" Nantan inquired.

Aguirre raised a hand to lightly touch his wounded shoulder. "With my injury," he said, "I cannot travel fast or far enough to overtake the men responsible. Clint here will lead four of our best men, but their numbers were depleted by the raid. They face perhaps ten times as many enemies."

"You come for warriors, then," Nantan observed.

"If you can spare them, old friend. No men pledged to wives and families. I am prepared to pay in gold and any other form of compensation that you may require."

Nantan turned to the other Mescaleros, village elders by the look of them, and whispered conversation passed between them. Clint could not keep up with it, simply observing as the chief and his advisers spoke among themselves. Aguirre seemed to catch the gist of what they said but kept his face composed, expressionless, until Nantan nodded and turned to face his guests once more.

"We can spare five men," he said, "but they must be volunteers. I cannot order them to risk their lives for you."

Aguirre nodded. Said, "My riders volunteered as well."

"Their pay depends on how long they are gone. One dollar each, per day, or the equivalent in food."

Clint did the math, came up with the equivalent of what Aguirre paid his hired hands on the hacienda. Figured it was not a bad deal, and significantly more than any peon earned across the border.

"And for a warrior who does not return?" Nantan inquired.

"Whatever you consider fair, *nitis*," Aguirre said.

"Five dollars."

Call it a month's wages, give or take a couple of days.

"Agreed," said Alejandro.

Nantan nodded. Said, "Then let us smoke on it before I call for volunteers."

WHEN THEY HAD finished with the smoking ritual, passing around a feathered pipe loaded with *kinnikinnick*—a mixture of regular tobacco with assorted herbs and barks from desert shrubbery—Nantan led his three elders from the tipi with his guests in tow. Outside, the Mescalero villagers stood waiting to discover what would happen next.

Clint and Alejandro watched and listened while Nantan explained the situation to his people in their native language. Parnell followed little of it, speaking next to no Ch'laandé, but he reckoned that the chief was spelling out Aguirre's offer, putting out a call for volunteers. It was instructive in a way, watching the older Mescalero braves whisper among themselves, most looking dubious, while womenfolk and minors huddled closer to their parents.

When the chief had finished, five young men stepped up, forming a line of volunteers. From the varied expressions on their faces, some of them were eager for the hunt, while others kept their feelings hidden behind bland postures, revealing little or nothing.

Nantan seemed satisfied with the selection ranged before him and he introduced them to Aguirre, starting on the left end of the lineup. Kuruk was the first, with hair of medium length, broad shoulders, and a half smile brightening his face. Clint pegged his age as somewhere in the early twenties, though he held himself with confidence that spoke of greater age. His name, according to the chief, meant "bear."

Next up, to Kuruk's right, was Goyathlay, translated to "yawner" from Ch'laandé. Clint supposed that might explain his vaguely sleepy look, but there was something in his eyes that let an adversary see he was alert, in spite of any seeming outward lassitude. He wore his hair in braids and had large hands that seemed a tad ungainly at the termination of his slender arms.

The third in line was Nantan Lupan—"gray wolf"—and he proved to be the chief's son. Parnell wondered that Nantan did not prefer to keep him safe at home, then thought the young man might have seen that as an insult to his manhood and rebelled against a well-intentioned bid to make him stay home.

The next to last in line was called Itza-chu, meaning

"great hawk," although Clint saw nothing birdlike in his face or build. Of all five volunteers, he was the stockiest and seemed most eager to embark upon their quest. Whether that attitude derived from yearning for adventure or just waiting to get paid, Parnell could not have said with any certainty.

And finally, the chief identified Bimisi, translated as "slippery" in English or *resbaladizo* in Spanish. Nothing about him seemed to justify the name per se, and Parnell hoped it would not indicate a tendency to slip away and hide when things got tough out on the trail.

When Nantan finished with the introductions, Alejandro moved along the line of volunteers from right to left and shook each of their hands in turn, spoke briefly to them, verifying his intent to compensate the volunteers or reimburse the tribe if they should not return. It was agreed for the five warriors to arrive with ponies, guns, and ammunition at the hacienda by first light the next day, ready to depart.

Clint and Alejandro mounted their buckboard after a final round of thanks and shaking hands, starting for home, while Nantan huddled with the volunteers who would be joining them. This time tomorrow, they should be across the Rio Grande into Mexico, and no one could predict what happened next—or who would live to see the journey through.

CHAPTER SIX

The Aguirre Hacienda

THE KITCHEN STAFF served breakfast well before daybreak, at trestle tables set up in the yard. A few older vaqueros looked askance at the young Mescaleros, ancient enmities remembered from a time when things were bloody on the borderlands and racial warfare was the order of the day, but no one stared too long or risked their jefe's wrath by upsetting the plan he had in mind.

If it came off, there would be blood aplenty, but no more spattered across the doorsteps of their homes.

The Mescaleros had arrived on unshod ponies, using blankets in place of saddles, set for double duty as their bedrolls when they camped at night. None came with saddlebags, knowing a packhorse had been set aside for hauling food and other necessaries on the trail, but all were armed for manhunting. All five carried long guns, mostly Sharps carbines, while Goyathlay and

Itza-chu had six-guns tucked under their beaded belts. All carried knives of varied lengths, fine honed. Kuruk and Nantan Lupan also carried tomahawks with brightly painted handles, heads of polished steel.

Clint Parnell watched the Mescaleros on arrival, taking note of their selected mounts. Kuruk's horse was a blood bay, Goyathlay's a smoky cream. Nantan Lupan straddled a cremello. Itza-chu managed a skewbald, while Bimisi sat astride a rabicano. Spirited but well behaved, the animals reminded Parnell of their riders, stuck somewhere between the wild times of their ancestors and what passed now for civilized society.

The morning meal was fried eggs, ham, and biscuits under sausage gravy. Strong black coffee washed it down, and every member of the hunting party went for seconds, knowing that the best part of the day might pass before they ate again. Across the river to their south, even for those who had completed journeys into Mexico or hailed from there, lay terra incognita now. The world had changed for all of them over the past two days and nights. Once they had crossed that borderline, they would be cast in deadly dual roles, as both hunters and prey.

Of those assembled at the outdoor tables, Alejandro spoke the least. His Mescalero reinforcements talked among themselves, their language barely understood beyond their small circle of five. Aguirre's riders told old jokes and stories many had heard before, most talking with their mouths full. Seated to their father's right and left, sisters Dolores and Sonya restricted conversation to their absent brother, letting Papa Alejandro understand their need to make things right.

As if they ever could.

Clint listened, taking in what he could overhear and translate, wondering if he had bitten off more than he might be capable of swallowing. Not breakfast, but its aftermath in Mexico, where every face they saw would be an enemy's or a suspicious stranger's, wondering if it was best to just ignore the interlopers or betray them for the prospect of a small reward.

Clint did not relish this new undertaking, would have gladly palmed it off on someone else if that were possible, but he was cornered now, with no choice but to forge ahead. He still was not at ease with the Aguirre sisters joining in the hunt, and more particularly not Sonya. Although the sisters were supposedly identical, he felt more warmth for Sonya than Dolores, even knowing that he should not have a favorite between his jefe's daughters or aspire to any more between them than a friendship spanning years.

Despite his elevated rank as foreman of the hacienda, he would never be a member of the family, could not replace Eduardo in his role as Alejandro's son. But if he could retrieve the stolen herd, or most of it at least, while meting out a taste of vengeance to the *bandidos* responsible . . .

What then?

Was there a chance he could find greater favor in his jefe's eyes, perhaps enough to compensate for having been born Anglo on the north side of the Rio Grande?

Don't jump the gun, he thought. *The first thing that you have to do is get your job done and come back alive.*

PEARL-GRAY DAWN WAS breaking in the east as the assembled diners finished mopping up their plates and started making ready for the trail. Clint and the twins were mounted on their normal horses. Joaquín Cantú rode a brindle gelding. Paco Yáñez settled comfortably on a liver chestnut stallion, while Ignacio Fuentes was mounted on a buckskin mare, and a piebald gelding served Arturo Lagüera.

Each vaquero packed a rifle or a shotgun, all wearing at least one pistol. The Aguirre sisters, in addition to their gun belts, each had extra holsters stitched onto their saddles, Sonya sporting one on each side of the saddle horn for three in all. The riders had canteens, lariats, and spare ammunition in their saddlebags. The pinto packhorse showed no strain under their food, cooking utensils, and spare water bags.

The last nightjars were winging home from insect hunting, bound for gullies where they nested on the ground, as Alejandro moved among the dozen riders, making his farewells. He lingered longest with the twins but made no last attempt to talk them out of joining in the hunt. There would have been no point beyond delaying their departure, and he felt it had already been stalled long enough.

The little caravan of thirteen horses headed southward, with the rising sun off to their left. Watching them go, Aguirre wondered whether they could manage to perform the task he'd set for them or if it was already doomed to failure from the start.

But most of all, he wondered whether he would ever see his girls again.

The Rio Grande

At first glance, the river separating Mexico from the United States is not the most impressive waterway. Granted, it winds for nearly nineteen hundred miles between New Mexico and Texas, frequently disputed on the grounds of natural course changes, but the Missouri and the Mississippi both are longer, wider, deeper. The Rio Grande's greatest measured depth is sixty feet, but other places find it only inches deep, while droughts may dry it to a creeping trickle.

The Aguirre posse chose a point where they could wade their animals from one bank to the other without having to dismount. The danger there was not in being swept away and drowned.

Instead, the peril came from being seen.

It was full daylight, with the desert heating up around them, as they scanned the river's length as far as human eyes could see, alert to any sign of a patrol on either side.

The risk, as Clint Parnell knew, was threefold.

Six years earlier, mounted watchmen from the U.S. Department of Commerce and Labor had begun erratic patrols of the river from their base of operations at El Paso, Texas. Fortunately, they never numbered more than seventy-five men in total, spread out across 724 miles between their headquarters and San Diego, California, assigned primarily to head off Asian laborers trying to circumvent the 1882 Chinese Exclusion Act. They rarely bothered Mexicans unless an untaxed pack train crossed their path, and the patrols had zero interest in whatever Americans might haul across the border, headed southward.

On the other side, Díaz's *federales* stood watch, and while there were more of them—some thirty thousand on official rolls—they were dispersed throughout Old Mexico's 762,000 square miles, pursuing bandits, smugglers, and determined rebels against *el porfiriato*. Clint knew that his party's *federale* problem would depend not only on random encounters with the troops, but on *which* troops they met.

Díaz's army was a patchwork quilt including old men in the ranks, incompetent commanders, and some units that were little more than bandits in their own right. Those extorted tribute from wayfarers headed north or south, had nasty reputations for assaulting women, and sometimes looted whole villages, stealing whatever came to hand, from food to meager hoarded cash.

And then, there was the *other* threat, from roving parties of *bandidos*, who might loot and kill for profit or pretend they served some higher cause, whether political or religious, as "liberators" of the peasant class they generally preyed upon. When bandits struck a group of travelers, survivors were a rarity. Those who survived the first encounter generally wound up without horses, weapons, even clothes in many cases, left to roam the desert waste until its lack of water, heat by day, or cold by night eventually finished them.

Apaches, in particular, were often slain on sight by either *federales* or *bandidos*, from race hatred or in hopes of claiming a reward for scalps.

All that passed through Clint Parnell's mind as he approached the river, but he wasted no time moping over it before he led the team and their packhorse across, the Rio Grande's murky water barely rising to their horses' knees at midstream. No one barred their way, but every member of the posse kept a firearm cocked and ready, just in case.

Once on the other side, their search began in earnest, and Chihuahua threatened to obstruct them every mile along the way—assuming they could even find their way at all.

They had no trail to follow through the state named for the much larger Chihuahuan Desert, which sprawled over 194,000 square miles from Albuquerque and El Paso southward to Durango and the northern part of Zacatecas. And if broiling desert were not adequate impediment, Chihuahua also featured mountains—the Sierra Madre Occidental—and the Copper Canyon system, larger and deeper than Arizona's Grand Canyon.

To that, add more forestland than any other Mexican state, plus vast prairies of short yellow grass, much of it under year-round cultivation. Politically, Chihuahua had been a major battleground for the Mexican-American War of 1846–48, the Reform War of 1854–67, and the Second French Intervention in Mexico, lasting from 1861 to 1867. Its ground had swallowed endless seas of blood and waited placidly for more.

And if all that were not enough, Clint's party had no pointers toward their human quarry or the stolen horses they were hoping to retrieve.

Ascensión, Chihuahua, Mexico

Zapata's messenger arrived as Pancho Villa and his aides were sitting down to lunch in a cantina, ringed by bodyguards. Arriving out of breath, his stallion lathered, he risked life and limb through his insistence that he must see Villa instantly and pass along his master's words.

Villa called for cerveza for his unexpected guest and watched the rider guzzle it before he asked, "What is so *importante* that you manage to forget the common courtesies?"

"Señor Zapata wishes you to know that he will be delayed," the young man answered, remembering to add jefe at the last instant.

"Delayed longer than he has been up to now?" Villa inquired, pretending that he did not hear his chief lieutenants sniggering.

"An unexpected clash with *federales*, jefe."

"As opposed to an expected skirmish, then?"

More laughter from his men, half of them with their mouths full of tortillas and frijoles.

"There was an informer," said the messenger, "but he has been identified."

"Belatedly," Villa surmised.

"It was his last betrayal."

"So, a little present for the *federales*, then."

"*Sí*, jefe."

"And the horses that we have procured for him? When does he plan to take delivery?" Villa inquired.

"As soon as possible. Señor Zapata is redoubling efforts to accommodate you."

"Better late than never, I suppose."

"He asks for your indulgence, jefe."

"Does he? And for how long might that be, pray tell?"

"A few more days, at most."

"He realizes that we may be forced to relocate at any moment or risk losing everything?"

"*Sí*, jefe. That is understood."

"I hope so," Villa answered. "Or I may be forced to find another buyer for the animals I cannot use myself."

"Señor Zapata means to keep his bargain with you. He is counting on it, jefe."

"As am I," Villa replied. "But if he cannot reach us soon . . ."

The messenger shifted upon his bench seat. Said, "Perhaps if I might be permitted to observe the animals and count them . . ."

Villa's full-throated laugh cut short the young man's words. When the hilarity had passed, Pancho replied, "*¿Por qué no?* Why not? I can show you where we keep them safe and then dismiss my guards while you ride back and tell Emiliano where to find them, ripe for taking. Would you find that satisfactory?"

The young man's eyes flared, and he might have paled if he had not been so dark skinned. "No, jefe," he replied, half stammering. "I had no such idea, I promise you!"

"In that case, do you carry gold? Have you authority to finish our negotiations?"

"No, jefe," the rider almost whispered in reply.

"Then ask me no more foolish questions, *niño*. This is man's work, not a game for children."

The answer came back sounding almost strangled. "*Sí, señor. Por favor discúlpame.*"

"You are forgiven, naturally," Villa answered, smiling. "This time only, mind you."

"And what should I tell Señor Zapata, jefe?"

"That our deal is still in place, provided he arrives in timely fashion. As a knowledgeable man, he must know that I cannot wait indefinitely for him to appear."

"I will convey your words precisely," said the young man.

"And I will expect," Villa replied, "that my next conversation on this matter shall be with Emiliano, speaking for himself. *Vaya con Dios, chico.*"

Los Tríos, Chihuahua, Mexico

The village of Los Tríos was not large, but after miles of empty desert since Clint Parnell's party crossed the border, it seemed like a fair first stop, where they could fill canteens, water their horses, and perhaps obtain some useful information. In a settlement that size, the recent passage of *bandidos* driving more than fourteen hundred stolen horses should have been remembered until something more exiting came along.

The foremost question in Clint's mind was whether any locals would see fit to speak with strangers, particularly when an Anglo rider led the group and it included five Apaches.

Clint reined in his dapple gray gelding atop a low ridge spiked with cactus, signaling the others do likewise. No one spoke as he reached back into his saddle-bag and retrieved a small spyglass, extending it before he raised it to his right eye, squinting with his left.

He knew nothing about the settlement beyond the fact that its name translated to English as "The Three." Three *what*? It might be anything from streams of water, precious in the desert, to enumeration of the first explorers who had put down roots and built adobe structures on the spot. From what his telescope revealed at half a mile distant, Clint saw the settlement consisted of two dozen buildings with a dirt road passing through the midst of them, the town divided roughly into halves.

Its central feature, like so many other villages in Mexico, was a well built out of stones. The largest structure was a weathered church, across the central square from a cantina and a blacksmith's shop that opened on the dusty thoroughfare. He saw no townsfolk on the street, but instantly picked out two dozen *federales*, presently dismounted, beating dust out of their khaki uniforms while watering their horses at the fountain.

"Soldiers," he told the other members of his team. "Looks like we won't be stopping here."

"Can we not wait until they leave?" Dolores asked him.

"Two problems there," Clint said. "First thing, we don't know if they're passing through or staying overnight. It could be hours yet before we figure that out, one way or another, then we've wasted half a day and have to circle round them in the dark."

"But if they *do* leave soon," Sonya chimed in, "we could ask questions, *¿sí?*"

"We could," Clint granted, "but we might be stirring up a hornet's nest. These villagers aren't stupid. They could take one look at us, riding with Mescaleros, looking for a bandit gang and lots of horses, then they think about the *federales*. All we need is one guy tipping off the soldiers, maybe hoping for a small reward, and they'd be hunting us. Might even have some kind of deal with the *bandidos*, given how things are down here these days."

"So, what then?" asked Dolores.

"Best idea that I can think of is to ride around Los Tríos while the *federales* are distracted. It's a couple miles out of our way, but maybe we can happen on a farm, even another settlement, and ask our questions there."

Nobody argued with Clint after that. The Mescaleros riding with his party did not have to understand Clint's words to realize that soldiers dawdling in their path meant trouble, and the rest—aside from the Aguirre twins—were long accustomed to obeying orders from the hacienda's foreman.

Clint flipped a mental coin, deciding that it made no difference whether they circled to the west or east in circumnavigating Los Tríos. He chose the latter, reined his dapple gray back down the far side of the ridgeline, placing it between his riders and the settlement. The others followed him, unspeaking, hands on weapons casually but prepared for anything.

Clint reckoned that the best outcome for this encounter with the army would be no contact at all. The time might come, and soon, when they would have to face down soldiers, bandits—anyone at all, in fact—and when that happened, Parnell was prepared to join the bloodletting. But if they could avoid it for the moment, even put the killing off until they overtook the raiders who had stolen Alejandro's herd, so much the better.

On the other hand, what if they *never* found the horses or their rustlers in the vastness that was northern Mexico? What would he tell his jefe then?

Forget that, Parnell thought.

He was not going back without the herd, some part of it, or at the very least an explanation of his failure to perform as planned. In that case, he would quit and leave his job, the rancho, all of it behind.

And in that moment, Clint decided he would rather go down fighting than to turn back empty-handed, knowing Alejandro's trust in him had been a hideous mistake.

CHAPTER SEVEN

Laguna de Guzmán, Chihuahua

TWELVE FIGURES LAY concealed in shadows cast by a long row of Texas pinyon pines, watching the lake below them, to their north. Fed by the Casas Grandes River, Lake Guzmán—located at an altitude of some 3,885 feet, between the Sierra Tapalpa and the Sierra el Tigre —was glassy flat under the late afternoon sun. Its waters would be clear and cold, the perfect draw for varied species of high-desert prey.

The band of Chiricahua hunters, led by one Alchesay ("warrior chief"), had waited since midmorning for a bear or deer to show itself, and the Apaches were becoming restless, though a stranger could not have divined as much from simply watching them. Young men, they had learned patience during boyhood, hunting small game for their families, but gladly tackled larger targets when they were available.

The warning, when it came, was whispered to the

others by Sahale, whose name translated to English as "falcon," a tribute to his keen long-distance eyesight. "Riders!" he alerted his companions, pointing off to the northwest of Alchesay's selected hiding place.

The rest followed Sahale's gesture and beheld a line of thirteen horses, twelve with riders, the thirteenth laden with what could only be supplies. Along the line of prostrate bodies, eyes narrowed and muscles tensed, each man weighing the odds and wondering whether they could take the travelers, how many of their own would suffer wounds or worse before the issue was resolved.

The other Chiricahuas in the band were Bodaway ("fire maker"), Cassadore ("angry"), Taklishim ("gray one"), Diablo ("devil"), Tarak ("star"), Jlin-Litzoque ("yellow horse), Calian ("warrior"), Illanipi ("amazing"), Elan ("evergreen"), and Baishan ("knife"). All had been hunted by the *federales* in their time, and all had managed—so far—to survive.

Alchesay scanned the line of riders, noting that a white man led them, followed by six Mexicans, two women and four men. The women instantly intrigued him—both attractive and apparently identical—twins being rare among his own people. The last five riders—clearly Mescaleros, the ancestral enemies of the Chiricahuas, although white men generally lumped them all together as Apaches—made Alchesay scowl. The final red man in the lineup held the reins of the approaching party's packhorse loosely in one hand, the pinto mare obliging him without resistance.

"What should we do, Alchesay?" Bodaway inquired.

"We have one more rifle than they do," Alchesay replied. "And two of them are women."

With a sneer, Diablo added, "Half of them are Mescaleros," spitting his contempt onto a bed of pine needles.

"It is decided, then," their war chief said. "Be ready on my signal."

For Alchesay, being ready simply meant he had to cock his venerable Henry lever-action rifle, drawing back its hammer with his thumb. The forty-five-inch weapon weighed nine and one quarter pounds with fifteen .44-caliber rimfire rounds in its tubular magazine and one more ready in the firing chamber. Unlike the newer Winchesters, it had no wooden forearm to protect a shooter's left hand if the barrel overheated during combat, but the under-barrel magazine served well enough in that regard, provided Alchesay used normal caution.

His companions carried a motley collection of rifles—Sharps carbines, stolen Winchesters, and a breech-loading Remington Rolling Block model that Diablo carried, taken from a settler's homestead, chambered for the .45-70 Government cartridge, capable of dropping man-sized targets at six hundred yards. Lake Guzmán lay within effective killing range for all of them, but accuracy was required, as much as for the targets they desired to miss, as in the case of those the warriors meant to kill.

The *mexicana* women, for example, interested Alchesay. Although both carried weapons, he was not convinced that they could hold their own in battle. And if captured, they could offer brief amusement to his fighters before they were bartered in Juárez as slaves.

But first, the men must be eliminated.

Staring one-eyed down the Henry's twenty-four-inch barrel, over open sights, Alchesay slipped his index finger through the rifle's trigger guard, drew in a breath, and held it as he started taking up the slack.

*Y*OU NEVER HEAR *the shot that kills you.*
Clint Parnell had heard that statement uttered time and time again, keeping his peace although he

knew it was not true. Most individuals who died from gunshot wounds, in his experience, were not killed instantly by bullets ripping through their hearts or brains. Gut wounds, particularly, were renowned for causing slow and agonizing deaths. Even a bullet to the arm or leg could bleed a body dry if it severed a major vein or artery, and sepsis from neglected wounds might claim a victim's life days later—sometimes even weeks, if gangrene should set in.

The first shot angled toward his riders from a nearby tree line, therefore, made Clint flinch, before he heard a cry of pain behind him that told the foreman someone else was either hit or startled badly by the gunfire's echo. Seconds later, even as Clint turned his dapple gray toward the lake's shore and the cover he had spotted there, made up of silver spruce, Durango juniper, and jumbled boulders, gunfire was crackling around him, bullets humming through the air like hornets swarming to defend their nest.

"Follow me and go to ground!" he shouted to the others, without looking back immediately to find out if they obeyed. Some of his party were returning fire without clear targets, but the hoofbeats closing in behind his gelding told Parnell that most of them, at least, were following his lead.

He thought about the sisters, glancing back just as he reached the screen of rocks and trees he hoped would shelter them, and saw both twins stampeding toward the lake, hunched over their respective saddle horns, to make their bodies smaller targets for the unseen snipers. Close behind them, his vaqueros followed, galloping, with Nantan's Mescaleros and their packhorse bringing up the rear.

No, wait! One of the tribesmen's horses ran without a rider on its back. It was a rabicano, meaning that Bimisi, whether wounded or just clumsy, had lived up to his slippery name and tumbled from his mount, lost somewhere in the rush for cover.

Clint dismounted, found cover behind a man-sized boulder, crouching with his Browning Auto-5 in hand. Before departing Alejandro's hacienda, he had switched the shotgun's normal buckshot load for full-bore slugs with rifling stamped into the nine-ounce lead projectile, compensating for the Auto-5's smooth barrel interior. Fired through the Browning's twenty-eight-inch barrel, slugs transformed the gun into a deadly hunting rifle, accurate out to seventy-five yards, more than doubling the weight of a standard .30-06 projectile.

Thus armed—his other riders crouched along the tree line to his right and left, their horses trotting toward the lake's shore—Parnell settled in, awaiting the assault that would decide whether they lived or died.

S ONYA AGUIRRE KNELT beside her twin, their shoulders almost touching, staring toward the tree line opposite where gun smoke rose like wisps of lake mist, sending rifle bullets crackling overhead. Their cover was the trunk and upthrust branches of a lightning-struck Tarahumara oak, fallen sometime last winter from the state of its decay, but still a decent bullet stop.

"I count a dozen rifles," Sonya told Dolores. "You?"

"The same."

Outnumbered by a single sniper, then, since they had lost one of the Mescaleros to the first barrage. His body lay exposed in no-man's-land, where he had tumbled from his mount, facedown in yellow grass with fresh blood soaking through his buckskin shirt. They could survive those odds, perhaps, assuming that their unknown enemies got restless soon and risked a foray toward the lake across the intervening open ground.

Sonya was ready for them with her Springfield Model

1903 rifle, Dolores sighting down the twenty-eight-inch barrel of her Winchester Model 1895, loaded with .30-30 rounds. Both sisters had the skill to pick off riders at one hundred yards, but only if their enemies were visible.

So far, no luck on that.

Sonya decided she could spare an aught-six round to test their would-be killers, but with no clear view of them, she had to count their puffs of rifle smoke again, selecting one almost directly opposite her hiding place, and sighting on a point where she surmised the shooter must be hunkered down.

Calculating range, she raised the Springfield's flip-up rear sight, waited for her unseen enemy to fire again, and stroked her rifle's trigger before she could hear the sharp crack of the shot fired from the tree line toward Lake Guzmán. Riding out the Springfield's recoil while her bullet flew downrange, Sonya could not be sure if she had hit her man or only frightened him, but after one full minute counting puffs of hostile rifle smoke, she could have sworn that there was one less on their adversaries' firing line.

She kept that supposition to herself and shifted for another try. Sonya had learned throughout her life that boasting of uncertain victories often resulted in embarrassment and endless teasing by her two siblings.

Only *one*, of course, now that nameless enemies had killed brother, Eduardo, robbing Sonya's father of his cherished heir.

Determined not to let that loss go unavenged, she heard her sister's Winchester unload a shot beside her, to her right, while lining up her Springfield's sights to see if she could score another long-range hit.

Perhaps a hit, she instantly corrected in her mind, hoping their unseen enemies would tire of dueling from a distance and either attack in force across the open ground before her or retreat to lick their wounds and wait for other prey.

In Sonya's heart, she hoped that they would charge and let her have a chance to repay blood with blood.

ALCHESAY HALF TURNED from his prone position on the tree line, glancing to his left, and saw Diablo twitching on the grass where he had fallen, bleeding heavily from a wound in his upper chest. His fellow Chiricahua's tremors were already fading, telling Alchesay the gunshot had been fatal or had stunned Diablo to the point where he was losing consciousness.

In either case, the steady outpouring of blood marked his companion for an early death.

Off to Alchesay's right, a yelp of pain distracted him. He spun in that direction to find Calian clamping a hand against his scalp above his left ear, rivulets of crimson trickling from between his fingers where they pressed against his skull.

That was a graze, survivable, but Alchesay guessed that his war party would only suffer further injuries by staying where they were, exchanging gunfire with the party marked as easy victims, only to be proven wrong.

As leader of the band, Alchesay had a choice to make within the next few moments. They could either slip away defeated, carrying their dead and wounded from the field, or else attack their chosen adversaries in a screaming charge against their fortified position by the lake. The first choice was humiliating and might jeopardize his place as war chief, while the latter could amount to suicide.

But if they charged and pulled it off . . .

Before he fled from the San Carlos Apache Reservation up in Arizona Territory, slipping into Mexico and living as a renegade, Alchesay had been no one, going nowhere. Twelve braves had dared to follow him, two of them killed before this morning's hunt, while prowling through Sonora toward Chihuahua, raiding isolated farms, and killing solitary *mexicano* travelers. The ten survivors—nine now—had accepted him as their leader and pledged to follow him as long as he proved worthy.

Now, however . . .

Alchesay decided he would put it to a vote, rather than forcing his companions who were still alive to sacrifice their honor by retreating, or to throw their lives away on what might prove to be a foolish move. Calling along their ragged line, he managed to achieve a momentary ceasefire, speaking in their native tongue and confident that even if his enemies might overhear some of his words, the meaning would escape them.

There were Mescaleros on the other side, of course, but variations in their dialect reduced the sometimes hostile tribes to using Spanish or sign language on rare occasions when they tried communicating with each other.

"Brothers, we have lost Diablo," he informed the warriors who had thus far failed to notice. "Calian is injured, but perhaps can fight."

On hearing that, Calian nodded in agreement, wiped his bloody hand along his buckskin pants, and scowled his willingness to carry on.

"Shall we retreat?" Alchesay asked his braves. "Or shall we finish what we've started, even at the risk of life itself?"

He scanned the firing line, meeting nine pairs of eyes in turn. Each nodded toward their chief, although a couple—Bodaway and Taklishim—delayed just long enough to make Alchesay wonder whether they would vote to cut and run. At last, though, all agreed to join his bold action that would either leave their band victorious or else give inspiration for a warrior's song no other living voice might ever sing.

Accepting their decision, Alchesay ordered, "Mount up! We ride to victory or death!"

THE ATTACK BEGAN with shrieking war cries from beyond the tree line where Clint Parnell's enemies had opened fire ten minutes earlier. If it had been Clint's call, he would have had his fighters try for a surprise assault, instead of telegraphing their intent, but when the riders broke from cover, quickly recognizable as Chiricahua, their technique was easily explained.

Scanning the field before him with his Browning Auto-5 shouldered, Clint saw ten riders charging out of cover, toward the jumbled rocks and fallen trees where his party had taken shelter under fire. The horsemen rode with skill and courage, rifles blazing as they closed the distance from their chosen enemies, their painted faces howling in a bid to terrify the travelers they had mistaken for a group of easy marks.

"Wait for my signal to open up," Clint called to his companions near the lake's shore. When you fire, make each shot count!"

It took a certain strength of nerve to watch the mounted Chiricahuas charging forward, firing long guns in an effort to expose their enemies. Clint wondered how it must have felt to the attackers, galloping headlong with no immediate response. When they had crossed the midway point between their first position and Lake Guzmán, right around the line of no return, Parnell decided they had traveled far enough.

"Now!" he bellowed, and depressed the trigger of his Browning Auto-5, his deer slug drilling one of the advancing Chiricahua, spilling him backward across the taut rump of his pony, landing crumpled on the yellow grass now stained crimson with blood.

Along the shoreline, ten more long guns joined the deadly fusillade. Their firing did not last long, since each shooter was a fair hand and only a couple of them had to fire a second time. By then, the grassy field was littered with corpses and dying braves, some of their ponies bolting from the battleground while others trotted aimlessly about, as if seeking their fallen riders. Clint's Mescalero volunteers moved out from cover then and passed among the wounded, speeding up their deaths with knives or tomahawks to keep from wasting any further ammunition.

That done, Nantan's tribesmen claimed the body of their fellow villager, Bimisi, and prepared to bury him. Unlike some other Native tribes, most nomadic Apaches preferred to bury their dead underground without protracted rituals. When tribesmen died near home, their lodges and other belongings would be torched to ward off evil spirits, but that aspect of Bimisi's funeral would have to wait until his fellow Mescaleros had arrived back in their village.

If they ever did.

One day across the Rio Grande, and Clint had lost one of his party, whittled to eleven members now. He was relieved that Sonya and Dolores had emerged unscathed from the engagement, but it worried him that losing one Apache early on might sow dissension among the remaining four. Would they desert him now that one of them was gone, an object lesson in the danger of their quest?

Clint hoped not, but he never had been able to predict the future and was not beginning now. If the remaining Mescaleros chose to leave, he would not risk the lives of the Aguirre sisters or their ranch hands trying to prevent a rift within their company.

He left that up to fate, hoping that it was past time for his luck to change.

CHAPTER EIGHT

Southeast of Ascensión, Chihuahua

Pancho villa sat astride his black stallion, left hand shading his eyes beneath the brim of his sombrero, staring skyward as a red-tailed hawk circled a hundred feet above his head in clear blue desert sky.

"A hunter much like us, eh, Javier?" he asked his chief lieutenant seated to his left side on a grulla mare.

"*Sí*, jefe," Javier Jurado answered, "but we hope for bigger game."

That much was true beyond the shadow of a doubt. At best, the hawk might bag a kangaroo rat or a desert cottontail, but Villa and his men were after gold. Specifically, they had been tipped by an informer to a *federale* payroll shipment moving through their territory, passing by the point where they were staked out on this very afternoon. The troops were running late, but that was customary for the quality of officers and men Porfirio Díaz employed these days.

Villa removed a watch from his vest pocket, opened it, and saw that it was well past two o'clock. Frowning, he put the watch away and reached down for a leather case that dangled from his saddle horn. Unbuckling its lid, he lifted out a pair of French binoculars made out of brass with a scratched-up black enamel finish.

Thinking of the former *francés* officer he'd slain to get them, with a Lebel Model 1886 rifle that soon ran out of ammunition and was useless to him, Villa had to smile. At least the field glasses had served him well enough over the past few years, and no one to his knowledge ever missed their first owner, a rootless mercenary hired to train Díaz's *federales* in pursuing bandits.

Clearly, he had failed to learn that lesson well enough to save himself.

Scanning the long road southward from his place atop a bushy rise, Villa saw dust rising around a short column of horses—possibly a dozen but no more— advancing toward the point he had selected for his ambuscade.

"At last," he told Jurado. "I'd begun to think the *tontos* might have lost their way."

"How many packhorses, jefe?" Javier asked.

"I only see the one, but it is carrying two wooden chests."

"So, not a wasted effort, then."

"Let us hope not," Villa replied, turning away to rouse his other men where they sat dozing in the desert heat. "*¡Arriba, muchachos!*" he ordered, and his riders scrambled to their feet, leaving whatever shade cactus and spiky Joshua trees had offered for their wait. They drew rifles from saddle boots, pistols from holsters on their belts, and formed a skirmish line below the sandy crest, awaiting Villa's order to proceed.

Villa alone did not reach for a weapon. He was the commander of this operation and would supervise in case it started to unravel unexpectedly. His force was nearly triple the eight *federales* sent by Díaz to defend his rural payroll, and he estimated half the soldiers would be killed or suffer wounds during the first barrage of fire his men unleashed upon Villa's command. Beyond that they would stop the army packhorse one way or another, either leading it back to Ascensión or off-loading the treasure from its carcass, opening the chest, and doling out the riches waiting inside.

In that case, Villa had no fear that any of his caballeros would attempt to pilfer from their take. All knew the penalty for stealing from the gang. All had observed the punishment for that infraction and would fear it more than God's wrath from on high.

"*¡Prepárense!*" he commanded, answered by the click-clack sound of rifles being primed and cocked. "Hold your fire until instructed otherwise."

He did not have to glance along the line to see them nodding in agreement. These were good men. Villa trusted them at least as far as he could see them—or, if need be, to the distance of his pistol's range.

SUBLIEUTENANT RIGOBERTO VALDÉS de Castillo eyed the winding track in front of him through the oval green lenses of fragile sunglasses that were designed to cut the desert's glare but were useless when it came to sparing him from heat. Sweat glistened on his forehead underneath the bill of his peaked cap and streaked the dust he could not escape upon his cheeks.

Valdés was recently promoted through the efforts of an uncle who did business with the government in Ciudad Juárez. The single brass bar on each of his red-rimmed khaki epaulets was still untarnished, but Valdés knew that he must soon begin the nightly ritual of polishing them, with his riding boots and the buttons on his tunic, to present himself before superiors in the best light available. Later, say when he had been promoted to first captain, there would be a lowly private to perform such tiresome chores on his behalf, but in the meantime he knew that appearances were everything.

The payroll transfer was his first significant assignment, and it worried Subteniente Valdés, conscious as he was of brigands wandering around Chihuahua, sometimes exercising more influence on the peasantry than any *federales* fielded by Porfirio Díaz. He had no reason to believe any should be waiting for his party on their journey to Nuevo Casas Grandes, but the sheer uncertainty of it was grating on his nerves.

Valdés was leading nine men, seconded by a grizzled corporal in his midforties who had spent a lifetime in the army, mostly chasing hostile Native tribesmen or abusing hapless campesinos when he had the chance. The rest were privates, two of them first class, the latter placed in charge of managing the packhorse and its precious cargo in four-hour turns.

Each private carried a Mondragón Modelo 1908 rifle chambered for 7×57mm Mauser ammunition, the first self-loading semiautomatic combat rifle adopted by an army. Corporal Eugenio Elias packed a venerable Sharps carbine older than he was, while Valdés wore a holstered 9×19mm Parabellum Luger P08 designed in Germany. In a firefight, Valdés knew the military saber sheathed on his left hip would be no use to him at all.

There was no reason why he should expect an ambush, but superiors had warned him that the moment when he *least* expected trouble might be the most dangerous of all.

"*Un momento, subteniente,*" Corporal Elias called out from his place a yard or two behind the leader's horse.

Valdés reined up, half turning toward his second-in-command. "What is it?" he demanded.

Peering toward a nearby ridgeline, Elias frowned through the stubble of a three-day beard and answered, "There is something—"

But he never finished, as his whiskered face imploded, spewing blood and mangled tissue, while his rumpled campaign hat took flight with a good portion of his scalp inside it.

A split second later, when the echo of a rifle shot reached Valdés, he could almost smell his dreams of swift advancement through the army's upper ranks evaporating into gun smoke.

O VER GUNSIGHTS, PANCHO Villa watched the nearly headless *federale* slither from his saddle, dead before his body flopped onto the sand and gravel surface of the narrow road. The officer in charge, a young sub-teniente, recoiled from the sight of sudden death, then fumbled for his holstered sidearm as Villa's *bandidos* raked the army column with a storm of rifle fire.

"*¡El oficial es mío!*" Villa shouted to be heard above the crackling fusillade. "The officer is mine!" He waved his smoking rifle overhead for emphasis, to make sure his guerrillas understood.

Downrange, some of the *federales* tried returning fire with their Mondragón rifles, but some immediately jammed, perhaps from shoddy maintenance or careless loading of their ten-round magazines. The soldiers who managed to operate their guns were poor shots under pressure, and their Mauser bullets, traveling at some 2,700 feet per second, fired at awkward uphill angles, barely grazed a pair of Villa's snipers before those behind the guns sprawled into dusty death.

Only the young lieutenant still remained upright

astride his mount as Villa galloped down the sandy incline toward him. Grappling with his awkward full flap holster, situated backward on his left hip for a cross-hand draw, the officer was clearly having trouble with it until Villa fired his rifle from a range of thirty feet and pitched the *federale* from his horse, into the dirt.

It was not meant to be a killing shot, but rather left the sublieutenant squirming on his back, reminding Villa of a capsized tortoise. Khaki cloth was going crimson from a shoulder wound, disabling the officer's right arm, putting his pistol permanently out of reach unless he tried to draw it backward with his left hand.

And he had no time to try that now, as Villa cantered up to him and leaned across his saddle horn, assessing the damage he had inflicted on his enemy.

"You are finished I think," he told the wounded officer.

"I'll live to see you face a firing squad," his victim answered back, words rasping from between clenched teeth.

Villa could only smile at that. "Your courage does you credit, but your mission is a failure. Díaz would not thank you for it, had you lived."

The sublieutenant's eyes widened when he heard that, and he made another fumbling effort at his holster, cursing, before Villa got there first. Francisco did not waste another rifle bullet on the *federale*, going for his Mauser C96 "broom-handle" pistol instead.

The weapon was a semiautomatic made in Germany and sold worldwide, to governments and individuals alike. Chambered for 7.63×25mm Mauser rounds, it held ten cartridges in an internal magazine set forward of the trigger and could empty out that load in under fifteen seconds flat, with an effective firing range around 150 feet.

Today, Francisco fired it only once, at a barely eight-foot distance from his target.

When the bullet struck, it punched a dark hole in the sublieutenant's forehead, just above his left eyebrow. The *federale*'s head bounced off the roadway's surface, then the third eye at his brow line filled with blood that ran in streamers down his face and up into his hairline, painting him as if he were a clown made up for *Día de los Muertos*. His recumbent form went slack and he was simply . . . gone.

"Retrieve the packhorse," Villa ordered no one in particular. "And do not touch the payroll chests. We open them together in Ascensión, and anyone who tries to crack them earlier *está muerto. ¿Me escuchan?*"

None of his riders answered, but they heard and understood their leader well enough.

It would be close to sundown when they reached their temporary headquarters, and they could well afford to wait.

Hidalgo del Parral, Chihuahua, Mexico

"It is a miracle that we have come this far, jefe," said Alfonso Soberon.

Sipping cold coffee at his chief lieutenant's side, Emiliano Zapata Salazar nodded his agreement silently. Although raised by ardent parents to revere the Holy Mother Church, Zapata had no faith in miracles these days. He and his men had reached the farthest southern border of Chihuahua more by luck and cunning than by any help from God on high. Along the way, they'd fought two skirmishes with *federales* serving President Díaz, and they would all be sleeping under blankets without any fire tonight in case the soldiers were still hunting them beyond sundown.

Tomorrow was another day, if they survived that long, and they were still some eighty miles southwest of Ascensión, where Pancho Villa was supposed to meet them with the horses he had stolen from New Mexico. Zapata's solitary scout had found him on the road, reporting back that Villa had the animals but grew impatient waiting for Zapata to arrive.

That was unfortunate, but with his thirty-odd riders, Zapata would still need the best part of a week to reach his destination, even if his men were not ambushed by *federales* while en route. And if they were . . .

In that case, he might have no further use for horses in this life—or any life at all.

At thirty years of age, Zapata sometimes felt like an old man. The previous year, he had succeeded aged José Merino as chief elder of Anenecuilco, a village in Morelos, elected by a landslide over two competitors. His pledge had been continuation of Merino's budding land reforms, but he was blocked at every turn by the aristocrats supporting *el porfiriato* and Díaz. Finally, in desperation, he had opted for another course of action, hoping that some of the country's leading brigands, Pancho Villa first among them, might be converts to his revolutionary cause.

But first, Zapata had to meet with Villa personally, close their deal for horses, and take a reading of the man himself. A late arrival in Ascensión—or failure to arrive at all—would not be an auspicious start for their relationship.

The other side of that scenario was that if soldiers met Zapata on the road north, executing him on orders from *el presidente*, then he had no future and it would not matter anyway.

"More coffee, jefe?" Soberon inquired.

Zapata shook his head, dumping the dregs from his tin

mug into the desert sand. "I've had enough," he answered. "We should try to get some sleep before sunrise."

"I'll just sit up a little longer," Alfonso replied.

"*Como desees, amigo*," said Zapata, rising from the rock where he was seated. "As you wish, friend. Our caballeros must be ready at first light."

Ascensión, Chihuahua

Pancho Villa was no fool. He recognized that his *bandidos* were primarily in business for themselves but followed him as long as he put money in their pockets and did not appear too greedy when he cut his own slice of the pie. Accordingly, when he was counting out the *federale* payroll they had liberated, he formed thirty stacks of Caballito pesos on a weathered table outside a run-down café.

Each coin was solid silver, weighing twenty-seven grams. Stamped on the front side was the year and a depiction of Miss Liberty holding a torch and olive branch, riding sidesaddle on a stallion. In the background, framing her, a rising sun dispersed its rays. On the back side was an eagle with its wings spread and a snake clutched in its talons, perched upon a mountaintop or boulder—Villa could not say with certainty—beneath an arch of words reading ESTADOS UNIDOS MEXICANOS.

Villa was irritated that his native country's coins were cast to mimic silver dollars minted in the USA. In time, when Mexico was truly liberated from all foreign influence, he hoped the men in charge might demonstrate greater originality. But in the meantime, he was happy to relieve the Díaz government of any cash it handled carelessly by placing it within reach of his hands.

Francisco formed the stacks of coins methodically, on terms his caballeros had agreed to in advance. From each pile of sixty-three coins he kept four as his own, stacked three for Javier Jurado, and left two for each of his twenty-eight riders. By the time he finished counting, each vaquero walked away with sixty-four pesos, his second-in-command had ninety-six, and Pancho kept one hundred forty-four. He thought that fair enough, since his share bought supplies to feed his men and horses, as well as information for the planning of their future raids.

Meanwhile, under President Díaz, a Mexican father of four would count himself fortunate to earn fifty pesos per year from backbreaking labor, most families having lost 90 percent of their ancestral land to wealthy planters under the corrupt *porfiriato* system's banner of *orden y progreso*—"order and progress."

To Villa and like-minded others, that meant Díaz gave the orders and his cronies monopolized the progress, while the campesinos were abused and robbed by venal *federales*.

But a change was coming. He could smell it on the desert wind.

"Not bad, jefe," Jurado said as Villa finished doling out shares to his gunmen.

"All right for fifteen minutes' work," Villa agreed, "but we should do much better from the horses."

"*Sí,*" Jurado answered. "If Zapata ever gets here."

That could be a problem, Villa realized. The longer he delayed in selling off the stolen herd, the greater were his odds of being run to ground and killed or captured. He could spare another day or two, perhaps, but after that he would be forced to relocate the herd or make other arrangements for its sale, and that would drive a wedge between Zapata and himself.

Villa had enemies enough already, as he realized, to

last him for a lifetime—or to end it, if he ever dropped his guard.

The next few days were critical, but he could not hasten Zapata's pace across Chihuahua, where no end of dangers lay in wait.

"Enough talk of Emiliano for today," he told Jurado.

"Then perhaps tequila, eh?" his strong right hand replied, smiling.

Villa returned the smile, saying, "I thought you'd never ask."

CHAPTER NINE

"WE SHOULD CAMP SOON," Clint Parnell told the Aguirre sisters, after glancing westward, where a radiant sunset was burning down in shades of pink fading toward violet.

"I'm ready," Sonya said, and Parnell saw Dolores nod silent agreement, though she wore a frown.

"Got something on your mind?" he asked the slightly older twin.

"You mean besides the killings? Or the fact that we've achieved nothing today?" Dolores answered.

"Nobody ever thought we'd find the herd our first day out," Parnell reminded her. "As for the rest . . . well, everyone signed on with eyes wide open and expecting trouble."

"I *know* that." Her tone stopped just a fraction short of being bitter. "But I thought if someone died it would have meaning for the task we've undertaken."

Parnell could have said the obvious, that they'd been ambushed by Apache raiders, had fought through it in the end, and that their Mescalero volunteers were not complaining of the battle's outcome. He refrained because Dolores knew all that without being reminded and she didn't need to hear it. She was venting her frustration that they had no solid leads on the *bandidos* they were hunting, and Clint didn't mind—unless a spirit of defeatism infected the surviving members of their team.

Clint reined his dapple gray and turned to face the men strung out behind him. Raised a hand to signal for Kuruk, the leader of their four remaining Mescaleros. When Kuruk caught up to him, Parnell said, "We'll be camping soon. It's time to call the scouts back in."

He had dispatched two of the Mescaleros earlier, Nantan Lupan and Goyathlay, to ride a couple miles ahead and search for any useful tracks or obstacles across their path. Kuruk nodded but did not urge his blood bay on or call Itza-chu forward to run the errand Parnell had requested.

Rather, with the bare ghost of a frown, Kuruk announced, "They are returning now. Both riding hard."

Frowning himself, Parnell turned in his saddle, facing southward. In another moment he could see the two outriders raising dust, both bent over their ponies' necks and racing back to join the team they'd left behind. Clint wondered whether that meant they had found something, some trail suggesting that a herd had passed, or—

Kuruk cantered forward now, to meet his fellow tribesmen. One of them, Nantan Lupan, spoke urgently to him in muted tones, accompanied by hand gestures. Some thirty seconds later, Kuruk doubled back toward Clint and the Aguirre sisters, scowling as he said, "There is a troop of *federales* heading this way, possibly a mile behind."

"How many?" Parnell asked Kuruk.

"A dozen, maybe more."

Clint swore under his breath and scanned the desert, looking for a place where he could hide eleven riders with their mounts and loaded packhorse. There were no gullies nearby, and he could barely glimpse the closest range of weathered hills, perhaps two miles away to their southeast.

No place to shelter, then, and that meant trying to avoid the troops on open ground. Even with nightfall coming on, Clint did not like their chances of success for that.

"Okay," he said at last. "We can't outrun them on the flats. The best thing we can hope for is to bluff them. Have some kind of story ready for their *comandante*."

Sonya spoke up, reminding him, "That might work for the three of us and our vaqueros, but the Mescaleros . . ."

Parnell had already thought of that. The odds against a squad of *federales* letting armed Apaches pass them by were slim to none.

"You're right," Clint granted ruefully, "but there's a chance . . ."

He faced Kuruk. Said, "If you take your men and lag behind a bit, while we ride on, hang back until you're nearly out of sight, you can be ready when we need you."

Thinking of the sisters foremost, and the likelihood that *federales* would try something with them, in the guise of an arrest or a flat-out assault, Parnell was counting on another fight, hoping that strategy could see them through.

Or most of them, at least.

Up close, at point-blank range, there would be casualties. Clint could only hope to strike with greater speed and force than his opponents, hoping that before they glimpsed the trailing Mescaleros it would be too late.

It was a half-baked battle plan at best, but all he could come up with at short notice. When the smoke cleared, if he was alive to see the end of it, Parnell reckoned more ghosts would haunt him during the remainder of their journey.

And if this turned out to be the end, he would have failed his boss and friend, likely cost Alejandro his last two surviving children and the herd Aguirre counted on to keep his spread running through winter and into spring.

Failure would mean the end of everything.

Clint's only consolation was that if disaster came to pass, he would not live to see its brutal end.

A RE YOU CERTAIN they were Mescaleros?" asked Lieutenant Jesús Ahumada of the *federales*. He did not entirely trust his sergeant's eyesight, even though the man was only ten years older than himself, a fairly youthful-looking forty-two.

"*Estoy seguro, teniente*," Sergeant Lázaro Velázquez answered with a hint of irritation in his gravel voice. "I'm sure of it. There is no mistaking Mescalero war paint."

"But we've lost them, then, *sargento*?"

"No, not lost, *señor*. They turned and ran. If we make haste, I'm confident that we can overtake the two of them."

Lieutenant Ahumada, for his part, was not convinced of it. Worse yet, considering his rank, he was not sure that they should even try. Regardless of their tribe, Apaches were well known for laying traps for *federales* on patrol, as they had done for generations with unwary travelers. The two Velázquez had seen—assuming he was right when he identified them—might have parted company by now, expecting Ahumada to divide his meager force, or else they might have joined with reinforcements waiting up ahead to spring an ambush.

If Ahumada failed to follow up and overtake the stray Apaches, Colonel Gaspar Islas would find out about it when the squad returned, and he would have no end of questions about Ahumada's failure to pursue and kill or capture them.

To that end the patrol was galloping after the riders he had barely glimpsed, uncertain in his own mind whether they were *indios* or campesinos *mexicanos*. Either way, once he caught up with them, Lieutenant Ahumada meant to seize their horses and any weapons they were carrying, along with anything else that he deemed worth confiscating.

There would be no protests from his victims after they were dead and left as carrion for vultures.

Suddenly, at a distance of two hundred yards or less, Lieutenant Ahumada saw riders raising a pall of dust in front of him. From the hats they wore, the horsemen did not look like Native tribesmen, nor were they attempting to evade his men. In fact, they were advancing on a hard collision course with the patrol.

"So, who are these?" he challenged Sergeant Velázquez. "Not Mescaleros, surely."

Suddenly uncertain, Velázquez craned forward in his saddle, using his right hand to shade his narrowed eyes. "I would say *mexicanos*," the sergeant replied, forgetting military courtesy, "except their leader seems to be a gringo. And the two who ride on nearest beside him are *mujeres*."

"Women!" Ahumada made no effort to disguise his skepticism. "Now I know your eyes are failing you, *sargento*."

"Wait and see, *señor*," Velázquez answered.

A long, tense moment later, Ahumada knew his second-in-command was right. The leader of the group approaching his patrol was certainly a gringo, flanked by two young women whose faces seemed precisely to resemble one another's.

Was Ahumada going mad? Had riding all day through the desert heat and skimping on water from his canteen addled his brain?

The *teniente* pushed those thoughts aside and concentrated on the riders drawing closer to him, even as he signaled with a raised hand for his troops to halt in place. He counted seven riders, including the women, all but the leader being *mexicanos*. The four trailing horsemen all wore wide sombreros, but the slanting sun from Ahumada's left still clearly showed their faces underneath. Two of them cultivated horseshoe mustaches, a third wore the Vandyke style with a moustache and goatee, while the last one in line had been clean-shaven prior to going on the road, some two or three days earlier. The young women wore their hair tied back, while matched serape shawls did little to conceal the ripeness of their pulchritude beneath.

It was the gringo leader who concerned Lieutenant Ahumada most, however. Why would half a dozen Mexicans be trailing him through the Desierto de Chihuahua, southward bound on such a fading day as this? What was his business with them when he so clearly was not a *mexicano*?

Noting the long gun braced across the leader's pommel, even though he did not recognize its caliber or model, Ahumada half turned toward Sergeant Velázquez, ordering, "Prepare the troops, *sargento*. Cautiously."

Without raising his voice, Velázquez called back

down their line of *federales*, ordering them, *"Prepárense."*

Be prepared.

Lieutenant Ahumada heard his men drawing their rifles clear from saddle scabbards, cocking them, but knew that none of them would raise their weapons. They were mostly young recruits, but none of them were fool enough to give the game away.

At least, the *teniente* hoped not, because when shooting started—and he felt a nagging certainty that they were in for some—he would be caught between two groups of blazing guns.

T**HEY'RE GETTING READY** for us," Clint Parnell advised, voice muted, speaking from a corner of his mouth.

"We see them," Sonya answered, using a hand gesture, down beside her right leg, to alert the trailing riders if they had not seen the *federales* drawing rifles from their dusty saddle boots.

Clint knew the moment was approaching that sharp tipping edge where planning yielded to frenetic action, blood was spilled, and lives not ended in the first exchange of fire might still be changed forever. He was tired of all the recent killing, going back four nights to the attack on Alejandro's hacienda, but it was not over yet.

And would not be until his mission was completed or he died in the attempt.

Holding the dapple gray's slack reins in his left hand, Clint braced the Browning Auto-5 across his thighs, snugged up against his saddle horn. He had reloaded it with buckshot rounds after their skirmish with the Chiricahua at Laguna de Guzmán, a whim

that he had not fully considered at the time but now
saw might be helpful with the *federales* waiting for
them up ahead.

In Parnell's mind, there was no question of avoiding
conflict with the soldiers. He knew the army's sordid
reputation: cruel at best, no more than uniformed *bandidos* at their worst. The officer in charge was bound
to question Clint and his companions, asking where
they'd come from and where they were headed, eye-
balling their mounts and weapons, focusing particularly on the twins who flanked him as the gap narrowed
between his party and the khaki-clad patrol.

Whatever else occurred, he could not leave the two
Aguirre women in the *federales'* hands.

From fifty feet or so, the officer in charge of the patrol called out, "*¿Cuál es tu negocio aquí?*"

Clint understood him well enough but offered up a
lie, still closing in on the patrol. "Sorry, but I don't
know much Spanish."

The lieutenant frowned, translating his query. "What
is your business here?"

At thirty feet, Parnell replied, "Looking for horses
on the cheap. Some breeding stock."

His answer was not wholly false that time, it simply
dodged their true purpose for being in Chihuahua. If
Clint told the *federale* they were chasing rustlers from
New Mexico, the next step would be shouted orders to
arrest them all.

But if he bought a little time by talking, while he
closed the gap a few more yards . . .

"Where do you hope to find these horses?" The
lieutenant almost sneered his words.

Parnell shrugged casually, wearing a bewildered
smile as might befit a gringo facing down armed soldiers in the fading light of dusk. "Still looking," he re-

plied. "I don't suppose you'd know of any nearby ranchos that might have a few to sell?"

"Our people need their animals, *señor*. Where have you come from on this *búsqueda inútil*?" Calling it a futile quest and letting Parnell know that he could recognize manure when a gringo shoveled it his way.

"A ways up north of here," Clint said, the knuckles of his right hand blanching as he tightened up his death grip on the Browning Auto-5.

"How far north, gringo?" the lieutenant pressed him.

"Since you ask . . ."

Clint raised his shotgun, angling its muzzle toward a point midway between the troop's commander and his sergeant, bracing for its recoil as he squeezed the trigger. Buckshot pellets spewing from its muzzle caught both *federales*, toppling the sergeant from his saddle, while the officer in charge managed to keep his seat somehow, despite blood soaking through the right side of his khaki uniform.

Parnell's shot sent one empty cartridge spinning from the Auto-5's ejection port and fed a live round to the firing chamber in the split second before gunfire exploded all around him, *federales* and Clint's riders all unloading weapons in a blaze of close-range fire. Bullets swarmed around him in the dusky desert air, one plucking at Parnell's left sleeve, his dapple gray gelding trying to turn away before Clint gripped its reins and held them fast while lining up another hasty shot.

S ONYA AGUIRRE LEFT her Springfield rifle in its saddle scabbard when the shooting started, whipping out a Smith & Wesson Model 1899 revolver from its quick-draw holster fastened to the right side of her saddle horn instead. The double-action weapon with its four-inch barrel held six rounds of .38 Special hollow-point ammunition, with its rate of fire restricted only by the strength of Sonya's hand.

The hollow points were specially designed to "mushroom" upon impact with a target, peeling back each bullet's soft indented nose, causing extreme internal damage as they churned through flesh and bone, rarely opening an exit wound, disabling her chosen mark without harming whoever stood nearby.

Her first shot, fired a heartbeat after Clint's initial shotgun blast, traveled no more than thirty feet before it slammed into a slender *federale* private's face, drilling his cheek beside a small flat nose and punching his head backward as if he'd been smitten by a sledgehammer. The soldier tumbled over backward, sprawling from his saddle, managing to fire a wasted rifle shot into the graying sky before he landed on his back, immediately trampled by his rearing horse.

The sharp crack of a rifle shot behind Sonya and to her left told her Dolores had decided to use her Winchester. Distracted by her own part in the battle, Sonya did not see whether the .30-06 bullet from her sister's rifle found its mark, but she trusted her sister's marksmanship as being equal to her own. Their little band's vaqueros, fanning out to keep from shooting one another by mistake, had joined the melee with their own rifles or sidearms, while the soldiers still alive returned fire from their semiautomatic Mondragón Modelo weapons, most of them too startled for precision aiming.

Sonya chose another mark and fired her .38 again, a gut shot this time, doubling the *federale* over in his saddle as he clutched at his wounded abdomen and cried out before he spilled into the dust. He landed on his head, stifling that wail of pain, just as raised voices from the north began to shriek out battle cries.

The Mescaleros had arrived to join the fight.

They charged into the breaking rank of *federales*, whooping as they fired at point-blank range, one of them—Sonya thought it was Nantan Lupan—flailing at his adversaries with a tomahawk instead. She saw the hatchet's blade slice through a peaked cap, opening the wearer's skull, bathing his face in crimson as he died.

At the same time, Sonya heard another blast from Parnell's shotgun, saw one of the army horses going down, pinning its wounded rider underneath its thrashing weight. The young man, also wounded, screamed as his left leg was crushed and ground into the sand. Grimacing, she fired a mercy round into his head, and that left three more .38 Specials before she had to switch that revolver out for the second pistol tucked inside a left-hand saddle holster.

Time slowed to a crawl in Sonya's mind, and she could almost see herself, as if standing outside her body on the battle's sideline. She was barely conscious of her actions as she aimed and triggered her revolver once again, rushing the shot and barely grazing her intended target. Yelping at the pain, that *federale* swung around to face her with his rifle shouldered, but he never got the chance to put her down. A bullet fired by someone else ripped through his jaw just then, twisting his whole face out of shape, and sent him tumbling to the ground, unconscious if he was not dead on impact.

Cursing in Spanish, Sonya wheeled her varnish roan around and sought another target in the midst of swirling dust and gun smoke.

DOLORES PUMPED THE lever on her Winchester, three aught-six rounds already gone, with one remaining in the rifle's chamber and another next on tap from its internal magazine. Of three shots fired so far, she'd definitely hit two *federales*, likely killing one who'd fallen from his mount and failed to rise, with one clean miss counting against her.

Shooting in the maelstrom of close-quarters combat was a hazard, bullets flying everywhere, some fired in panic with no serious attempt to aim. Her snowflake Appaloosa was not gun-shy under normal circumstances, but this chaos, with horses and their riders racing back and forth, exchanging shots or savage blows at arm's length, would have taxed the bravest man or animal.

She had already seen two of the *federales* try to flee, deserting under fire, and had dropped one of them herself, the other blasted from his saddle by some shooter she could not identify. Gun smoke had formed a patch of fog around the duelers, worsened by the rising dust from horses' hooves and bodies dropping to the arid ground. Her ears were ringing, as if she were trapped inside a giant bell with someone on the outside hammering its sound bow till her head was ringing and the shouts of fear or fury rising all around her sounded muffled to her ears.

The fight was too intense to last, and while it seemed that time slowed down around Dolores, moving with a nightmare sluggishness that cast each bloody detail into sharp relief, she knew that only moments had elapsed before the gunfire ceased, its echoes fading out across the desert flats and into dusk. Clutching her horse's reins, she swung it in a counterclockwise circle to survey the battleground, littered with human corpses and the bulky carcasses of animals caught in the crossfire.

There were no surviving *federales*, all of them shot down or finished off with knives and tomahawks once they were on the ground. Checking the members of her own team, she saw two of them had dropped to rise no more. One was a Mescalero, Goyathlay, a fragment of his skull detached by impact from a Mondragón Modelo's Mauser bullet, spilling brains.

The second body took a moment longer for Dolores to identify, before a pang knifed through her chest. She had been fond of Paco Yáñez—more than fond, if truth be told, remembering his gentle kiss on recent moonlit nights, although they'd gone no further than propriety and Papa Alejandro would permit. Paco had fallen from his liver chestnut stallion, both gunned down while on the gallop, laid out on his back with sightless eyes staring into the lowering blue shades of nightfall.

Could those soft brown eyes see anything beyond the earthly plane? Dolores hoped so, prayed that the religion of her youth was accurate in promising good men a place in paradise, but it was not for her to say while she remained alive, somehow unscathed.

Clint Parnell's voice cut through the ringing in her ears, distracting her from Paco and the grief she felt.

"We need to get our people out of here and underground," he said, "then patch the wounded up as best we can and put some miles behind us while there's still enough daylight."

Glancing around once more, Dolores saw that two more members of their party—Joaquín Cantú from the hacienda and Kuruk, leader of their Apache allies—had received flesh wounds that ought to heal with proper treatment, if they could prevent infection from setting in. Putting her private thoughts away, Dolores joined in wrestling their two dead aboard surviving horses, then mounted her snowflake Appaloosa once again and joined the remnant of their band on a southeastern route of march.

"Where are we going?" she asked Clint, when she was close enough to speak without raising her voice.

"Should be a village up ahead called Agua Fria," he replied. "After we finish with the spadework and the patching up, I'm hoping we can stay there overnight."

Agua Fria, Chihuahua

"You know the people of this village?" asked Dolores.

Clint understood her doubt, the hesitancy after what they'd been through recently, and did not want to raise false hope. He gave it to her straight.

"I passed through some years back," he said, "before your father took me on. Stayed overnight and had a home-cooked meal. I can't swear anybody will remember me, but if they have the same headman, an old guy named Guillermo Alcazar, there is a chance he might. Don't know how he or any of his people feel about Apaches, though."

"You think that it is worth the risk?" Dolores pressed.

Clint mulled that for a moment. Said, "I think we run a greater risk by camping in the open, on our own. Those *federales* may be overdue somewhere, for all we know. How fast their officers start looking for them will depend on when and where they were expected back in camp."

Dolores said no more, but Clint could feel her eyes upon him, with unspoken questions hanging in the air. As foreman of her father's hacienda, he had known about her closeness to Paco Yáñez and could imagine what Dolores must be feeling now, at least to some extent. Parnell had never lost someone he cared about in that way to an act of violence and hoped he never would. With Yáñez's death coming so close behind her brother's death and Papa Alejandro's injury, Clint hoped the anguish would not break her down.

And if it did, what then?

That was another worry weighing on Clint's mind, despite the fact that he could do nothing about it. Only time healed wounds like those, and who knew how long the remainder of their party would survive in Mexico?

So far, they had lost three men on their first day in Chihuahua. Whatever might follow on the heels of that bloodshed remained a mystery.

For now, only Clint's pledge to Alejandro kept him on the trail, hoping tomorrow's sunrise would illuminate some path to the *bandidos* who had looted the Aguirre rancho and the horses they had stolen, threatening the family with poverty if they were not retrieved.

Agua Fria, when they saw it standing on the edge of night before them, looked like what Americans might call a one-horse town. In fact, as Clint recalled from his brief visit there, the village had no horses, although he remembered several burros kept for hauling carts or drawing plows through arid desert soil.

A cry went up from somewhere in the village as Clint's party closed their distance to a quarter mile, some sharp-eyed lookout already on duty for the night. Before the party reached the first of ten to fifteen squat adobe buildings, most of Agua Fria's population had turned out to meet the new arrivals, half a dozen of the men carrying hoes and axes as if they were just proceeding to a day's work in the nearby cultivated fields.

Out front stood a familiar couple, old Guillermo Alcazar and his wife Beatriz, the village elders, neither one elected to a formal post but honored for their wisdom drawn from life experience. Parnell suspected that if he could add the venerable couple's ages they'd be working on their second century.

But would their memories hold any trace of him from years ago?

Clint doffed his hat as he approached the line of villagers, a gesture of respect, and spoke directly to the man in charge. "Don Guillermo," he said, "I don't know whether you remember me . . ."

"Of course, amigo," the old man replied. "You spent a night with us some time ago. The date, I must admit, escapes me now."

"And me as well, jefe."

"You were alone last time, but now arrive with friends," Don Guillermo observed. "Including three young Mescaleros."

Parnell nodded. Said, "If that creates a problem for you, we can move along."

"No problem comes to mind," Guillermo said. Then asked, "How long might you remain with us this time?"

"Same as the last," Clint said. "Just overnight. And we can pay for food, for water."

Guillermo frowned slightly, as if Clint's offer insulted him, but Beatriz spoke up before her husband could reply. "Nonsense," she said. "We give freely, expecting nothing in return for Christian charity."

"That's mighty kind of you," Clint said. "We're out tomorrow at first light, I promise you. People to see and business to conclude."

"You all look weary from the road," Don Guillermo advised. "I see two of your friends have suffered injury."

"A little disagreement with *bandidos* on the trail," Clint lied.

"We can attend to them," said Beatriz. "Then *una comida caliente* while the young ones take care of your horses."

"Much obliged, *señora*," Parnell answered for his crew at large. "A hot meal sure would hit the spot."

Agua Fria, Chihuahua

A coward at heart, Diego del Paso was trembling with fright but determined to proceed regardless of the risks his plan entailed. He dared not think of how the gringo visitor and his companions might react—let alone the Mescaleros—if they knew about his treachery, much less the other people of his village, if and when they learned he was responsible.

Greed drove him forward, even though his hands were trembling as he led one of the village burros out of its corral and crept through darkness toward the south side of the village, waiting until he was well beyond its limits before mounting up and pressing out.

The plan had come to him full-blown while Diego eavesdropped on a private conversation held between Guillermo Alcazar, the gringo, and the two young women who had ridden at his side when their strange group arrived suddenly. Spying was not difficult in Agua Fria for a lifelong sneak, although del Paso had missed certain details of the story when voices were lowered, nearly whispering.

It was the women who had drawn him to the headman's home initially. Diego, just turned twenty years of age, had never laid his eyes on twins before, much less a pair that stirred his loins so strongly, giving him sharp visions of desire. At first, he'd merely hoped to shadow them, perhaps catch glimpses of them partially undressed as they prepared for sleep, but once he overheard their words, Diego understood that it was time for thinking bigger, reaching out to grasp a prize he would not have to share with any of his fellow visitors.

Indeed, it might just be his key to getting out.

The gringo and his friends were from New Mexico, across the Rio Grande. They were riding through Chihuahua seeking vengeance and a herd of horses stolen by *bandidos* from an hacienda there, and they had suffered hardship on the trail so far, ambushed by a Chiricahua raiding party first, then clashing with a troop of *federales*, wiping out the small patrol and taking losses of their own.

That told del Paso there was money to be made, and he did not intend to share it with his fellow villagers.

He knew a place where soldiers camped, a few miles south of Agua Fria, and Diego reckoned they would pay for information that would lead them to the slayers of their comrades. If Diego asked them nicely, groveled properly, their *comandante* might allow him private time with one or both of the beguiling twins, before they faced the mandatory firing squad.

But if need be, Diego would be satisfied with gold, enough for him to reach a major city—Ciudad Juárez, perhaps, or possibly Victoria de Durango—where he could make a fresh start and the villagers who looked upon him with disdain in Agua Fria could not track him down.

That is, if any of them should survive once *federales* learned they were responsible for sheltering a gang of killers from *el norte*.

Determined not to fail, Diego climbed aboard his stolen burro, flicked its rump with a Texas persimmon switch, and moved on through the desert night.

CHAPTER TEN

CAPTAIN ISIDRO LÓPEZ-DÓRIGA smiled to himself as he pictured his *comandante* pinning a Medal of Military Merit on his tunic, or perhaps even a gilt-edged, red-enameled Decoration for Heroic Valor for tonight's action. He might even be promoted if he pulled the mission off successfully, perhaps to wear a major's golden star or two for a lieutenant colonel.

On the other hand, if he should fail . . .

Captain López-Dóriga pushed that thought aside, determined that he would succeed in tracking down and punishing the outlaws who had traveled to Chihuahua from New Mexico and killed a dozen *federales* while pursuing horse thieves. He had brought along the stool pigeon from Agua Fria, under guard in case he tried to break away, and anything that happened once López-Dóriga's men reached Agua Fria would be based upon the information that Diego del Paso had sworn to at gunpoint and under oath.

The whining campesino had resisted coming with

López-Dóriga to his native village, but the captain needed him to single out the fugitives and finger those who'd made them welcome when they turned up on the cusp of sundown. In López-Dóriga's mind, all residents of Agua Fria shared in that complicity, and if he had to wipe their village off the map, so be it.

Those who made bad choices suffered the consequences.

And sometimes those who just got in the way must suffer, too.

That was the state of life in Mexico today, and all around the world, from what Captain López-Dóriga understood.

Riding to the captain's right, Lieutenant Jacobo Ferriz asked, "How much farther to the village, *comandante*?"

López-Dóriga answered with a question of his own. "Have you not been there before?"

"There has been no occasion for it until now, *señor*."

"Five miles, perhaps. No more than six. You'll find it much like any other clutch of campesino hovels in Chihuahua." Turning toward Diego del Paso, the captain said, "Remind me of the headman's name in Agua Fria, pig."

Cringing, the *informador* replied, "Guillermo Alcazar, jefe."

"I thought he would have died by now," López-Dóriga sneered, remembering the old man whom he had confronted on his last pass through the village.

"Not unless he's passed on since I left tonight," del Paso said, forcing a smile.

"You find humor in this?" López-Dóriga snapped at him.

"No, jefe! Not at all!"

The traitor's mood had switched in a split second from attempted jocularity to cringing fear. López-

Dóriga liked the latter more, and he could not resist adding, "That's good, because tonight may yet turn out to be your last."

Del Paso nearly whined as he replied, "I came to you in good faith, *capitán*, to help you and report the murder of your men."

"You came to help yourself, hoping there would be a reward," López-Dóriga countered. "If you're *muy afortunado*, that reward may be your worthless life. If not . . ."

"I only wish to serve you, *capitán*," del Paso fairly whimpered.

"And you shall," López-Dóriga answered back. "In one way or another."

The captain left del Paso sniveling and fighting not to show it. Truth be told, he would have no use for the spy once he was finished with the night's business in Agua Fria and had already determined that whatever else might happen in the village, his informer would not live to see another sunrise. There were two reasons for that: López-Dóriga personally hated tattletales, although he made use of them in his work, and it would look better for him—improve his prospects for promotion—if he solved the massacre of troops himself, without an intervening middleman. His *coronel* at headquarters need never know that fate had dropped that gift into López-Dóriga's lap without a hint of work on his part.

Heroes were not made that way, and he had learned during his first year with the *federales* that they did not share the credit for their deeds with anybody else who might detract attention from themselves.

So be it, then. Whatever else transpired in Agua Fria on this night, however many enemies were slain, Diego del Paso was taking his last breath beneath a pale moon whose light made the desert seem an alien landscape, where mortal danger lurked in every shadow.

Suppressing a brief shiver down his spine, Captain López-Dóriga called an order back along the marching column to his men. "*¡Preparen sus rifles!*"

They responded instantly, in unison, snapping the bolts back on their Mondragón self-loading rifles, each man chambering a Mauser round that would soon find its way into some human target's flesh.

Agua Fria, Chihuahua

Despite her weariness after a day of riding through the Chihuahuan Desert and the battles she had fought, Sonya Aguirre found that sleep eluded her. She could not stop her mind from racing, haunting her with images of combat, the companions she had lost that afternoon, and strangers she had helped to kill.

Guillermo Alcazar had made room for the sisters in his own home, shared with his wife Beatriz. They had no children living in the village any longer, while their age and status in the village made them perfect chaperones for two young women they assumed were maidens, thus subject to separation from the male riders they had accompanied across the Rio Grande. The spare room where they slept was small but clean, their straw-filled pallets soft enough to insulate them from the ground beneath.

Prepared for anything, Sonya was wrapped up in a blanket with her Springfield rifle and her brace of Smith & Wesson pistols, ready to defend herself if need be. No more than a yard away, Dolores slept with her Winchester and the Colt she favored when it came to potting targets and for self-defense. Unlike her sister, though, Dolores, softly snoring, had found respite from their tiring day in dreams.

Sonya, for her part, was afraid of dreaming as she

lay in strange surroundings, thinking of her brother and the men whom she had sent to join him in the after-life that day.

Before that week, her mother's death aside, she had not given much thought to wherever souls wound up once they departed from their earthly shells of flesh and bone. The church she had been raised in offered four options. Aside from paradise and hell, it spoke of limbo, set apart for spirits of unbaptized infants, and purga-tory, an intermediate state after physical death where marginal souls lingered during expiatory purification. That arrangement seemed unnecessarily complex to Sonya, and she did not like the thought of being trapped somewhere, perhaps for centuries, after her death.

Where would the bandits and the *federales* she had helped kill over the past few days wind up, if all of that were true? What of the Chiricahua warriors and the Mescalero volunteers her group had lost so far? Were any of them Christians, or did Native tribesmen wind up somewhere else, sent to some other place that Son-ya's people could not understand?

It was too much for her to ponder in the darkness of their strange bedroom, but while those thoughts in-creased her weariness, they did nothing to help her fall asleep. She thought of counting livestock leaping over fences, something that had helped lull her as a child, but now, at half past midnight, that only reminded Sonya of the horses stolen from her father's hacienda and the pressing need to take them home again.

Disgusted, she was on the verge of rolling over, hoping that a shift might help her, when a rifle shot tore through the night outside. A heartbeat later, as she scrambled to her feet, prodding Dolores close beside her, Sonya heard a man's voice bellowing, "*¡Despierta y sal afuera!*"

Who was demanding that the villagers awake and go outside their homes?

Two possibilities immediately came to Sonya's mind, *bandidos* or marauding *federales*. And just now, between the two, that seemed to be no choice at all.

"Who do you think that is?" Dolores asked her sister, whispering.

"There's only one way to find out," Sonya replied.

Their bedroom had no window, but there were two exits from the Alcazar home, front and back. Before the sisters left, choosing the rear exit, they heard Guillermo and his wife departing from the front door, facing on the village square. Outside, the same male voice was now shouting, "*¡Rápido ahora! ¡Fuera de sus casas!*"

Quickly now! Out of your homes!

The sisters hastened to obey, holding their weapons ready for whatever happened next.

CLINT PARNELL SLIPPED from the adobe hut he had been sharing with vaqueros Arturo Lagüera and Ignacio Fuentes. He held his Browning Auto-5 shotgun, Colt Peacemaker riding leather on his hip. The other two Aguirre riders carried rifles, backed by handguns of their own.

The outdoor gunshot, followed by barked orders, had supplied a rude awakening from fitful sleep in strange surroundings. Now, outside the small house where he had been lodged, Clint saw a troop of mounted *federales* formed up in the village square, their Mondragón Modelo rifles covering the town's surprised inhabitants. Up front, an officer wearing captain's three gold bars upon his epaulets was brandishing a Luger pistol vaguely angled toward Guillermo Alcazar.

Clint cursed under his breath, counting the soldiers, seeing that his people were outnumbered by their enemies in uniform. He knew their party's three remaining Mescaleros had preferred to camp outside of Agua

Fria, but he could not see them at the moment, wondering whether they would stay to fight or slip away into the darkness while they had the chance.

As for himself, Lagüera, and Fuentes, it seemed they had no choice.

And what of the Aguirre twins? Clint looked for them but could not pick them out among the shadows lying black between the huddled houses and the small church where the local campesinos pledged their faith at Sunday morning mass. He hoped the *federales* would not see them, fearing that the scene would quickly take a more disturbing turn.

Would the remaining villagers—civilians, if you like—join in a fight against the soldiers, or were they too long accustomed to subservience, bowing and scraping in the presence of authority? In any case, Clint knew he couldn't wait for them to make a move if the intruding *federales* started searching house to house for him and his companions.

Parnell was pondering what to do next when someone from the crowd of villagers shouted a name he did not recognize. "*¡Mira, es Diego!*"

Parnell looked as he had been directed, following a single pointed finger, quickly joined by others and an angry growling in the central square of Agua Fria.

"*¡Traidor!*" someone shouted. Other voices joined the chorus with "Turncoat!" and "He's betrayed us!"

Clint's eyes picked out a small man slouching on a burro, close behind the captain of the *federales*, head ducked down as if he hoped the brim of his sombrero might conceal his face. Clint did not recognize him, but the angry shouting told him that the lone civilian rider, dressed in peasant garb, had slipped away sometime during the night and led the soldiers back.

For what? To Parnell it could only mean that he had run to spread the tale of strangers in his village, hoping for some payoff in return, but now he found himself before a jeering mob.

In the front rank of the gathering, Guillermo Alcazar shook a bony fist at the defector, shouting, "*¡Desgracia!* You have no home here any longer. We spit on your name and memory!"

Some of the villagers were doing that exact thing when the *federale* captain bellowed out at them, "*¡Silencio!* I give the orders here! Give up the murderers or suffer for betrayal of your government!"

In answer to his shout, a rock flew out from somewhere in the raging crowd, sailed past the captain's face with mere inches to spare, and struck the huddled villager behind him on one shoulder, jolting him but failing to dislodge him from his mule.

Outraged, the captain half turned toward his men, keeping his Luger trained upon the crowd before him as he ordered, "*¡Fuego, hombres!*"

All along the line of mounted soldiers clad in khaki, rifles snapped into position, shouldered, aiming toward the village crowd that had been rousted out of sleep into a waking nightmare.

Clint Parnell could think of only one response that fit the situation. Whipping up his Browning Auto-5, he squeezed its trigger, blasting buckshot pellets toward the *federale* firing squad.

DOLORES AGUIRRE SWUNG her Winchester Model 1895 toward the *federale capitán* but missed him by a second, maybe less. Somebody else had fired a shot before her and had either grazed the officer or frightened him enough that he fell over backward from his saddle and hit the ground while her .30-06 slug passed through empty space where he had been a heartbeat earlier.

The shot was not a total waste, however. The projectile traveled on to strike a *federale* private in the shoulder, impacting at 2,500 feet per second, nearly ripping the *soldado*'s right arm from its socket with 3,036 foot-pounds of energy, flinging his Mondragón Modelo rifle off to strike another startled private in the face. That soldier toppled from his horse as well, stunned as he hit the dusty ground.

Two *federales* dropped with one shot, although neither of them had been killed. One would most likely bleed to death in minutes, while the other would be groggy as he struggled to his feet and tried to retrieve his weapon, making an attractive target with his back turned to the crowd of villagers.

Those were dispersing now, running for cover, their initial anger at a traitor from their own community lost in the boom and crackle of gunfire. The frightened *federales* still apparently had no idea of who was firing at them, and in consequence were blasting Mauser rounds into the fleeing campesino ranks. Dolores saw Beatriz Alcazar go down, shot in the back, her husband turning to help her if he could, at least two soldiers sighting down the barrels of their Mondragóns in his direction.

She was faster, pumped the lever action of her Winchester and fired again, shifting her aim a trifle to the left and toward the closer of the two infuriated riflemen. The Model 1895 bucked hard against her shoulder, but she held it steady, saw her target crumple from the horse he sat astride, blood spurting from his khaki-covered chest.

A kill or a disabling wound, which would amount to the same thing.

Dolores swept on, cranked the Winchester again and fired almost without aiming this time, her rifle firing at the same instant when smoke burst from the

muzzle of the second *federale*'s Mondragón. Her bullet
struck this one beneath his jawline, snapped his head
back with sufficient force to send his peaked cap flying.
Glancing farther to her left, she saw Guillermo Alcazar still on his feet, assisted by another man in hoisting
Beatriz, retreating toward their squat adobe home, but
she could not tell whether the dying soldier's bullet had
flown on to find another mark.

How many enemies remained before her? Counting
quickly, making an allowance for the leaping horses and
the rising dust their hooves stirred up, Dolores estimated that a dozen still remained, firing wildly among
the frightened villagers. Their *capitán* was on his feet
and had retained his pistol somehow as he fell, now
pumping random shots at strangers running for their
lives.

Dolores pinned him in her rifle's sights, but once
again she was too late. A shotgun blast thundered from
somewhere to her left, perhaps Clint's Browning Auto-5,
and the captain received a charge of buckshot in his
chest, hurled backward as if unseen puppeteers had
yanked his strings. He landed on his back, spread-eagle,
shuddered once, and then lay deathly still.

A second later, chaos in the village was compounded
as their party's three remaining Mescaleros joined the
battle, running in among the *federales*' horses, whooping war cries, firing rifle shots at point-blank range.
Their entry to the fight appeared to turn its tide, even
Kuruk—despite his wound from earlier that day—
dispatching one *soldado* with a stomach wound, then
pouncing on him as he fell, swinging a tomahawk to
crush the young man's skull.

Dolores now felt giddy, from inhaling dust and gun
smoke, dropping to one knee and finding better balance as she cocked her Winchester once more and

sought a target in the swirling knot of enemies. Among them, trying to escape aboard a frightened burro, she beheld the villager Guillermo Alcazar had vilified as their betrayer. Shoulders hunched, he was retreating from the battle line, kicking the burro viciously to make it travel faster.

Deadeye and coldhearted now, Dolores sighted on the turncoat, steadying her aim. She did not wish to shoot the burro by mistake, as it was innocent, nor did she wish to kill the coward outright if he could be saved for questioning. She drew in a breath and held it, hands rock steady as her index finger found the rifle's trigger and she fired.

LIEUTENANT JACOBO FERRIZ was terrified. He'd seen his *comandante* fall, first from his horse, then blasted into grim death after he regained his feet and tried to fire his pistol at the raging villagers. Ferriz himself had fallen when his mount reared, panicked by the roaring gunfire all around it, and had lost his rifle in the process, kneeling helpless while the young *soldados* serving under him were cut down one by one.

It crossed his mind that they had found the killers they were seeking on the ride to Agua Fria, and that notion almost made him laugh hysterically until Ferriz choked on the sound emerging from his throat and clapped a hand over his mouth.

The only goal remaining for him now was to survive whatever happened next, and from the nightmare scene surrounding him, the *teniente* reckoned that might be impossible.

A bolting stallion, riderless, brushed past Ferriz and knocked him sprawling in the dust. He cursed it impotently, even as it galloped out of earshot, knowing that his words were wasted on an animal. While struggling to his knees, he saw the stallion trample a wounded corporal, its shod hooves fracturing the young man's ribs and face, sending his body into spasms as the horse rushed into outer darkness and was lost to sight.

What now?

The *teniente*'s eyes fell once again upon Captain López-Dóriga's corpse, sprawled on its back, no further use to anybody with his orders and contemptuousness. He might still help Ferriz in one way, though, his limp right hand stretched out beside him, fingers pointing toward his fallen Luger pistol on the ground.

As an *oficial* in the army of Porfirio Díaz, Ferriz was trained to use all the weapons recently acquired from Germany and elsewhere. While no pistol had been issued to him, he had practiced firing it until he was proficient and familiar with the Luger P08, properly designated Pistole Parabellum in the land where it was manufactured. Parabellum meant "for war" as Ferriz understood it, and also described the weapon's 9×19mm ammunition, eight rounds slotted into a detachable box magazine that loaded through the Luger's butt for semiautomatic fire. A unique toggle-lock action on top relied upon a jointed arm to lock, unlike the slide actions of other semiautomatic pistols, with an estimated rate of fire in practiced hands reported as one hundred sixteen rounds per minute.

That, of course, depended on how many magazines a shooter had available and how much time his enemies allowed him for reloading. Still, Ferriz saw that he had no other options at the moment and should settle for whatever slim chance fate had offered him.

He scrabbled toward Captain López-Dóriga's body, leaned across it, groping for the Luger, nearly sighing with relief as he took hold of it. Ferriz had no idea how many cartridges remained inside the pistol's magazine and could not check without removing it, a waste of precious time that might well cost his life. Instead, he simply checked the Luger's safety switch, relieved to find it in the "off" position, and turned back to bring his adversaries from the village under fire.

Instead, he found a tall, broad-shouldered gringo rushing toward him, glaring down the barrel of a semiautomatic shotgun aimed at the lieutenant's face. Squealing, Ferriz almost released his captain's pistol then and there but knew he could expect no quarter from his enemies after the blood they had already spilled today. The gringo and his various companions had to know they would be hunted to extinction in Chihuahua or wherever they went next, after annihilating two army patrols.

In short, Jacobo Ferriz had nothing to lose and saw no prospects of survival if he should surrender, pleading for his life.

Instead, he could at least attempt to take one of the outlaws with him as he died.

Bracing the Luger in both hands, the *teniente* found its curving trigger with his index finger, was prepared to squeeze a round off, when the shotgun's muzzle belched a cloud of smoke, flame, and buckshot no more than two feet from his face. Ferriz was conscious of a stunning pressure from the impact, then his world dissolved into a cloud of swirling atoms, fading swiftly into deepest everlasting black.

DIEGO DEL PASO imagined he was dying when the rifle bullet creased his skull, plowing a bloody furrow just above his left ear, and he tumbled from his burro, landing in a slack heap on the ground. It took another moment, hearing shouts and gunfire all around him, watching *federales* fall, before he realized that he was somehow still alive.

Alive but wounded, warm blood spilling down his face into one eye from his scalp wound. It was miraculous, but he had no spare time for thanking God, the saints, or anybody else while he was in harm's way, with bullets hissing all around him, finding other targets, rending flesh, unleashing screams.

Unarmed and stuporous, Diego struggled to all fours and started crawling off haphazardly across the battlefield. He sought escape, perhaps a dark gully where he could hide, but then an eerie silence told him that the fight was over. Glancing to his left and right, del Paso calculated that the *soldados* had lost.

Tears streaming from his eyes to mingle with the blood from his head wound, Diego had not traveled far on hands and knees before the sound of rushing footsteps overtook him and he was surrounded. Looming legs in trousers and concealed by peasant skirts surrounded him as if a sturdy fence had dropped from heaven, cutting off his progress.

From above, a man's voice speaking English asked, "Is he the one?"

A second man, familiar sounding, answered in Spanish. "*Sí. Este es el traidor.*"

They had him now, the traitor in their midst who had brought death and misery upon them. As his stomach suddenly convulsed, surrendering its meager contents, spattering his dusty shirt and hands, Diego knew he had run out of time.

He had lost his sombrero in the fall from his burro, and now felt bony fingers clutching at his hair. Their owner drew Diego's head back, forcing him to stare into the anguished visage of Guillermo Alcazar.

"My wife is dead because of you!" the village headman snarled. His free hand rose before del Paso's eyes, clutching a butcher's knife.

Diego's hopeless babbling for mercy was cut short when someone else—the gringo who had led the mismatched riders into Agua Fria around sundown—stopped Guillermo's hand from plunging steel into del Paso's throat.

"Hold on," the gringo urged. "We need him to find out who else he told about us at the army base."

Reluctantly, Guillermo took a step back, lowering his knife. "*Bien*," he said. "But I can help you make him talk."

"I had another thought on that score," said the gringo, turning to his right and gesturing to someone whom Diego could not see.

Del Paso felt his stomach turning over as a trio of Apaches stepped up to surround him. Two of them were holding tomahawks, the third a skinning knife. Another urge to vomit overtook him, but his empty stomach merely curled into a painful knot.

"We need to know whatever he knows," the gringo advised his Mescalero friends. "Can do?"

One of the Natives, with a bandage wrapped around one arm, replied in English, "When we finish, you will know him better than he knows himself."

The two uninjured Mescaleros grabbed del Paso underneath his arms and started dragging him away toward outer darkness. Sobbing now, his vision blurred, Diego saw the village headman staring after him with hatred in his eyes, his weathered face a mask of disappointment that he had to miss out on the show.

Before they cleared the village square, before the three Apaches had a chance to work on him, Diego del Paso began to scream, a helpless sound that echoed through the desert like a dying night bird's mournful cry.

* * *

THE *FEDERALE* RAID had claimed four lives in Agua
Fria, with another five villagers wounded. Funerals would have to wait for sunrise, but removal of the
fallen soldiers was the top priority. Crude litters were
constructed, large enough to haul two corpses at a
time, and they were dragged a half mile from the
settlement, three teams of two men each repeating
round trips by moonlight while selected women bearing tree branches followed the litters, wiping out their
tracks.

The destination was a ragged gully that sporadic
rainfall sometimes turned into a rushing stream. Upon
arrival, the transporters dumped their loads into the
quebrada, piling tumbleweeds on top of them until such
time as the ever-hungry vultures and coyotes sniffed
them out.

Four *federale* horses had been killed as well, the
rest dispersed by gunfire while the battle raged. Given
the dearth of food available, the village butcher and
his young apprentice were assigned to clean the carcasses and slice them into pieces that could be explained away as food stores once the meat was smoked
and aged.

Dolores and Sonya Aguirre helped the villagers
clean up as best they could, aware that certain residents of Agua Fria must be blaming them for the attack. Diego del Paso had stopped screaming by then,
his three interrogators coming back and huddling with
Clint Parnell to share what they had learned up to his
dying breath. The sisters watched Clint nodding,
frowning thoughtfully, before he joined them by a bon-
fire in the central plaza.

"Well?" Dolores prodded him.

"The *federales*' base is roughly eight miles east of

here," Clint said. "The captain who ran out of luck tonight was *comandante* of the post. Whatever men he left behind will wait for him, likely the best part of tomorrow, till they figure out that he's not coming back. Before they start another search, we need to get away from here as far as possible."

"And go where?" Sonya inquired.

"I'm hoping Kuruk and his men will have a lead on that," Parnell replied.

As if on cue, their party's three surviving Mescalero volunteers approached the fire. Dolores tracked them with her eyes, pretending not to see the streaks of blood drying on Nantan Lupan's hands.

"What did he say?" Clint asked Kuruk, the commander of their dwindling Apache allies on the journey through Chihuahua.

"The traitor told us everything he knew," Kuruk replied, the past tense verifying what Dolores had surmised about his fate. "He came to hate the other people of his village, thinking they despised him, but he was afraid to leave without making some profit from it. When we came in seeking shelter for the night, he saw his chance. The *federales*, as they always do, deceived him."

"What about the other?" Clint inquired.

"He had no knowledge of our mission," Kuruk answered, "but a rumor reached his ears from strangers, *mexicano* riders passing through, about . . . how you say it, jefe *militar*?"

"'Warlord' in English," Clint translated.

"Yes. Same thing," Kuruk agreed. "A warlord of *bandidos* who supposedly acquired a herd of horses in *el norte* earlier this week."

"This warlord have a name by any chance?"

"The coward only called him by the Spanish word for a small town. *Villa*."

Dolores interjected, "Pancho Villa?"

Kuruk shrugged. "He did not say, *señora*."

"That is name enough," Dolores said. Turning to Clint, she asked, "You've heard of him?"

Parnell nodded. Stories of Pancho Villa's banditry across Chihuahua and Sonora were reported, possibly exaggerated, even in New Mexico, although there had been no accounts so far of him crossing the Rio Grande with his men.

"I don't suppose he told you where to find this Villa?" Clint inquired.

"They were his last words," said Kuruk, "though not precise. Somewhere northwest of where we stand, around Ascensión."

"Sounds like our next stop," Clint replied. "Assuming that we ever get that far."

CHAPTER ELEVEN

ASCENSIÓN LAY THIRTY-ODD miles to the north-northwest of Agua Fria. Clint Parnell had mixed feelings as his riders departed from the village, leaving fresh graves in their wake and misery that would endure long after they were gone. Ahead of him lay nothing but uncertainty, the risk of more lives being thrown away.

Since they had crossed the Rio Grande, his team had lost three men and killed some forty enemies including the first Chiricahua band that had waylaid them. Add to that five dead in Agua Fria, with the traitor factored in, and five more suffering from wounds. Toss in the dead and injured from the bandit raid on Alejandro's hacienda that began all of the bloodletting, and Parnell felt the butcher's bill trying to smother him, as if it were a shroud.

Against that stood his solemn promise to retrieve Aguirre's stolen herd and save the family that he had served with pride for years.

But at what final human cost?

And if Aguirre's daughters fell along the way, how would Clint live with that?

The simple answer: he would not. If it came down to his life or those of the twins, he was prepared to die for them without a second thought. In fact, after all they had been through in their first day on the trail, Clint wondered whether that might not come as a relief.

Stop it! he thought, scolding himself. Defeatist thinking never helped in any situation, and the worse Clint's troubles seemed, the more he had to focus on the goal of ultimate success.

Sonya's unexpected voice beside him, on his right, drew Clint's thoughts from himself before he had to ruminate upon them any longer. "What's your plan for finding Pancho Villa?" she inquired.

"I haven't worked the details out," he said. "It's obvious we can't just ride into Ascensión, asking if anybody's seen him lately."

"Not if we plan on riding out alive," Sonya agreed.

"The farthest that I've thought it through so far, we could send one man in who claims he wants to be a part of Villa's outfit. Ride the outlaw trail, whatever. That removes suspicion of a whole group passing through and questioning the locals."

"Did you have someone in mind?" she asked.

"I've ruled out the Mescaleros," Clint replied. "With Cantú injured, that leaves Fuentes or Lagüera who could likely pass inspection."

"I could go along with one of them," Sonya suggested.

"As what, exactly?" Parnell challenged.

"Well . . ."

"Forget about it. I'm not sending you to look for Villa, putting you in any further danger. That goes for Dolores, too."

"But—"

"No!" he cut her off. "Your father's lost enough already, and there's still a good chance that we may not get his horses back. You want to sacrifice yourself down here, at least be kind enough to shoot me first, will you?"

That silenced Sonya for a somber moment, then she smiled, turning away, and said, "I'll think about it."

Parnell glanced over his shoulder, saw her riding back to join sister Dolores in the line of march, and wondered how the other twin was holding up after their bloody day crossing Chihuahua. He had been aware of her attachment to Paco Yáñez, had seen the looks exchanged between them, and had caught them sneaking off for private moments on a few occasions, though he didn't know whether Alejandro was aware of what was going on under his very nose around the ranch. It was not part of Clint's job to report on Alejandro's children to their father, and he'd kept that to himself, but he understood that she was grieving for Yáñez, although she tried to cover it.

He only hoped that grief would not lead to Dolores being killed before Clint finished up the task that he had been assigned—the deadly job for which both twins had volunteered over their father's sage advice.

In any case, it was too late for them to turn back now. The only thing their team could do was press ahead, attempt to do their job, and somehow make it home alive.

West of Ascensión, Chihuahua

Pancho Villa stuffed the final bite of a *chile verde* burrito in his mouth, slowly chewing the chunks of pork shoulder slow cooked in a green chile sauce of jalapeño peppers, garlic, and tomatillos, wrapped in a corn tortilla. The mixture set his mouth on fire but in a good way, helping to distract him from the problem foremost on his mind.

Finally, after he'd washed the last bit of his spicy breakfast down with cold *cerveza*, Villa asked his second-in-command, "Do you believe we're wasting time here, waiting for Zapata?"

Javier Jurado thought about that, shrugged, and then replied, "I don't think so, jefe. He wants the horses, certainly. But as to when he might arrive or whether he will have enough *dinero*, well . . ." Jurado shrugged again and let the still-unfinished sentence trail away.

"He could be dead by now for all we know," Villa surmised. "The *federales* have been hunting him, and with reports of trouble yesterday, I wonder if he's finally run out of time."

Sipping coffee generously flavored with tequila, Javier considered that, then slowly shook his head. "I doubt that," he said at last. "Díaz would surely make it known if he had bagged Emiliano. It would make him feel *muy valiente*, even though he had no hand in it himself. Good for the old fool's withering machismo, eh?"

"So, if the soldiers weren't fighting Zapata's men, then what was happening?" Villa countered.

During yesterday afternoon and earlier this very morning, close to dawn, had come reports of two engagements where *soldados* had been killed. One had occurred at Lake Guzmán, the other at a flyspeck of a settlement called Agua Fria. Villa had sharp eyes and ears throughout Chihuahua, some across the border in Sonora, who kept track of information that might possibly concern him, passing it along and pocketing some pesos in return. Around two dozen *federales* had been slain in widely separated incidents, and if they had not tangled with Zapata's men, what did it mean in fact?

Jurado drained his coffee cup, set it beside one of his dusty boots, and then unleashed a wet belch as he straightened up again. Villa scowled at him. Asked his aide, "Is that your answer, then?"

"No, jefe," Javier replied. "The fighting could mean anything or nothing. At Laguna de Guzmán I understand that Chiricahuas were involved somehow."

"Apaches." Villa spoke the tribe's name like a curse and spat into the sand.

"As for the other thing," Jurado forged ahead, "it could be possible the Agua Fria villagers were smuggling."

"Smuggling what?" Villa challenged. "They barely have a pot to cook *un pollo* in."

Jurado forced a laugh at that, adding, "If they could find a chicken. Still, could be anything."

"If they were smugglers, we would know about it," Villa said. "They would be paying tribute for the privilege."

"Then something else," Jurado answered back. "It's said they fired upon the *federales*, who killed several of the villagers in turn."

"And that's another thing," said Villa. "You have been to Agua Fria, *¿sí?*"

"I was not much impressed," Javier said.

"Which is my point, exactly. Did they strike you as a group that would attack *soldados*? And if so, attack with what?"

"Guns are not difficult to find, jefe," Jurado said.

"Not if you have *dinero*, Javier. But Agua Fria? Seriously? They must rank among Chihuahua's poorest of the poor. It would surprise me if they had one decent rifle in the village, and they could not overcome a troop of *federales* with their rakes and hoes."

"What, then, jefe?" Jurado asked his leader, frowning.

"*No lo sé*," Villa replied. "I don't know, Javier, and that's what troubles me."

Jurado rolled a cigarette as he responded. "Let me put your mind at ease, Pancho. The Agua Fria campesinos know nothing about us that could not be heard in any other village. Whatever the *federales* wanted with them, they are dead now and the secret died with them."

"I hope that you are right," Villa replied. "If not . . ."

He let the sentence trail away, thinking, *It could mean death for all of us.*

D OLORES SAW HER sister riding back from where she had engaged in conversation with the foreman of their father's hacienda. Sonya reined in as her twin caught up to her, glancing along the shortened line of vaqueros and Mescaleros trailing them.

Three dead so far, out of the dozen riders they had started with—one out of four—and two more wounded but still capable of fighting. How many would remain to bring the stolen livestock home, assuming that they ever found the herd at all?

"Well?" asked Dolores as Sonya's varnish roan fell into step beside her snowflake Appaloosa.

"He's devised a plan, if you can call it that," Sonya replied.

"And . . . ?"

"Send one of the hands into Ascensión, pretending that he wants to work for Villa. Bring back word of whatever he learns, where he is hiding out or has the horses stashed away. Then make another plan for the attack."

Dolores recognized her sister's skepticism, knew it sounded vague, but what more could Parnell have said before they reached the desert city where Diego del Paso, dead now, claimed that Pancho Villa could be found? She reckoned that the traitor had shared everything he knew, if only to relieve the pain inflicted on him by the Mescaleros, but that did not mean his words were true.

Even a dying man in agony could only spill the information he possessed, and if del Paso had been wrong about where Villa spent his time . . . well, they could wind up wasting days on end with further searching, while more *federales* caught their scent and rode to intercept them.

"Who will he send?" Dolores asked.

"Arturo or Ignacio," Sonya replied. "Joaquín is still recovering and might appear suspicious." With a sidelong glance, Sonya added, "He would not hear of sending us."

"Why would he?" asked Dolores. "It is only *sentido común.*"

"I know it's common sense," said Sonya. "Still . . ."

She let the statement die there, but Dolores knew her sister understood the folly of dispatching women to Ascensión with questions about Villa and his hideaway. The men who rode with Pancho Villa were the kind who married late or not at all, spending their time with prostitutes whenever brothels were available, more likely to assault a woman traveling alone—much less a pair of twins—than to sit down with one or both and spill the secrets of their outlaw gang.

Dolores understood that Clint was looking out for them and honoring the promises he'd made to Alejandro when his last surviving children insisted on joining the trek to save their horses and the hacienda's future.

"Maybe—" she began, then stopped.

"Maybe what, *hermana*?" Sonya prodded her.

"I was about to say maybe we should have stayed at home and taken care of Papa."

"Bite your tongue!" Sonya hissed back at her. "Who else remained to represent the family?"

"Clint represents us. All of the vaqueros riding with him represent our family."

"But it is not the same. You know it's not."

"I know we're killers now," Dolores answered back.

"I'm not sure that confession and a few Our Fathers ever washes that away."

"You doubt the church now?"

"I've begun to question everything," Dolores said. "It's one thing, doing man's work at the rancho, but to hunt down other men and kill them . . ."

"Only if they try to kill us first," Sonya cut in.

"And what about the *federales*? Here we are in their country, killing *soldados* who enforce the law."

"What law?" The scorn in Sonya's voice was obvious. "They are no better than *bandidos*, thieves, and rapists, killing their own people for Díaz."

"I know that," said Dolores. "Still . . ."

"Still nothing," Sonya cut her off. "If they knew Villa had our horses, they would take them from him for themselves."

"Of course, you're right," Dolores said.

"But you feel sympathy for them? I think the sun has baked your brain, *hermana*."

Or my heart, Dolores thought, but kept it to herself.

What worried her the most was that she felt herself becoming hardened to the killing, skipping past excuses for it and accepting it as something more or less routine.

And that, in turn, made her surmise that she had lost a portion of her soul.

WHEN THEY WERE four or five miles short of entering Ascensión, Clint called a halt and everyone dismounted, closing in around him while their horses grazed on yellow grass and Clint laid out his plan, such as it was. He saw the skepticism written plainly on the faces of Ignacio Fuentes and Arturo Lagüera, neither one of them eager to play a spy's role even as they nodded their grudging acceptance of the scheme.

"It's risky," Clint acknowledged as he finished. "If somebody has a better idea, I'm all ears."

He scanned the ring of faces, half expecting Sonya or Dolores to speak up, but all around the circle there were only negative head shakes. Lagüera and Fuentes looked sour at the prospect, but they raised no options.

"Right, then," Parnell said at last. "We're short on straw. I guess the only fair way to decide is by tossing a coin. Okay with both of you?" he asked the two vaqueros who were now the central focus of attention.

Both nodded without enthusiasm. Clint removed a Barber half dollar from his vest pocket, eyeing the two riders as he said, "Somebody call it."

After they exchanged a cautious glance, Lagüera shrugged. Fuentes told Parnell, "I take heads."

Clint tossed the coin and watched it spin above him, made no attempt to catch it as it fell to earth. Eleven pairs of eyes peered down at Lady Liberty's profile, featuring a wreath atop her crown, hair ribbons dangling down her nape.

"And heads it is," Clint said. Across from him, Fuentes nodded, the brim of his sombrero wobbling slightly, as he forced a smile.

"*Sí*, jefe. What am I to do?" the wiry cowhand asked.

"First thing," Clint said, "is play it safe. Don't try to rush things. Pick out a cantina, have a drink and get a feel for it. If it's too high-class, move on to another one. You're bound to hit a place where low-life types kill time."

"Lowlifes like us," Lagüera quipped, then watched his joke fall flat when no one laughed. "*Lo siento*," he amended, nearly blushing underneath his suntan. "Sorry."

Clint ignored it, forging on with his instructions to Fuentes. "Don't make it obvious," he said. "Just sidle into it. You're out of work and game for anything.

You've heard there was an outfit in the area that might need extra men. Don't mention Villa on your own. Wait for somebody else to bring him up."

Fuentes nodded in agreement. Clint picked up the coin, returned it to his pocket as he asked, "Your buckskin doesn't carry the Aguirre brand, right?"

"No, jefe," Ignacio replied. "I had it when Don Alejandro hired me."

"Good. There's nothing to connect you with the hacienda, then," Parnell confirmed.

"How many *tabernas* should I visit?" Fuentes inquired.

"As many as it takes to hit pay dirt," Clint said. "Just watch how much cerveza you throw down and keep your wits about you."

"Since my life depends on it," Ignacio replied.

"Exactly right. We'd hate to lose you or whatever information you dig up."

"And if I make a good impression? What then?" Fuentes queried.

"That's a good point," Parnell granted. "If they want to take you somewhere right away, make an excuse. You have to break it off with someone you've been working for, let's say. A job you're tired of, going nowhere with it, looking for advancement. You can meet them later, but you need to get your final payoff first."

"And if they wish to come with me?" asked Fuentes. "To be sure I speak the truth?"

Clint thought about that for a moment, felt the others watching him before he said, "In that case, bring them back to us. We'll get the drop on them and verify where we can find their boss, then plan our moves from there."

He did not have to add the postscript that if one or more *villistas* followed Fuentes back to meet his hypothetical employer, it would be the last thing that they ever did on earth. That was a given, even if he had to do the gun work on his own, and there was nothing to be gained by rubbing anybody else's nose in it.

"*Está bien*," Fuentes replied, nodding resignedly. "I should be going, then."

Lagüera and Cantú walked with their friend and coworker until he reached his horse and mounted up and then rode off toward Ascensión without a backward glance.

Ascensión, Chihuahua

Ignacio Fuentes achieved his destination ninety minutes later, riding down a central thoroughfare that seemed to have no posted name. His pulse was elevated and his stomach felt uneasy, but he did his best to keep a poker face intact and bury any signs of nervousness.

It seemed to work with locals on the street, few of them paying any more attention to him than they might to any other stranger riding through. A man alone, he posed no threat to anyone he passed along the way and scrupulously kept his eyes from lingering on any woman walking with a man or children.

Checking out the shops and offices downtown, Fuentes swiftly determined that he'd have no trouble finding barrooms in abundance where he could enjoy a drink and make a cautious try at tracking down his enemies.

But one wrong word, one misstep, could turn out to be his last.

Passing along the unpaved street, avoiding eye contact with the townsfolk whenever possible, Ignacio took stock of the equipment he was carrying, aware that some of it might be required to save his life. His rifle, in a saddle scabbard, was a Winchester Model

1873, loaded with fourteen rounds of .44-40 ammunition. On his right hip, with a hammer thong securing it in leather, sat a Colt Peacemaker manufactured in the same year as his rifle, chambered for the selfsame rounds to help conserve the weight of ammunition that he carried on the trail. A hunting knife, its eight-inch blade honed to a razor's edge, resided in a scabbard on the left side of his pistol belt. Draped on his saddle horn, a lasso and canteen were ready for emergencies. His saddlebags, aside from extra ammunition, held a change of clothes, a compact shaving kit, and hardtack to sustain him when no hot meals were available.

With any luck, Fuentes would need no more supplies before he left Ascensión, reporting back to Clint Parnell with Pancho Villa's whereabouts.

The lone alternative he saw to that scenario of sudden, bloody death.

The first cantina Fuentes spotted, El Escorpión, stood to his left beside the city jail and marshal's office. He passed by that one on principle and traveled two more blocks, then veered off to his right. The second was a dive simply called Pepe's, on his right beside a narrow alley strewn with trash. Fuentes saw that it had a hitching rail outside, with access to a water trough, and made his first stop there.

His buckskin mare drank deeply once Ignacio dismounted, then he looped her reins over the rail and stroked her neck for reassurance while the horse regarded him with seeming skepticism. Fuentes nearly took his rifle with him, then decided that he did not want his first impression among strangers to be that of someone on the prowl looking for trouble.

Pepe's was dark inside, no windows facing the street, with smoky air diminishing the light from lamps that the proprietor rarely took time to clean. Directly opposite its entrance, half a dozen men were bellied up against a bar, chasing tequila shots with beer. The place boasted four gaming tables, three of them unoccupied, while at the fourth a quartet of vaqueros focused on a game of *la viuda*, similar to whiskey poker in the States. Its name, translated as "the widow," referred to a special good-luck chip in the pot that players were eager to win.

Ignacio felt sharp eyes boring into him as he passed by the table but avoided looking back at any of the players, anxious not to give offense by any wayward glance or deed. Arriving at the bar, he ordered beer and found it warm but offered no complaint, focused on how he should begin his quest for information without winding up a corpse dumped in the alley.

Outside El Fresnal, Chihuahua

"They are leaving, jefe," said Alfonso Soberon, before he passed his pocket telescope to Emiliano Zapata. His master palmed the looking glass, peered through it, and released a weary sigh.

"At last," Zapata said, half whispering.

He understood there was no need for speaking softly, since the squad or *federales* were the best part of a mile away and riding farther by the second, northward bound. Still, to be safe, Zapata and his men would have to wait another quarter of an hour to be sure that no sharp-eyed *soldado* might glance back and see them coming out of cover from the tree line near Laguna el Fresnal. Zapata had already spent enough time hiding from them without touching off a running battle on the open flats below.

Rising stiffly, knees cracking, Zapata said, "By now Villa is wondering what's happened to us. I don't trust him not to sell the horses out from under us since we are late."

"We've done our best, jefe," Alfonso said.

"But that is never good enough for him," Zapata countered. "He lacks patience and would sell the animals to anyone—even Díaz, I think—if he believed that he could get away with it."

"He made a deal with you," Soberon said. "He shook your hand."

"I don't care if he swore upon his mother's grave, assuming that he ever had one."

That produced a chuckle from Zapata's chief lieutenant, but he offered nothing more.

"*Todo bien*," Zapata said, when he had lost sight of the khaki uniforms retreating in formation. "Gather the men. We need to make up for lost time."

"You intend to ride all night, jefe?" Alfonso asked.

"I would prefer it," said Zapata, "but we can't risk running into any more patrols." He checked the sun's position overhead, already westering, and said, "Until *puesta de sol*, at least."

Sundown, approximately three more hours, and Zapata knew that even staying on the trail that long would pose a risk. Chihuahua's *federales* seemed to be in turmoil, agitated, scouring the land in greater numbers than Zapata was accustomed to around Morelos, but he had no explanation as to why. He dared not stop and ask at any settlement along their route of march, for fear of having someone tip the soldiers, leading to a showdown that his men might lose.

If he wound up a prisoner—or worse, a bullet-riddled corpse—so far from home, all of Zapata's work to that point would have been in vain.

But if he reached Villa in time to close their deal, obtaining horses that his men could train for war while he sold off the rest for cash, it just might make a crucial difference to his crusade against Porfirio Díaz.

Zapata's riders took the best part of ten minutes

mounting up, and while he felt an urge to shout at them, Emiliano knew better. His fighters were all volunteers, presumably invested in the coming revolution to the same extent that he was, but Zapata understood that most of them had been simple *bandidos* prior to enlisting with his private army. Most were easing into personal acceptance of the military discipline required to wage and win a war where victory depended on support of campesinos in the countryside. By that same token, if he pressed his men too far, too rapidly, desertions would increase and he might find himself standing against his enemies with only Soberon beside him.

That was if Alfonso did not leave as well.

Zapata climbed aboard his sorrel gelding, pushed his pessimistic thoughts aside, and concentrated on observing his guerrillas as they formed up into ranks, ready to ride. He wondered how many of them would still be with him by this time next month. Thinking about next year was too much of a stretch when all the odds seemed stacked against him at the moment.

Only time would tell the fate of his attempt to change life for the better in his homeland, gradually benefiting all its people through reforms the ruling power structure would resist with every means at its disposal.

That meant war, and while Zapata knew that he might not survive it, he could be the visionary with a dream who set its torch ablaze.

Beyond that only fate or Jesucristo could predict what happened next.

JOAQUÍN CANTÚ, ON lookout duty, found Clint standing by a small campfire, sipping a cup of coffee. Seated on the ground beside Parnell, the twin Aguirre sisters spoke in muted tones, while Arturo Lagüera finished mopping up his plate of rice and beans with half of a tortilla.

"Ignacio is back, jefe," Cantú announced.

Clint did not need to check his watch, as he'd been keeping track of time since Fuentes first rode out of camp to search for answers in Ascensión. The last time Clint had pulled the timepiece from his pocket it had been four and three quarter hours. Now he estimated that it must be ten o'clock, perhaps ten minutes more.

All things considered, it was a relief to see Ignacio returning in one piece at all, but if he came back without answers, all that night was simply wasted time.

Fuentes dismounted, led his buckskin mare close to the fire, and dropped its reins to let it graze on grass and scattered wildflowers nearby. Clint noted that his spy carried a scent of alcohol, but that was not surprising, since his job had been to look for answers in Ascensión's saloons.

"Something to eat?" he asked Fuentes.

"*No, gracias*," Ignacio replied. "I ate tamales with a couple of new friends at a *taberna* called Lagarto de la Suerte."

"Lucky Lizard?" Sonya translated from her position near the fire.

"You would not know to look at it," Fuentes replied. "The patrons seemed to have no luck, at least with cards, but I *did* see a lizard crawling on a wall behind the bar."

"Your new friends." Parnell brought him back on track. "Would those be Villa's men?"

"*Sí*, jefe. One calls himself Jesús Zarita. His friend is Enrique Rocha."

"Did you have a chance to ask them about joining up?" Clint asked.

"After a few tequilas and cervezas, *sí*. They both enjoy their alcohol."

"And you kept up with them," Clint said, not asking this time.

"*Pero por supuesto,* jefe. But of course. "I had to prove my stamina, *¿verdad?*"

"As long as you remember what they told you," Parnell said.

"*Perfectamente.* They are sleeping over at the tavern, which has women upstairs for renting. In the morning, they are riding back to Villa's camp west of Ascensión while others take their turn in town."

"You didn't get around to mentioning the horses?" Clint inquired.

"I dared not bring it up directly, jefe. But Zarita let it slip that Villa has some livestock that he plans to sell within the next few days. A customer is coming from Morelos to collect them, bearing gold."

"No deadline on that sale?" asked Clint.

A shrug from Fuentes as he said, "They cannot say for certain, but he is already late."

Good news for us, Clint thought, *if we can show up in his place.*

And if they somehow managed to appropriate the gold earmarked for Pancho Villa in the process, well . . .

Clint did not want to press his luck when they'd already lost three members of their team. He had to focus on Aguirre's horses first, and winning back as many of the fourteen hundred eighty-seven as he could, then getting them across the Rio Grande, back into New Mexico.

"I don't suppose your new friends mentioned when they would be riding back to camp?" Clint asked Ignacio.

"Rocha said after breakfast, but with all that liquor in them, plus exertion with the ladies"—there he cast a glance toward the Aguirre sisters, frowning as if to apologize—"I think they won't be leaving early in the morning."

"And headed west, you say?" Clint asked.

"Oeste, sí."

"Okay, so that's our plan. Stake out the road ahead of time and pick 'em off. Take one of them alive, at least."

"And then?" Dolores asked.

Clint drank a final swig of coffee, dashed its residue of grounds into the fire.

"Then," he replied, "we start to pay them back with interest for running off your father's herd."

CHAPTER TWELVE

Ascensión, Chihuahua

ENRIQUE ROCHA DID not let his hangover, throbbing behind his blurry eyes, prevent him from enjoying a breakfast of huevos rancheros with garlic and ancho chile peppers, with frijoles and an enchilada on the side. Instead of using beer to wash it down, he drank black coffee strong enough, in his opinion, to remove the rust from hinges in a long-abandoned house.

Rocha had always been a man who struggled to suppress his appetites where liquor, food, or women were concerned. From age sixteen or thereabouts, he'd relished anything he could afford, and if he came up short of cash . . . well, there was always someone else burdened with more than he could comfortably spend at any given time. He had begun his life of crime by rustling livestock, fled his village in Campeche when he was discovered, then began living on the run, stealing a pair of guns, and using them to rob shops, small-town banks, and the occasional stagecoach on both sides of the Rio Grande. He had slain his first traveling salesman on the night before his seventeenth birthday, surprised to find that it had no seeming effect on him as the old priest in his home village had declared from his pulpit.

If anything, it made Rocha feel powerful, an *hombre valiente* set apart from others by his willingness to kill. Potential victims, he believed, could see that in his eyes and willingly surrendered their belongings—even giving up their wives and daughters for an hour's dalliance—if it kept them from losing any blood.

This morning was just one more of a thousand days when he had overslept and risen from a harlot's crib unwashed, smelling of sweat and other things, achy and with his stomach knotted, but still knowing he must eat and then get back to camp, where Pancho Villa would be waiting for him, ready to dispatch another team for rest and recreation in Ascensión.

Across the table from him, Jesús Zarita was looking green around the gills. His breakfast order was a lone fried egg, and he had barely touched it but was on his second cup of coffee, sipping timidly instead of gulping it as Rocha did. Some of the fresh stains on his shirt were obviously vomit, but he had not brought a change of clothes with him to town, and thus would spend the day's ride back to camp looking and smelling like an alcoholic hobo from the city's slum.

"You need to ride downwind of me today," Rocha taunted his friend. "You smell like a hog in muck."

"No one is likely to mistake you for a blossom either," said Zarita.

"But the difference would be that I don't care." Eyeing his comrade's plate, Rocha asked him, "Do you intend to eat that egg?"

Zarita made a sour face, and Rocha took that as a

negative response, spearing the fried egg with his fork and stuffing it into his maw as one lukewarm bite. That done, Jesús pushed back his chair and rose, left money for his own meal on the table by his plate, and told Rocha, "*Vamos*, amigo. We are late already."

"Thanks to you," Enrique muttered in reply.

Zarita brayed laughter, saying, "At least I left my woman satisfied. Can you say that?"

Cursing, Rocha followed him out and down the street, into the livery, where an old man with thinning hair and spotty whiskers was engaged in saddling their animals. The outlaws left him to it, since his fee was paid up in advance, but checked the girth and billet straps to make sure both were properly secured. Once mounted, they rode out into the morning sunshine, Rocha reaching up with one scarred hand to shade his eyes beneath the brim of his sombrero.

As they reached the outskirts of Ascensión, Enrique Rocha checked the pocket watch that he had stolen from a traveler outside of Torreón, some five or six years earlier. Its owner had no further use for it, since he was dead, and Enrique had admired the crisp engraving on the inside of its pop-up lid that read CON AMOR PARA SIEMPRE, ANNABELLA.

He had no idea who Annabella was or had been, much less how her everlasting love had ended or how long ago. Sometimes Rocha pictured her, a different woman each time, as he drifted off beside a campfire, needing help to fall asleep. It was all ancient history, of course, but sometimes Enrique fantasized that he might meet her one day, smiling as he let her see the watch and bent her to his will.

A half mile out of town and westward bound, he glanced back toward Jesús and found him slouching in his saddle like a man who could not quite decide whether he was sick or just exhausted. Enrique jeered at him,

"You should have had some *desayuno*. Were you never told that breakfast is the most important meal you eat all day?" Zarita produced a retching sound, Rocha laughing as he added, "Or you ought to hold your liquor better, eh, amigo? Set a good example for the rest of us."

T HEY SHOULD BE here by now," Sonya Aguirre said. "Be patient," her twin, lying in the desert grass beside her, answered. "They will have been up most of the night, drinking and whoring. We can start to worry if we don't see them by noon."

"I want to get this over with, Dolores."

"As do I. But we cannot control when two drunken *bandidos* stumble out of bed."

Sonya frowned at that. Replied, "But what of Papa? He needs us to care for him."

"He has the staff to deal with that," Dolores said. "Right now, he needs the stolen horses more, to close that army sale."

"And we have no idea yet as to where they are," Sonya retorted.

"Which is why we wait for these *gusanos* to arrive and point the way for us."

Gusanos. Maggots. Sonya thought that fit the raiders well enough. Perhaps one of them fired the shot that killed Eduardo, while his various amigos made off with their father's herd.

Although she had been raised on breeding horses, working daily at the rancho, Sonya never thought about the animals they raised and sold as being hers. Sometimes she wondered whether Dolores felt the same, as if they both were set aside, assigned to lesser roles than Papa Alejandro—who had built the hacienda up from scratch—and his firstborn, Eduardo, who as son and heir stood to inherit everything. It was expected, understood, that Sonya and Dolores would find husbands and that their *esposos* would team up with Alejandro and Eduardo at the ranch, or else remove their wives to some other location, where they would produce children in turn and pray for healthy sons.

But there was no Eduardo now, and that changed everything.

Their father, as a widower who showed no interest in marrying again, would likely never have another son and heir. Or, if he did, the boy would lag so far behind his half sisters in age that they would likely wind up running things while he was still a child of tender years. As much as it pained Sonya to admit it, Alejandro could not live forever, even if he still possessed the will to try.

There had been no chance to discuss the matter since the raid that turned the twins' lives upside down, though it preyed on Sonya's mind and she imagined that Dolores felt the same. From infancy, it seemed that they had shared most thoughts between them, often finished each other's sentences, and when Dolores broke her arm while falling from a horse at age nine, Sonya felt a corresponding stab of pain before she learned about the accident.

That was the way of twins, and Sonya reckoned it would never change, unless . . .

There had been so much killing on their trek across Chihuahua, with no end in sight, she had to wonder how she would react if something fatal should befall Dolores in their campaign to retrieve the stolen herd.

"*¡Dios no lo quiera!*" Sonya muttered, God forbid, then checked to make sure that Dolores had not heard her.

No. Her sister's eyes were still fixed on the east-west trail that served Ascensión and that should bring the two *bandidos* riding unawares into their trap.

What was delaying them so long? How much could two men drink in one night? How often could they perform with working women in a smelly two-bit crib? The waiting set her nerves on edge, no matter how she tried to calm herself.

Another thirty minutes passed before Dolores said, "Two riders coming." As she spoke, she passed her pocket telescope to Sonya. Through the glass, Sonya immediately saw the pair of horsemen drawing closer, magnified by the action of the spyglass's lenses.

Ignacio Fuentes had given them a short description of the men he called Enrique Rocha and Jesús Zarita, but drooping sombreros hid their faces for the most part, and since neither twin had glimpsed the two *villistas* previously, Sonya could not verify whether these were the right two men. She turned and signaled for Ignacio to join them on the rise and watched him crawling toward her on all fours, not wishing to expose himself against the skyline if the riders glanced in their direction.

"Take this," she instructed, passing the spyglass to Fuentes. "Are those two the men you met?"

Ignacio focused the telescope to suit his eye, taking a longer time than Sonya would have liked before he said, "*Creo que sí.*"

"You *think so*?" Sonya challenged him. "Keep watching and don't answer until you are certain."

Fuentes held the telescope in place against his right eye. Downrange, Sonya saw one of the riders draw a watch and chain from his vest pocket, open it, and raise his chin to check the time.

"*Sí, señorita,*" Fuentes said this time. "There is no doubt. The one in front is Rocha, so the other has to be Zarita."

"If we take the wrong pair by mistake," Dolores cautioned him, "it will go badly for you."

Handing back the telescope to Sonya, Fuentes said, "I'm certain. There is no mistake."

"*Bien*." Sonya spoke for her sister and herself as one. "Go and prepare to close the trap."

JESÚS ZARITA FELT no better for his time spent in the saddle than when he had left the Lucky Lizard sixty minutes earlier. The desert sun seemed bent on baking his tequila-addled brain despite the shade from his sombrero, and the warm wind blowing in Zarita's face served only to increase his nausea. The rocking of his horse with each step that it took was also sickening. If they did not reach camp soon . . .

"*Por el amor de Dios*," he called out to Rocha, leading their two-man parade by half a dozen yards. "How much longer?"

Rocha half turned in his saddle, glancing back, and cracked a wicked smile. "Do you remember nothing from our journey yesterday?" he answered in a mocking tone.

"I asked a simple question," groused Jesús.

"A simple answer for a simple mind, then, *mi* amigo. Two more hours at the very least."

"I don't believe it took that long before," Zarita came back at him, not quite whining.

"You were younger yesterday," said Rocha, laughing at him. "I believe Concetta stole the best of you away last night."

"She stole three pesos, I can tell you that." Zarita moped.

"And you did not complain, *cobarde*?"

"I decided she was worth it," Jesús said.

Another laugh at that. "Mingling with whores and sinners," Rocha said. "You should not try to match your namesake from *la Biblia*. Unless, of course, you can turn water into wine."

"That's blasphemy," Jesús protested feebly.

"Then I ask forgiveness in your name," said Rocha, laughing all the louder.

They rode on another hundred yards or so with Rocha chuckling to himself, Zarita muttering under his breath. He wished that he could think of some way to get even with Enrique, maybe slip a scorpion into his bedroll one night soon, then thought that with his own luck, he would be more likely to receive the deadly sting.

Perhaps, instead, he could—

Before another plan could take shape in Zarita's fuzzy mind, a voice cried out from somewhere up ahead. "*¡Deténganse donde están!*"

Stop where you are, that would have been in English, and Zarita reined up instantly, while Rocha walked his steed a little closer to a long, low ridge that lay before them to the west. At once, a rifle shot rang out. Zarita ducked his head and heard the bullet whisper past him. Even as he ducked, not trusting his sombrero to repel a rifle shot, he glimpsed a line of mounted figures on the ridgeline, etched in silhouette against a clear blue sky.

Bandoleros, Jesús thought, but would not highwaymen plying their trade in this part of Chihuahua know on whose toes they were stepping? Hard upon the heels of that thought, it was clear to him that transient robbers would not recognize himself and Rocha as *villistas*. To a stranger's eye, they might appear as simple travelers and ripe for picking.

Rocha must have had the same thought, as he called out to faceless riders, "*¡Estás cometiendo un error!*"

"There's no mistake," the man who had first spoken answered in English. "You are Pancho Villa's men. We need to have a word with you."

Jesús muttered a curse on hearing that. It meant a gringo barking orders from the ridge, backed up by others—eight of them now visible, five faces shaded and obscured by hats. The other three wore nothing on their heads except long hair tied back, which made Zarita wonder whether they might be *indios*.

And what could that mean for his chances of surviving the ambush?

If all they wanted was, in fact, to talk . . .

But how could he trust that?

Enrique Rocha plainly did not. Leaning to his right, he dipped a hand to reach his Henry rifle in its saddle boot, snatching the weapon free and raising it to fire. He did not pump the rifle's lever action, since he always kept a live round in its chamber for emergencies like this one, but Zarita did not like his chances of debilitating more than one or two of their opponents.

As it happened, Rocha could not manage even that.

Before Rocha had a chance to fire his Henry, Jesús saw a puff of rifle smoke rise from up range. A heartbeat later, he heard lead rip into flesh, propelling Rocha over backward, tumbling from his startled horse's croup and tumbling to the ground. Enrique was already twitching through his death throes as the echo of the shot that killed him reached Zarita's ears.

Slowly, not wishing to be slain in turn, Jesús hoisted his hands skyward, remaining mounted only by the pressure of his knees against his horse's ribs beneath the fenders of his saddle. Once the ambush party saw that he was not holding a gun, they galloped down to meet him, fanning out as they advanced, ready to fire if Jesús changed his mind and tried to draw a weapon.

As they closed the gap, the gringo leading them ordered, "Take off your pistol belt and let it drop. Then slip your rifle clear and toss it, nice and easy like."

"*Sí*, jefe," Jesús answered.

"Play your cards right," said the Anglo, "and you just might make it home alive."

C LINT'S RIDERS LED their captive to a deep arroyo that would flood during a heavy rain but posed no threat aside from lurking rattlers with a clear sky and a bright sun overhead. One of the Mescaleros dragged the other outlaw's corpse into the same ravine, while Kuruk claimed the dead man's mount.

That did not tip the scales much against fourteen hundred eighty-seven stolen animals, but Clint supposed it was a start—and partial payment to the Mescaleros for their losses up to now.

Jesús Zarita fessed up to his name and ties to Pancho Villa without any argument, while glaring daggers at Ignacio Fuentes, remembering their first encounter at the Lucky Lizard in Ascensión. When Clint inquired about the raid in Doña Ana County, Zarita denied that he was present, and it didn't matter much if he was lying or told the truth. In either case, the odds were good that he must know where Villa had stashed Alejandro's herd and what he planned to do with them.

On that score, though, their hostage balked. He seemed more frightened of his boss than any pain he suffered for refusing to answer—at least, he did before Kuruk stepped up behind him, yanked off his sombrero, tangled fingers in his hair, and laid the sharp edge of a skinning knife against the dark edge of Zarita's widow's peak. It took a bit of pressure, just enough to send a rivulet of crimson coursing down between his eyes, before he squealed and started pleading for the chance to spill his guts.

And once he started yammering, the challenge was to keep his train of thought on track, instead of veering off on dead-end sidings. Yes, he knew where Villa was—or where he had been yesterday, when Jesús and his dead amigo left camp for Ascensión. A herd of horses, likely stolen, was nearby, penned up in a box canyon that had grass aplenty and a flowing stream to keep them healthy while Pancho was waiting for his buyer to arrive.

Who was the buyer?

When Zarita spoke Zapata's name, Clint recognized it instantly, from stories printed in the *Rio Grande Republic* and the *Albuquerque Journal*. Writers for those papers disagreed on whether Emiliano Zapata was a revolutionary or a plain old everyday *bandido*, and the truth of it made little difference to Clint. Regardless of his trade or politics, he had a good-sized force of caballeros under arms who did his bidding—which reportedly included killing *federales* on occasion and relieving small-town banks of cash reserves.

A gang like that could always use fresh horses, and the ones they did not keep would bring more cash into Zapata's war chest at the point of sale.

Unless Clint and his people stopped them first.

"Okay, enough," Clint said, damming their captive's flow of words before he drifted off into confessing local crimes that Parnell cared nothing about. "Here's what we need from you. You'll lead us to the place where Villa keeps the herd, and if the animals are where you claim they are, we turn you loose."

Zarita's eyes turned shifty, peering at the ring of enemies surrounding him. He swallowed hard and said, "Maybe I draw a map for you instead?"

"No good." Clint's tone allowed for no further negotiations. "Even if you did that, we'd still have to take you with us all the way and make sure that you weren't lying."

"But, jefe, if Villa finds out that I betrayed him—"

"We don't plan on telling him," Clint said. "Show us

the horses—*all* of them—and we can tie you up some-where away from trouble while we get them moving."

"And if Villa finds me there, he knows what's hap-pened all the same!"

"We'll leave one of the Mescaleros with you," Clint replied. "We get the horses and he'll cut the ropes. Of course, he'll have to knock you out, keep you from run-ning to alert your friends. That can't be helped. You'll still be better off than Rocha. When you come around, skedaddle. Find yourself some other reprobates to waste your time with."

Zarita had another thought, frowning. "But what if he has moved the horses, jefe? Anything is possible."

"Was that part of his plan?" Parnell demanded. "Tell it straight now, if you want to keep on breathing."

"*No lo sé, señor.* How would I know? I am not Villa's *confidente.* He would tell such things to Javier Jurado, his right hand, not to a poor *lacayo* like myself!"

"Well, if you're just a flunky like you say," Clint an-swered back, "it's all the more reason that we can't trust your word. Odds are you wouldn't know a thing."

"But all the caballeros talk, jefe. Some of them placed the horses where I say they are."

"And we still need to see that for ourselves," Clint said. "You're going with us, so get used to it."

Zarita made an anguished face as he replied, "But what if Villa *has* removed the herd without my know-ing it, *señor*? What then?"

"Then you're a dead man," Clint assured him. "And it won't be quick. I guarantee you won't enjoy it."

DOLORES WATCHED AS two of their Apaches placed Jesús Zarita on his horse, one of them using raw-hide strips to bind his wrists securely to the saddle horn. Before he mounted up, another frisk revealed a penknife in his trouser pocket, Nantan Lupan removing it and tucking it inside a leather belt pouch for himself.

When she was mounted on her snowflake Appaloosa, Clint Parnell upon his dapple gray gelding, she asked, "Do you believe his story?"

"I won't know until we see that box canyon, if there is one," Clint said. "Short of having Kuruk's people skin the miserable wretch, I reckon that's the best that I can tell you."

"I think he was with the others when they hit our rancho," she replied. "He lies as other people breathe."

"Can't argue with you there," Clint said. "Still, he's the only lead we've got to find the herd and try to slip past Villa's people in the process."

"And if he plans on trapping us somehow?"

"Then he's the first to die. I'll take him down myself. You have my word on that."

Another thought occurred to her, not for the first time since they'd crossed the Rio Grande, although she had kept it to herself during their first long, bloody day crossing northern Chihuahua. Even now, voicing the notion made Dolores feel guilty, as if she were betraying Papa Alejandro, her late brother, and the very reason for their quest.

"You realize that only nine of us remain," she said.

Clint nodded. "Sure. I learned to count that high in school before I quit."

"And Villa had at least four times that number when he took the herd."

Another nod. "That's also true, and it's been on my mind."

"How can we drive them north across one hundred fifty miles with Villa's riders chasing after us and maybe *federales*, too?"

Clint smiled at her. Replied, "I'd say we'll likely need a miracle."

Dolores felt her cheeks flush, whether from embarrassment or sudden anger she could not have said. "Do you believe in miracles?" she challenged him.

"I never have before," Parnell said. "Never had a cause to, but I *have* seen things I can't explain that go against the normal odds. Remember you and Sonya argued with your father that you ought to come along."

"It is our duty."

"And it's my job," Clint responded. "What I'm drawing pay for if I ever see the ranch again. Besides, from where I sit, we're past the point of no return. Either I find the herd and try our best to get it home again, or I can slink away and crawl into a hole somewhere. As for you and your sister . . ."

"We have made a promise to our father. I will not betray him. Neither will Sonya."

"I guess we forge ahead, then," Clint replied. "Whatever happens next, we face it and fight through."

Or die trying, Dolores thought, but kept that to herself, internalizing the depression it elicited. Instead, she answered Clint, saying, "I'll do my part. Be sure of that."

"I never doubted it," he said, wearing a wistful smile. "Just keep your Winchester and pistols handy."

Raising an index finger to his hat brim in parting, Clint rode off toward the column's head, Dolores following and easing into place beside her sister's varnish roan. Ahead of them, but trailing Clint, Jesús Zarita rode slumped over, wrists bound tightly to his saddle horn. Two Mescaleros flanked him, Kuruk on his right, Nantan Lupan off to his left, holding Zarita's reins.

Between them, the Apaches could prevent him from escaping, but Dolores almost hoped that he would try. In that case, she had made a solemn promise to herself. Before one of his escorts could lash out with knife or tomahawk to finish him, Dolores meant to draw her Colt .38 caliber and put a bullet through his brain.

For Papa Alejandro and the brother she would never see again in life, she thought it was the very least that she could do.

And truth be told, the prospect did not bother her at all.

JESÚS ZARITA RECKONED that he must know how a hog felt, trussed up in a killing shed and waiting for a butcher's knife to open up its throat. He had survived so far—more than Enrique Rocha might have said, if a cadaver could express itself in words—but as for coming through the day and night ahead still living, Jesús did not like his odds.

Thinking about Rocha caused him to wonder where the brash *bandido*'s soul was at that moment. Visions of the afterlife, assuming such a thing existed, rarely crossed Zarita's mind, and then only to sneer at the idea of heaven with its rumored streets of gold. After the things that he had done, the many crimes he had committed in his thirty years on earth, it never had occurred to him that he might be made welcome at the Pearly Gates, wherever legend claimed they could be found.

And as for hell, with its eternal torment of the damned . . . well, Jesús blocked that from his thoughts, preferring to indulge in alcohol when teachings from his early childhood bubbled to the surface of his dissolute subconscious mind. Thinking of tequila and cerveza now, wishing he had some, set his upset stomach grumbling again, Zarita fearing that he might disgrace himself by spewing uncontrollably.

The moment passed, and he cast sidelong glances at the Mescaleros flanking him like bookends, seeming

to ignore him while their hands rested on weapons,
ready to eviscerate Zarita if he made a sudden move.
One of his second cousins had been murdered by
Apaches in Sonora, years before, and while Jesús had
never viewed the corpse, descriptions of it circulated
through his family, each telling turned more gruesome
than the last, and somehow always raised at mealtimes
when they killed Zarita's adolescent appetite.

In fact, he knew that if he tried to flee and the
Apache watchdogs did not kill him outright, others
from the party would be quick to blast him from his
saddle into dark oblivion. That fear immobilized him,
but his mind was racing at the same time, plotting ways
in which he might escape after the gringo and his riders saw the stolen horses, leaving Jesús to his own de-
vices while they moved in to reclaim the herd.

And things could only go downhill from there.

On one hand, his captors might execute him once
they found the horses in the canyon he'd described for
them—and if Villa had moved the herd sometime yesterday, while Rocha and Jesús were in Ascensión, his
fate would certainly be sealed.

Unfortunately, that was not the only danger to Zarita's life, as he well knew. Assuming that the gringo
and his mismatched team of riders found the stolen
horses as predicted, they would obviously leave him
bound to stop him from alerting his fellow *villistas* to
their plan. When they attempted to retrieve the herd,
outnumbered four or five to one, they would be massacred, and then Villa would ultimately find Jesús
wherever he'd been left, assuming rightly that Zarita
had betrayed him.

That meant certain death as well, and when it came
to punishing a traitor, Jesús knew that Pancho Villa
could be just as brutal as a tribe of renegades. Only
three months before, when Javier Jurado caught a

member of the gang deserting after sundown, sneaking off to summon *federales* in the hope of getting a reward, Villa had ordered the construction of a pyre and supervised the turncoat being set ablaze beneath the light of a full moon.

Sometimes, when he was standing guard at night or lying in his bedroll on the verge of sleep, Jesús imagined he could still hear the defector screaming his lungs out as flames devoured him, flesh blackening and crisping off his bones.

Zarita's stomach gave another bilious lurch and might have shamed him if he had consumed his meager breakfast at the Lucky Lizard. As it was, he could not bottle up a belch that made his Mescalero escorts laugh until the stale aroma of tequila reached their nostrils. Jesús could not understand the words that passed between them, but he needed no interpreter to realize that they were mocking him.

It was almost enough to set Zarita raging, make him try a break for freedom even if it cost him his life, but courage failed him at the final instant, as it had before, when Rocha tried to pull a weapon on the ambush party and was instantly cut down.

Jesús Zarita was a killer, knew that he was named on "Wanted" posters and that nooses waited for him in Chihuahua and Jalisco if Díaz's *federales* ever captured him alive, but he had never been much good at fighting in a manly way. Of course, he'd had his share of drunken barroom brawls, but that was alcohol posing as courage. He had never stood before another gunman in the street to fight it out at noon, always preferring to attack from hiding when he could, backshooting, or relying on a greater force of numbers to suppress unruly adversaries.

Faced with Pancho Villa's righteous anger, Jesús knew that he would crumble, weeping, begging for his life, screaming until his lungs at last could draw no breath.

And that was why he must attempt to flee as soon as possible, the first time that he saw even the slightest opportunity.

SONYA AGUIRRE HAD no faith in what their captive had revealed, but she was loath to say so openly, aware that there was no alternative to following his lead and hoping for the best. As for herself, Sonya had largely given up on hoping when the raiders struck her father's hacienda, and she'd seen her sister lose much of her normal confidence when Paco Yáñez fell in battle on their first day in Chihuahua.

As a twin, she felt the grief Dolores had endured after Paco's death, when both of them were still grieving brother Eduardo's loss and worrying about their wounded father, back at home. Leading the team that had been whittled down considerably, Clint Parnell felt duty bound to soldier on with his assignment, even unto death, and fear for his well-being amplified her own sense that their time was running out.

Sonya had seen the way Clint looked at her, the secret smiles he flashed at her from time to time, when no one else was watching, and while nothing more had passed between them yet, she had begun to see a future there—until Francisco Villa intervened to tear her comfortable world apart. Since then, she had sustained one loss after another, slaying strangers to the point where it began to seem routine, imagining a bloody end for all of them in Mexico that left her father childless, ultimately destitute.

With those thoughts brewing in her mind, Sonya briefly considered reaching for her Springfield rifle, executing their reluctant guide before he could betray them all, then caught herself, backed off from the insane consideration as Dolores rode back from her talk with Clint and took her normal place on Sonya's left.

"A penny for your thoughts?" Dolores said.

"You would not get your money's worth," Sonya replied.

"You do not trust the swine we captured," said Dolores. Not a question from her tone.

"Do you?" Sonya replied.

Dolores smiled at that. "Of course not. At the first sign that he's tricking us, I'll blow his brains out."

"You will have to get in line, *hermana*," Sonya cautioned. "But if he *can* lead us to the herd . . ."

"Then what?" Dolores asked her twin. "Villa is said to lead forty or fifty men."

"Minus the ones we killed at home," Sonya reminded her sister.

"So?" Dolores answered. "Suppose there are no more than thirty. We are still outnumbered nearly four to one."

"If we can take them by surprise . . ."

"And there is still the herd to think about," Dolores said. "Consider driving them across the border and back home again, with *federales* and *villistas* hunting us along the way."

"I've thought of little else," Sonya advised. "Our duty still remains."

Dolores frowned at that. "Do you suppose Papa would rather have his horses or his daughters safely back at home?"

"I think he would prefer that none of us go hungry through the winter and next year," Sonya replied.

"You think we have a chance then? Honestly?"

"I say we've come too far and sacrificed too much to simply turn around and run, *hermana*. Not that we could make it anyway, after the *federales* we have killed."

Dolores thought about that, frowning, finally agreeing with a desultory nod. "*Entonces, hasta el final*," she said at last.

Sonya echoed her twin, translating her words mentally. "On to the finish, then."

"And may the devil take whoever stands between us and our goal," Dolores said.

"From what I understand, the devil has already taken Pancho Villa."

Putting on a smile she did not feel, Dolores said, "Then we shall send him down to hell where he belongs."

And likely join him there, she thought, but kept that morbid postscript to herself.

CHAPTER THIRTEEN

West of Ascensión, Chihuahua

"WHERE ARE THOSE *idiotas inútiles*, Javier? Are they not hours late by now?"

"At least three hours, jefe," Javier Jurado answered with a nod of confirmation. He agreed with Villa that Enrique Rocha and Jesús Zarita were idiots, indeed, but had not found the pair of them entirely useless. They were sometimes fairly good at cleaning up around the camp, and adequate at standing guard by night, if they could stay awake and had no liquor close at hand.

"Four other men are nagging me about their turn in town," Villa explained, as if he thought Jurado might be unaware of that. "I have a mind to send them on and find the *absentistas*, possibly disarm them before sending them back here."

Jurado frowned. Said, "Jefe, that might cause an incident involving *la policía*. If they become involved, or summon *federales* . . ."

A weary sigh from Villa as he said, "You are correct, of course. That is the last thing that we need while waiting for Zapata to arrive. But I must punish them somehow if they ever return."

"It is a matter of some delicacy, jefe," his lieutenant ventured. "Rocha is the worse *borracho* of the two. He's always sneaking drinks and slipping off from work if he can manage it. Zarita is more pliable and would not leave Enrique drunk in town or laid up in some *puta*'s crib to ride back here alone."

"Perhaps a whipping," Villa said, a smile playing across his face.

"Perhaps."

"You disagree?" asked Villa.

"If we shame Rocha in public, he is likely to desert, jefe," Jurado counseled. "If he runs . . . well, who knows where he might end up, revealing secrets that may harm us in the end."

"So, you think I should kill him, then?" The prospect did not seem to bother Villa overmuch.

"Or possibly assign him to a dirty job like cleaning out the stables, eh?" Jurado said. "A month or two of that with no more trips into the city may encourage him to mend his ways."

"You trust in his intelligence?" Villa inquired.

Jurado stalled answering that. At last he said, "Not much. He's like a simple-minded child, but he can follow orders well enough if supervised."

"In which case, you'll be happy to ride with him if I ever let him go back to Ascensión."

Jurado managed to suppress a grimace and keep any skepticism from his tone as he replied, "As you see fit, jefe."

"*Bueno*. Go on and send the others who are waiting, with instructions for their tardy comrades to return immediately and report to me.

"And if they don't come back within the next two hours, we must reconsider executing both of them. Does twenty pesos for the head of a deserter seem a fair price, Javier?"

"It should encourage prompt response," Jurado said. "Once we have spread the word, they will find nowhere in Chihuahua safe to hide themselves."

"Now, if only we could speed Emiliano on his way," mused Villa.

"He is still beyond our reach, jefe," Jurado said. "We should not risk a scouting expedition at the present time."

"No," Villa granted. "We can only wait—but not much longer, eh? If there is still no word by day after tomorrow, we should look for other buyers. I obtained this herd to sell, not start a breeding rancho of my own."

Jurado sometimes marveled at the way Villa claimed credit for the deeds accomplished by his men acting together. Granted, he came up with most of the ideas, always consulting Javier, but nothing on the scale of their New Mexico incursion could be realized without seasoned *bandidos* pitching in.

That simple knowledge was not jealousy; far from it. Javier Jurado knew he lacked Villa's charisma when it came to handling others, mollifying and cajoling them into pursuing tasks that placed their lives at risk. Granted, they were compensated handsomely, but it was still the man in charge—backed by his ever-growing legend—who commanded their respect and loyalty.

When all else failed, Jurado played the role of hatchet man.

He knew his place and had no yearning to rise above it, to command a troop of raiders on his own with all of the attendant dangers. Javier was happy in his role as Villa's second-in-command, and if that forced him into dirty jobs from time to time, like playing nursemaid to a pair of negligent *villistas*, he could live with that.

It was the price of standing next to power, basking in his jefe's aura, elevated by that close proximity. But given Villa's volatility, standing *too* close meant that Jurado faced a risk of being burned—perhaps incinerated, so that there was nothing left.

As Villa's *teniente*, he passed orders down to their *soldados* and made certain they were carried out. But there might come a time when being privileged to speak with Pancho's voice was a handicap.

If Javier was careless in performance of his duties, it might even get him killed.

K URUK OF THE Mescaleros flexed his muscles as he sat astride his unshod blood bay pony, challenging his recent minor wounds to cause him pain. They did not disappoint him, but the sting and ache were manageable, nothing that would alter the expression on his stoic face.

Kuruk mourned in his silent way for Goyathlay, the yawner, and for slippery Bimisi, who had fallen and lay buried now where no one from their tribe would ever find their bones. Though neither man had passed through wedding ceremonies, both left young women behind to mourn their loss—Lilue, "hawk singing," for Goyathlay; Onawa, "wide awake," who must now wait in vain for affable Bimisi to return. Kuruk had shed no tears for either warrior, but he felt an empty place beneath his ribs and longed for vengeance if the spirits granted him that opportunity.

The captive *mexicano*, riding slouched between himself and Nantan Lupan, would be first to pay that price in blood if Kuruk had his way. Should he betray the team and fail in guiding them to reach their destination, it would be Kuruk's pleasure to leave him in the desert as coyote food, but not before the prisoner had suffered to his limit of endurance.

For now, Kuruk could do no more than wait. He had agreed with his selected tribesmen, those who still survived, to serve as Clint Parnell required and earn their stipulated pay. The next time they faced battle, though—and he could feel it drawing nearer, almost smelled it on a faint breeze blowing from the west, Kuruk would sate his hunger for revenge.

And if he ever saw his village once again, he just might call on nubile Lilue, console her in her grief.

Or maybe Onawa.

He glanced beyond the prisoner toward Nantan Lupan, riding his cremello pony. While his father was their village chief, Gray Wolf was younger by two summers than Kuruk and thus had not been chosen as their party's leader when selecting volunteers to cross the Rio Grande. So far, he had done well in combat and would doubtless make a fair successor to his father when that time came, but this trip was meant to be his trial by fire.

The last survivor of the five Apaches who'd begun that journey, Itza-chu, lagged back behind his tribesmen, ready just in case the *mexicano* tried to run amok and somehow save himself. That was impossible, Kuruk knew, but a man in desperation sometimes lost his mind and threw his life away.

Watching their prisoner, smelling the sour reek of alcohol that emanated from his pores, Kuruk found himself wishing that the man *would* make a move, but he quickly suppressed that feeling. If the captive did not keep his word and lead them to the stolen herd of horses, then the ragtag posse would be forced to start again and seek some other means of finding them.

Meanwhile, their enemies were doubtless scouring

the arid countryside, perhaps had found their trail already and would be advancing to attack them.

Kuruk had no doubts about his fate if they were overtaken and surrounded by the *federales*. Soldiers would not even try to capture living Mescaleros, vying for the honor of a scalp lifted that would put pesos in the slayer's purse. Their gringo leader and the *mexicano* twins might be arrested, if they were disarmed, disabled, but considering the women's beauty, Kuruk thought it might be better for them if they sacrificed themselves.

Although Kuruk had never lived in Mexico and rarely traveled there, he knew that so-called soldiers working for Porfirio Díaz were known for wanton cruelty toward rural villagers and to their females in particular. How would they treat a pair of *mexicanas* from *el norte* caught trespassing in Chihuahua with a makeshift posse of *bandidos* and Apaches? If they managed to survive the first encounter, Kuruk reckoned they would likely wind up in some low-rent brothel where Díaz's flunkies pocketed the cash and women suffered through their last years in a kind of wasting death.

The warrior shot another cold glance toward the prisoner who rode beside him.

That one, he could rest assured, was definitely living through the final hours of his miserable life. Kuruk himself would gladly see to that.

THE SUN'S POSITION overhead told Clint Parnell that it was noon or thereabouts. He checked that guess against his pocket watch and saw that he was right. The time read seven past twelve on the cusp of afternoon.

He tugged back gently on his gelding's reins, turning the dapple gray enough to let the three riders behind him close the gap. Looking past Nantan Lupan toward Jesús Zarita, he demanded, "How much farther?"

Glancing up from where his wrists were tied around his saddle horn, the captive shrugged. Said, "Eight or nine more miles. I can't be sure. I think no one has ever measured it."

"We're talking now about the canyon with the horses," Parnell sought to clarify. "Not Villa's camp?"

"*Es correcto*," said Zarita. "But there will be guards on watch, you realize? The animals are not left unattended."

"Do you know how many guards?" Clint asked.

"It varies. More at night than in the daytime. Three or four when there is light, and double that after sundown."

Clint did the calculations in his head. Traveling at their present pace, eight miles should take them roughly two hours; tack on another thirty, maybe forty minutes for a nine-mile ride at walking speed. That meant, if Jesús was not lying through his teeth, arrival near the box canyon sometime between the hours of three and four o'clock. The sky would still be clear and bright by then, but Parnell reckoned darkness would serve better for the job he had in mind.

Sundown meant twice as many guards—again if he could trust Zarita—call it six or eight *villistas* standing watch. That gave Clint's team the very slimmest of advantages, and he preferred striking under the cover of nightfall if possible.

A raid in darkness meant that most of Villa's pistoleros would be sitting down to supper in their main camp, wherever that was, relaxed and maybe with their mounts unsaddled for the evening. If shooting was required to deal with any guards watching the stolen herd, an armed response from Villa's camp should be disorganized, his men at least briefly disoriented in the dark. Before first reinforcements reached the canyon, Parnell hoped to have a firm defensive ring established and repel them.

Failing that, he might have to stampede the herd directly through the *bandoleros* who had stolen them, and if he lost some in the process, it was preferable to surrendering the lot of them. Whatever happened after that was anybody's guess.

"You understand what's waiting for you if you've lied to us? If you have any tricks in mind?"

Zarita bobbed his head, avoided meeting Parnell's gaze. "*Sí, entiendo*," he replied.

"I hope so," Clint advised. "Because you're out of second chances here."

With that, Clint rode back to the straggling column's point position, eyes scanning the landscape for potential danger. He already had a plan in mind to camp somewhere close by the canyon where Aguirre's stolen horses were confined, assuming they could find it acting on directions from their prisoner.

If they did not . . .

In that case, Clint would rid them of Jesús Zarita and attempt to spot the herd by other means. It required slipping someone into the outlaws' base camp after dark, one of his three vaqueros who could pass a casual inspection—that is if they could locate the camp itself.

And after that?

Parnell would simply have to keep his fingers crossed, or maybe take a fling at trying unaccustomed prayer.

With that in mind, he pictured Sonya and Dolores volunteering for the mission, hoping they could get past Pancho Villa's guards and mingle with the normal camp followers who attached themselves to such outfits. Both male and female, those nomadic souls traditionally serviced needs of armies on the move, providing goods and services not normally available, including meals and liquor, laundry, nursing, sutlery, and sexual favors. If they tried that, and never mind how they pleaded with him, Clint was dead set on refusing them.

His boss's daughters had already taken risks enough, and still more lay ahead for them, without jumping from a skillet, landing smack-dab in the middle of a raging fire.

Whatever sins he carried on his back already, Parnell knew he could not live with that.

JESÚS ZARITA RISKED a glance skyward, no sudden moves to spook his Mescalero guards and cause them to lash out at him with knives or hatchets. He had never been much good at telling time from the position of the sun, but he was certain that they must have traveled roughly half the distance from the point where he was captured to the spot where Villa's stolen herd was kept secure from prying eyes.

Betraying Villa did not haunt Zarita, since he reckoned that he had no choice. He feared discovery and punishment, but his preeminent concern was living long enough to make his getaway, first escaping from the posse that had killed Enrique Rocha, then putting sufficient distance between Villa and himself to guarantee that he was never found and brought to book.

Whatever else came out of this bizarre experience, Zarita hoped to make it through alive and in one piece.

That would require a weapon, and Zarita did not like his odds for laying hands on one with nine armed enemies surrounding him, each one clearly prepared to kill him if he made a move. In normal circumstances, Jesús might have thought the twin sisters least dangerous among his captors, but he had noted the way they glared at him, as if they had a score to settle that required spilling Zarita's blood. He guessed that they were from the rancho Villa's men had raided in New Mexico, but it was no good telling them that he had missed that action, left behind with others in Chihuahua after Villa chose his best men for the job.

At first, Jesús had viewed that as one time when being a slovenly *borracho* worked to his advantage, but it obviously did him no good now. Either his captors pegged him as a liar when he truthfully denied participation in the raid, or else they did not care. Whoever rode with Pancho Villa was their enemy, and there was no forgiveness in their stony hearts.

Zarita knew he must escape.

But how?

His best hope would be when most of them left him unattended, slinking off to liberate the horses Villa had obtained on his foray into *el norte*. Or if they returned, confirming that his information was correct, the gringo might release him.

No.

On second thought that seemed improbable. His captors would not trust him on the loose, afraid that he would rush to Villa's camp and warn his *jefe* of the raid impending or in progress. The alternative, leaving Zarita bound for Pancho to discover him when it was done, held no appeal, since it would surely mean his death at Villa's hands.

It was escape or nothing, then.

That was a daunting prospect with his hands bound, possibly his feet as well once he'd dismounted, and no cutting tool to free his hands. A rough stone might suffice, but that depended on where he was left, and scraping at the rawhide strips until they separated might take hours. If discovered in the process by whichever of his captors stayed behind to guard him, he would certainly be slain—and if his killer proved to be one of the Mescaleros, he would probably be tortured in the process.

Something else, then.

Like the cutthroat razor hidden in his boot.

It was a last resort in case of trouble, backing up his rifle, six-gun, and the folding knife that had been taken from his pocket. Zarita had never actually used it, but he kept the blade well stropped, folded inside its handle, shoved inside the stocking on his right foot with a hole worn in its tip from his big toenail. It remained snugly in place after he had been searched twice, safely out of sight.

The problem, once again: Zarita could not reach it while his hands were bound behind his back.

He would think of something when the time came, and would do his utmost to succeed.

It was too bad, Jesús thought, that his best never seemed to account for much. But he was motivated now, by fear and mounting anger toward the strangers who had killed Enrique Rocha and forced Jesús to confront his darkest fear of painful death.

On rare occasions when he had considered it before, Zarita thought that he would likely die from guzzling down too much tequila in too short a time, or maybe end his life with cataclysmic pain while rutting in a harlot's crib. Perhaps a horse would throw him, snap his neck, or he might take a bullet in a *federale* ambush. If worse came to worst, he might even be hanged or face a military firing squad.

But to be bound and butchered by a Mescalero or one of the gringo's riders? That was unacceptable.

Slowly, his mind began to work out means for getting to the razor in his boot when it was time. Within another mile, Zarita had begun to think that he might just surprise them all.

* * *

DOLORES AGUIRRE SIPPED water out of her canteen. It was tepid and had an earthy flavor to it, but fulfilled its necessary function, moistening her tongue and throat. Above her a relentless sun beat down on the Chihuahua flats, while up ahead, a range of rugged hills shimmered behind the insubstantial veil of a mirage.

She hoped that they would find the canyon that contained her father's horses soon. Clint planned to camp before sundown, when he judged they were near enough, sending the Mescalero called Itza-chu off ahead to scout the land and find out whether their prisoner had spoken truthfully or lied in a misguided effort to protect himself from harm.

If so, he had misjudged his situation fatally.

As if reading her sister's mind—a trait common with twins—Sonya asked, "Do you think we'll find them where he said?"

Dolores shrugged. Replied, "I hope so. We've been at this long enough."

"It is not over yet, *hermana*."

"No."

Sonya's reminder was unnecessary. Even if Great Hawk found the horses and reported back on their location, bloody work still lay ahead. There would be guards watching the herd, and they must be disposed of, which undoubtedly meant killing them. Add more lives to the butcher's bill of their excursion into Mexico, and if the sounds of battle reached as far as Pancho Villa's base camp, then . . .

More fighting, with their party or whatever still remained of it facing a force much larger than their own. Dolores pictured a last stand, like that of Texicans penned up inside the Alamo nearly three quarters of a century ago, one hundred eighty-nine of them facing two thousand soldiers under General Antonio López de Santa Anna, riding to suppress rebellion in what then was known as Texas Mexicano. Santa Anna's men had slaughtered every rebel in the mission-fortress outside San Antonio, then faced defeat at San Jacinto one month later.

But while Santa Anna had rebounded from that beating to become dictator of all Mexico, then to win election as *el presidente* of the Mexican Republic, there would likely be no happy ending for the members of Dolores's party.

She wondered now whether she would ever see her home or father's face again. If not, at least she would be spared the vision of him grieving over her, over her twin, presiding over services beside two empty graves.

There would be nothing left for transport to New Mexico if they were slaughtered in Chihuahua, no appeal through diplomatic channels to Porfirio Díaz or to the U.S. Department of State. With his last two children gone, what would remain for Papa Alejandro on the hacienda he had built through labor spanning years, destroyed within the space of one short week?

Nothing.

Still, she could not turn back now. Her twin would be the first one to condemn her for a show of weakness, and Dolores dared not face her father at their hacienda, trying to explain why she'd left Sonya in Chihuahua with Clint and the others, running from a fight that could have saved their family.

As for the odds of that succeeding, she refused to think about it on the eve of a battle that might leave them all dead, their bones bleaching underneath the desert sun. She might find it impossible to hold positive thoughts, but on the other hand, preoccupation with defeat made her feel guilty, as if she had cursed their effort with a *bruja*'s evil charm.

Dolores would remain and see what happened next because she had no other choice. She'd made a promise to her father, to Eduardo's memory, and to her comrades who had sacrificed their lives in Mexico so far.

She simply had no other choice.

Southeast of Ascensión

"*¡Más federales, jefe!*" said Alfonso Soberon, reining his rose-gray gelding to a halt and pointing northward, toward low-lying hills where horsemen clad in khaki had appeared.

Zapata saw the troops, some fifty of them, still the best part of a mile away, and snarled a bitter curse. Turning his sorrel back, he barked an order at the men strung out behind him.

"*¡Retiren!*"

They began retreating as commanded, asked no questions, doubling back in the direction of a straggling line of Rocky Mountain white pine that the farthest back in line had barely cleared so far. They did not panic, but all sensed their leader's urgency and the impending threat of contact with Díaz's troops.

Once relatively safe inside the cover of the trees, it came down to a waiting game. Zapata and his *teniente* had to watch the *federales*, see if they were riding due south and, more vitally, if they had glimpsed the party of guerrillas up ahead of them. They had Zapata's team outnumbered by a dozen, give or take, and while Emiliano would have played those odds in other circumstances, a pitched battle at that moment would have spelled disaster for his mission to Ascensión.

Zapata was relieved at length when the *federale* column turned westward, but that relief was short-lived. Their present route of march would lead his adversaries toward Ascensión unless they turned off to the north or south before reaching that city thirty-odd miles distant from the desert they were currently traversing. If they stayed on course, it meant Zapata's riders would be following their enemies, most of the journey over open ground, when any *federale* might glance back and see their dust rising.

And even if the soldiers did not spot them, did not change directions and attack, how would it benefit Zapata to arrive at Pancho Villa's stronghold once the troops had passed, driving him on to safer territory? How would the exchange of gold for stolen horses then take place at all?

A sinking feeling in Zapata's stomach cautioned him that he had made the long ride from Morelos to Chihuahua on a fool's errand. His growing band of revolutionaries needed horses, and the price quoted by Pancho Villa was a fair one, but with each mile that he traveled farther north, Emiliano came across another stumbling block. His grandmother would have regarded them as evil omens and advised him to turn back, seek livestock closer to his base of operations, even if he had to rustle up a herd himself and place himself beyond the law.

It would not be the first time he had crossed that line, and so far he had lived to tell the tale.

But if he followed *federales* to the very place where he intended to commit a crime—and one that might have repercussions in *el norte*—would it not prove him a fool?

Zapata loathed frustration, had since childhood, and impatience was something he had to guard against even today, when he was thirty-one years old and fully grown. It could betray him if he let it, and for one who planned to overturn the very government of Mexico, such rash behavior might prove fatal, to himself and to his cause.

Emiliano owed it to his men—and to thousands of the campesinos who had joined with him in spirit, even if they balked thus far at rising up against Díaz—to stay alive and lead them on to victory. Or, failing that, at least to a conclusion that would pave the way for his disciples to demand their freedom in the future.

Shoulders slumped in resignation, close to weeping now but fighting it, he told Alfonso, "*¡Es demasiado!* It's too much. We're turning back."

"What of the horses, jefe?" Soberon inquired.

"We can find others elsewhere, given time. We have already risked too much, even without the ride back to Morelos driving fourteen hundred animals."

Alfonso nodded, still watching the column of *solda-dos* as it drew away from them, westbound. "The men will not complain," he said. "At least they had an outing, eh?"

Zapata forced a smile. Replied, "And we shall live to fight another day."

"And Villa?"

"He will learn to live with disappointment as we all do," said Zapata. "To be fair, send out a rider with the message. He should reach Ascensión by midnight, or at least by dawn."

"*Sí*, jefe. I will see to it at once."

Sitting alone, Zapata wondered if it was a sin for him to feel relieved.

DUSK WAS STILL at least two hours off when Itza-chu rejoined the posse, bringing word that he had spotted the box canyon from a distance and had seen horses contained within it. Sonya felt a subtle lifting of her spirits when she heard that news, then settled back into a kind of funk, imagining the trials that still lay ahead of them.

First step, the party had agreed with Clint's sugges-

tion that they camp until night fell, no fire, hoping that
no one, whether *federales* or *villistas*, happened by and
spotted them.

Next up, they had to deal with their lone prisoner,
then move in on the stolen herd and try to wrest it from
the control of Pancho Villa's guards, ideally without
drawing reinforcements from the outlaw's main base
camp. Sonya, for her part, was not sure that would be
possible.

Part three, whether or not they faced enhanced resistance from the canyon, eight of them—or nine, if
they finished Zarita without leaving anyone to guard
him in the meantime—must maneuver nearly fifteen
hundred horses from their trap without provoking an
aimless stampede.

And finally, if all of those conditions were fulfilled,
they had to drive the herd one hundred fifty miles across
Chihuahua's desert and the Rio Grande, avoiding hostile contacts while en route, returning them safely to
Papa Alejandro's hacienda.

As Sonya reviewed the phases of Clint's plan, to
which she and Dolores had agreed, they now felt like
the trials of Hercules from Greek mythology. And
even Hercules, himself a demigod with powers far beyond the reach of mortal men, did not survive, slain by
an arrow tipped in poison from the multiheaded Hy-
dra that he had reputedly defeated earlier.

In short, the prospect of a happy ending for their
quest was faint, at best.

The place that Clint selected for their campsite was
a dry arroyo choked with yellow grass and tumbleweeds. The sky above was clear as the sun lowered,
ruling out the prospect of a flash flood to disturb them
while they waited for Clint's signal to advance. Sonya
found room to sit down with Dolores and their ani-

mals, after she'd checked the ground for rattlesnakes and scorpions, hoping she could relax a bit before they rose again and rode into the panther's lair.

"I don't like waiting, even if it's just for dark," Dolores said.

"Better than riding in where anyone can see and open fire on us," Sonya replied.

"*Supongo que sí*," her twin said. "I suppose so. But the stalling sets my nerves on edge."

"I feel it, too," said Sonya. "But you trust Clint's judgment?"

"*Cómo no.* Of course, but even if he's right, and we succeed, it means we either have to start the horses north tonight, or Villa's men rush over from their camp and trap us here."

"I wish we had more caballeros," Sonya granted, "but the rest were needed back at home."

"And here we are. Nine left to do the job of twenty, even thirty, in the middle of the night. How many of us do you think will finally survive, *hermana*?"

"I'm not counting anybody out just yet," Sonya replied. "If fighting is required, we are as good as any man, eh? And we've brought along some of the hacienda's best."

"Remember what the Frenchman said?" Dolores asked. "Some count, I think."

"Refresh my memory."

"He said, 'God sides with big squadrons against the small,' or words to that effect."

Sonya supplied the speaker's name. "Comte de Bussy-Rabutin. And Voltaire disagreed with him. *He* said, 'God does not side with the heavy battalions but with the best shots.'"

Dolores laughed at that. Both sisters had been tutored in the classics and in history, dividing time between their studies and working around the ranch. "What would you do, then, with our prisoner, *hermana*?"

"Kill him," Sonya answered coldly. "He is no longer of any use to us."

I'M TIRED OF waiting for those useless mongrels," Pancho Villa told Alfonso Soberon. "Send four men to Ascensión, the next in line to go. Tell them to sniff out Rocha and Zarita first, before they go to drinking. Send them back to me at once."

"*Sí,* jefe. But they may not wish to come," his second-in-command observed.

"I don't care what they *wish* for," Villa sneered. "When they return, I'll punish them accordingly, for wasting all our time."

"And if they don't return?"

"Then spread the word to all friends, near and far. Ten pesos for the head of each deserter. Twenty pesos for delivery to me alive, with only minor damage."

"I shall see to it at once, jefe."

Alfonso left Villa alone beside the campfire, sipping from a half-empty tequila bottle in between drags on a long, crooked cigar. Pancho had made his mind up that the two drunkards who had defied his orders would serve better as examples to the rest of his *bandidos* than they'd ever been on any raid for cash or livestock. He would hold court over them with all his other men assembled, looking on, to judge which slacker was primarily responsible. That one would die by Villa's own stern hand. The other might escape with simple flogging if he groveled and abased himself convincingly.

Spilling a little blood would fortify his other pistoleros and remind them forcefully of who would always be in charge.

At least as long as Pancho Villa lived.

His thoughts shifted, turned once again back toward Emiliano Zapata, the gold that he was carrying to close their bargain on the horses stolen from New Mexico. If he did not arrive tomorrow, or the next day at the very latest, Villa would be forced to change his plans, remove the horses to another hideaway and shift his camp's location likewise. Sitting still for too long in Villa's profession tempted fate and weak-willed human beings, threatening his freedom and life itself.

From his position near the fire, Villa saw four men riding out of camp, eastbound in the direction of Ascensión. At the same moment, Javier Jurado returned and sat beside him on a flat stone thrust up from the desert soil.

"It's done," Alfonso said. "They're going now."

"I see that," Villa answered. "And they understand their orders?"

Jurado nodded. "Find Rocha and Zarita first, before they start on the tequila and *muchachas*."

"And you trust them?"

That produced a shrug. "As much as I trust anyone," Javier said. "They are *bandidos* but not *idiotas*. They already know what's waiting for Enrique and Jesús."

"*Está bien*," Villa replied, letting it go. "I worry more about Zapata now."

Jurado frowned into the fire. "He would be foolish not to take the horses at the price you offered him. It will be good for everyone."

"If he can make it," Villa said. "Our eyes and ears report the *federales* out in force since Agua Fria. Still no word about whoever executed their amigos."

"They will be discovered and eliminated," Javier replied. He sounded confident.

"But in the meantime they could trouble us," said Villa. Swigging down a mouthful of tequila, waiting for the fumes to clear his sinuses, he said, "I have decided we should move the herd tomorrow."

"Move it where, jefe?" Jurado asked.

"Do you remember Juan Baillères?"

"*Sí*. The farmer with the ugly wife and daughters?"

"That's the one. His land is four or five miles from the canyon where we have the horses now," Villa replied.

"Does he have room to keep them for us? Will he do it?"

"I think he would do most things for *dinero*," Villa said. "Part of his land has wooded hills. There are corrals for livestock that he does not wish the *federales* to discover."

"Stolen?" asked Jurado.

Villa shrugged. "I've never asked him, but it's fairly obvious."

"He knows you are aware of that, jefe?"

"He showed them to me. There were longhorn cattle last time."

"Fifteen hundred of them?" Javier was clearly skeptical.

"I trust that he will make accommodations if the price is right. Also, we'll leave some pistoleros to assist him."

"For how long, if I may ask?"

"I tire of waiting for Zapata," Villa answered. "If he does not reach us by tomorrow or the morning after that, no later, I will find another buyer for the herd."

"Emiliano won't be happy," Javier observed, "after he's ridden all that way for nothing."

"Then he should have ridden faster, eh?" Villa winked at his second-in-command. "Time waits for no man in this world."

CHAPTER FOURTEEN

CLINT PARNELL CRAVED a cup of hot black coffee, but he settled for a drink from his canteen instead. Having imposed the no-fire rule on his companions, he could not be seen to violate it, and in fact, his nerves were tight enough already that he did not need a caffeine boost to keep him on alert.

Daylight was nearly gone, the desert's temperature dropping as late afternoon gave way to the oncoming night. Clint had put on his fleece-lined corduroy jacket while others in his party reached for dusters or serapes, some buttoning shirts up to their necks for greater warmth. Someone had removed the saddle blanket from their captive's horse and draped it over him so that his head and boots protruded, at the top and bottom, but his body was concealed.

No problem there, Clint thought. The prisoner was still secured by rawhide thongs, wrists bound behind his back, ankles hobbled. He was not going anywhere until Parnell decided whether he should live or die.

Before this journey south, that choice would have weighed heavily upon Clint's mind. Tonight, after the things he'd done, the men he'd killed, it mattered no more to him than the act of stepping on a *cucaracha*. Whether that should have concerned him in itself remained a question that he did not care to contemplate.

Not when he reckoned there was still more killing to be done.

Clint understood that Pancho Villa's guards, who had been posted with the stolen herd, would not stand idly by without resistance while the horses were reclaimed. Before he got to that point in his planning, though, he had to plan his next step if Itza-chu could not find the canyon where Zarita claimed that the Aguirre herd was being kept.

So, one step at a time, and that would guarantee that Parnell faced no risk of dozing off.

He spent time seeing to his guns, ensuring that the Browning Auto-5 and Peacemaker were fully loaded, extra cartridges secure in the loops around his pistol belt and in his jacket's pockets. When he'd finished that, Clint drew his hunting knife, tested its cutting edge against his thumb, and reckoned it was sharp enough to see him through the night ahead if things went worse than he was hoping.

Never mind the odds against eventual success. If Parnell had considered that, he likely never would have left the ranch in Doña Ana County—or, if leaving, would have handed in his resignation first and ridden off alone.

Now, having pledged his word of honor to retrieve Don Alejandro's herd from Mexico, Clint had no choice but to proceed and let the chips fall where they may. He might not see the ranch again, or even make it to the Rio Grande, but if he failed, Clint knew his main regret would be from leading Sonya and Dolores to their doom.

They were so young and should have had their lives laid out in front of them with no storm clouds on the horizon. Losing Paco Yáñez obviously pained Dolores, coming on so close behind her brother's death, but she was bound to meet *hombres* in due time.

Or should if she survived.

That morbid thought depressed Clint, and he reconsidered having coffee, then decided that he couldn't stand to drink it cold. At least one of the posse's caballeros likely had a bottle of tequila in his saddlebag, but none of them were passing it around, intent on staying clearheaded when they eventually faced their enemies.

Now, if Parnell could just confirm exactly where to find them and the stolen herd, wipe out the nagging fear that they were on a wild-goose chase.

As if in answer to his thought, a sound of hoofbeats rapidly approaching from the northeast reached Clint's ears. He rose, hefting his shotgun, and the other members of his party closed around him, weapons ready if the rider proved to be an enemy.

Sighs of relief greeted their recognition of Itza-chu, finally returning from his quest to find the canyon filled with horses that their captive had described. Great Hawk reined up his unshod skewbald pony and dismounted, stroked its neck to calm the animal, and stood before Clint to report.

"I found it," he announced, casting a sidelong glance toward where Jesús Zarita sat huddled beneath his saddle blanket. "He was off by half a mile or so."

"How many guards?" Clint asked the Mescalero.

"I saw three," Itza-chu said. "But if the *comadreja* was not lying, they increase the number after nightfall."

Comadreja translated to "weasel." Parnell thought it was a fair description of their prisoner, apparently still grappling with the ill effects of last night's hangover.

"All right," Clint told the other members of his

team. "We'll give them half an hour more to change the guards. I don't want to meet any of them on the trail and start a fight before we've seen the herd. For now, just finish packing up. Make sure you don't leave anything behind."

D OLORES CLOSED HER saddlebag, buckled its strap, and slid her freshly loaded Winchester into its scabbard. She had already checked the Colt revolvers, one holstered on each side of her saddle horn, and had the pockets of her duster loaded with spare cartridges.

However many guards Villa had posted on the canyon, she was ready to confront them.

"Are you frightened?" Sonya asked, walking her varnish roan up to her sister's snowflake Appaloosa, on the right.

"Concerned," Dolores said. "Not frightened."

"I am," Sonya countered. "We've come all this way to fight with strangers, and our lives depend on the outcome. Not only *our* lives, bur our father's and all others living on the hacienda."

"It's not fair, I grant you," said Dolores, "but there's no one else."

Sonya switched subjects. Said, "I half expected that Zarita lied to us about the horses, about everything."

"He knows the penalty and does not have the courage," her twin replied. "A so-called man like that, he's brave with *los viejos*, women, children, if he has a gun and friends behind him. Otherwise . . ."

Dolores let it go at that and spat into the sand.

"What will become of him?" asked Sonya.

"Clint promised him freedom if he spoke the truth, after we found the herd. If it were up to me, I'd treat him as a mad dog running in the street."

"Just kill him?"

"He would do the same to us if he were armed," Dolores answered. "And our backs were turned."

Sonya considered that and nodded, did not contradict her sister's words. "When will it end?" she asked.

Dolores, after wondering the same thing of her own accord, had a response prepared. "When we are safe at home," she said, "together with as many of the horses as we can recover. When Papa sees us and smiles upon us for a job well done."

"Do you suppose he still remembers how to smile, *hermana*?" Sonya asked.

"I hope he will," Dolores said. Sometimes, discussing it with Sonya, it felt as if she were arguing with her own mind, trying to smother stubborn doubts that would not die.

"But since he lost Eduardo . . ."

"Do not speak of that tonight," Dolores interrupted. "We *all* lost Eduardo."

"But his only son . . ."

"We are his only children now," Dolores said. "He did not raise us to be wallflowers."

"He did not raise us to be men," Sonya replied. "Only to mimic them when there is no alternative."

"If you are softening, *hermana*—"

"No!" hissed Sonya, eyes flashing, voice lowered so that it would not reach another's ears. "I only meant . . ."

"Perhaps you ought to marry Clint," Dolores said, one corner of her mouth forming a half smile.

"Now you're talking nonsense!" Sonya said.

"Am I?" The smile widened. "You think I am the only one who's seen the two of you together."

"We've done nothing inappropriate."

"But not from lack of *wanting* to. On your side, anyway," Dolores said.

The dusk had deepened too much for her to see Sonya blush.

After another moment Sonya asked her, "Who else knows? Not Papa?"

"Give him some credit, Sonya. He is not *un tonto.*"

"I would never say that he's a fool." Her shoulders sagged, and Sonya's hands covered her face as she muttered, "*¡Dios mío!*"

"Well, of course *he* knows," Dolores teased her twin. "He sees all, understands all."

"Do you still believe that?" Sonya queried. "Truly? Even since Paco . . ."

"He's gone," Dolores said. "No one can change that."

"And you will not forget him," Sonya offered. "But you will find someone else in time."

The smile Dolores turned upon her sister now had a chill to it.

"Do we have time?" she asked Sonya. "Perhaps you should not sit here wasting what is left of yours."

THE SADDLE BLANKET that his captors had draped over him supplied Jesús Zarita with the cover he required, trying to reach the razor hidden in his right foot's stocking. Still, it was an awkward position, hands still bound behind him, working up a sweat despite the chill of night on the high desert, straining every muscle in his torso as he tried to reach his boot.

At first, Zarita feared that it would be impossible. He was not a contortionist, not double-jointed like the young *muchacha* he had seen performing at a circus sideshow in Nogales two years earlier, before he had joined Pancho Villa's band. In fact, she had not been *that* young, rather a supple beauty ripe for picking by a man who knew his way around *mujeres*, and Zaria had imagined all the things that she could do in bed if motivated properly. He knew that every *hombre* in the audience had wanted her, watching the way she tied herself in knots, did splits and handstands, undulated on the stage as if she were a serpent.

Sadly, he had been distracted by a tent serving tequila and had drowned his momentary lust in alcohol, but Jesús still remembered her and wished he had her talent now.

If only he could somehow reach his boot. Was that so much to ask?

It would require twisting his torso at the waist, he understood, while simultaneously lifting up his knees. The second set of rawhide thongs binding his ankles made the task more difficult, but in his mind's eye it did not appear impossible.

If only he were not an aging drunkard who had let himself decline to a condition where his muscles sometimes failed him lifting heavy weights in camp, or even mounting to the saddle of his horse after a night of drinking in some low cantina. Even so, what *hombre* worthy of the name could not reach his own ankle if his life depended on it?

Me, Zarita thought. *Pathetic creature that I am*.

His job was doubly complicated by the saddle blanket draping him from shoulders to the scuffed toes of his boots. If he disturbed it in his struggling, then it would be obvious to all his enemies that he was striving to escape. In that case, one of them would surely summon others or, if it were one of the Apaches, simply cut Zarita's throat or split his skull and spill his liquor-sodden brains onto the soil.

"*¡Dios ayúdame!*" he whispered to himself, but even as he spoke those words, Zarita knew that God was not about to help him, even though he bore the holy Savior's name. Rendered unworthy by his life of sin and crime, Jesús knew he would have to help himself.

It finally occurred to him that he must first slump over to his left side on the ground, keeping the blanket

snug around him to conceal his movements underneath it. Lying down, as if trying to sleep, he might be
able to raise his feet and knees while groping for his
right boot top, striving to dip his fingers down inside it.
Yet another problem was the numbness spreading
through his hands and forearms from the thongs around
his wrists, and stiffness in his shoulders from remaining
bound for hours.

Still . . .

There was no other option, even if Zarita had to
dislocate a shoulder in the process. If that happened,
would the arm be useless to him, or could he succeed,
retrieve the razor from his sock, and then snap the
shoulder back in place before he went to work slicing
his bonds?

Collapsing to his left was not as difficult as Jesús had
imagined, although his sombrero snagged against the
bank of the arroyo as he slumped. A tilting of his head
kept it from falling off entirely, and a sudden cramp
knifed through the left side of Zarita's neck, shooting
pain through his trapezius and down beneath his shoulder blade. Clenching his teeth, Zarita breathed slowly
until the pain began to ebb and he could move his arms
again.

Now to begin the final series of contortions that
would either set him free or end his life.

KURUK, NANTAN LUPAN, and Itza-chu sat on the
ground together, singing softly to their Mescalero
ancestors. Each tribesman held a different image in his
mind, of forebears lost to passing time or violence, along
with thoughts for gods whom they revered.

Kuruk particularly sang to Shotokunungwa, god of
sky, lightning, war, and the hunt, and to Mosau'u, god
of death, the underworld, and fire. They seemed the

most appropriate of deities for this night when his life might end, and he beseeched them both for strength to face his enemies with honor, striking fear into them as they tried to bring him down.

He also kept in mind an image of his grandfather, Calian—meaning "warrior" in the white man's tongue—who fought beside Victorio of the Mimbreño clan until their last stand against *mexicano* soldiers at the Tres Castillos battle in Chihuahua, in October 1880. Over the span of two days' fighting, sixty-two bold warriors fell, along with sixteen women and children, another sixty-eight women and children captured and sold into slavery. It was a grim defeat but still recalled with pride by Mescalero men and boys.

Kuruk did not fear death, and he assumed that Itzachu and Nantan Lupan felt the same. Whatever happened to them next was written in the stars, known to their long-departed ancestors beforehand, and was nothing Mescalero men had not experienced before. The fact that none of them were married or had children lent a certain freedom to their enterprise, an almost cavalier adventure before they returned—should they survive the trek—and settled down as honored members of their tribe.

For those who made it home—and those who died along the way as well—the record of their deeds would live in song and stories, suitably embellished over time, until they gained heroic status. Maidens would vie for their affection, yearn to bear their sons. From young bucks seeking an adventure, they would graduate into respected members of the tribe. The living would have proved themselves for all time, and the slain would be revered.

In other circumstances, Kuruk might have swallowed a peyote bud or two, hoping for visions, but he needed all his wits about him for the fight ahead. He had no doubt that the *villistas* would resist any attempt to liberate the stolen herd, and there was no point in attempting to negotiate with them. The quickest way of ending opposition was by killing them to the last man, along with any reinforcements their *bandido* leader sent to safeguard his four-legged loot.

How many gunmen would their party face in all? Kuruk had only estimates to work from. Thirty men or more had raided the Aguirre hacienda, and the leader of their posse, Clint Parnell, believed that Pancho Villa had more fighters in reserve at his base camp. Imagining a number did Kuruk no good, but only played to his anxiety. It would be better, he decided, to face danger as it came, one pistolero at a time.

And leave them dying on the battlefield.

Thinking of which, they already had one close by.

Villa's cohort had led them to the canyon where Aguirre's stolen horses were confined. For that, gringo Parnell had promised the *villista* his freedom, but Kuruk had made no such promise and he seriously doubted that releasing the *bandido* was a sound idea. To his suspicious mind, the captive was more likely to rejoin his former comrades, angling to save himself from Pancho Villa's wrath, and lead them in pursuit of the Aguirre party on its flight back to New Mexico.

But he could not do that if he were dead.

With that in mind, Kuruk knew he could not simply rise up and slay the prisoner without infuriating Clint Parnell and possibly the twin Aguirre sisters, too. There must be some excuse for killing him. If he escaped and tried to seize a weapon, for example, no one could complain that he was slain unnecessarily.

Frowning in concentration even as his song wound down, Kuruk glanced over toward the prisoner and found him lying on his side beneath the saddle blanket someone had tossed over him for warmth. The tilt of his sombrero hid the outlaw's face from view, but he was clearly moving underneath the blanket. Trying for a bit of comfort on the stony ground, perhaps, or else . . .

Rising, Kuruk strode out across the dry arroyo toward their prisoner, with one hand dropping to the decorated handle of his tomahawk.

SONYA FOUND CLINT checking cinches on his dapple gray's saddle. He had his back turned toward her as she led her varnish roan to join him, but he heard her coming, turned to face her as he slid his Browning Auto-5 into its saddle boot.

"All set?" he asked her, with an almost wistful smile.

"As ready as I'll ever be," Sonya replied.

"I wish there was some other way around this but . . . you know . . ." He let whatever else he'd meant to say trail off into thin air.

"It can't be helped," she said. "We both made promises."

"How is your sister holding up?" Clint asked.

Sonya knew that he was referring to the death of Paco Yáñez, though the lost vaquero's name remained unspoken.

"She'll survive," Sonya replied.

"I hope we all will," Clint amended.

"Yes, but just in case . . ."

She paused a beat too long, perhaps. It put a cautious frown on Parnell's face.

"What is it, Sonya?" he inquired.

Though normally loquacious, Sonya suddenly had difficulty forming words. It was embarrassing. She cleared her throat and tried again. "You know—that is, I *hope* you know . . ."

"Know what?" Clint urged her, with a sudden softness in his voice that was not often heard around the hacienda in his dealings with the hired hands.

Sonya blinked, swallowed, and took the plunge. "Know how I feel about you. How I've come to care about you over time."

Her cheeks were flaming now. Sonya was thankful that the dusk concealed her fevered blush.

Clint stared at her with rapt attention. For a moment, Sonya could not tell if he was shocked, humiliated, even mortified. If she'd surprised him, how would he react? Parnell's first loyalty was obviously to her father and the rancho. Would the pressure of her revelation make his working life untenable? Would he feel driven to reject her out of hand, perhaps even resign and travel on, riding out of her life for good?

Did any of that matter if they rode to meet their deaths tonight?

She was surprised when Clint moved closer to her, one hand raised to lightly touch her arm beneath the drape of her serape. "Sonya," he began.

"You don't have to say anything," she blurted out. "And please forgive my speaking out of turn. Forget this ever happened and—"

"I don't want to forget it," Parnell said.

"*¿No?*" she said, then quickly translated.

Clint shook he head. "Truth is, I care about you, too, and not so much as Alejandro's daughter. Working for him, though, I was afraid to say. How it would sound and look to him."

Sonya blinked away a startled tear, before it had a chance to reach her cheek. "My papa loves you like a son," she said. "You know that."

"But I'm *not* his son, and he just lost the only one he had," Parnell replied. "What would he think, at a time like that, if I tried keeping company with you? Suppose he took me for a leech trying to batten on his family and fortune?"

"He would never think that," Sonya answered earnestly. "And should you not be more concerned with what *I* think?"

"I would have been," Clint said, smiling, "but you just told me."

More heat in Sonya's cheeks. "Forgive me if I'm acting like a *mujer desenfrenada*."

Parnell laughed at that, softly, without drawing attention from the other riders making ready for the raid ahead. "Nobody would mistake you for a wanton woman," he assured her. "Or at least they'd never say it around me, if they wanted to keep their teeth."

It was her turn to laugh. "So, I have not repulsed you, then?" she asked him not quite teasingly.

"Not even close to that," Clint said. "You give me hope. What some might call reason to stay alive."

"I think we should not kiss now," Sonya wistfully replied. "Not with the others . . ."

"No. But I'll be looking forward to it," Clint said.

"As will I," she said, and slowly turned away.

What some might call reason to stay alive, he'd said. And while his words lifted her spirits, Sonya knew that was the essence of their problem now.

Not what her father thought of Clint as a potential fiancé, but whether either one of them would manage to survive the night.

Villa's Base Camp

Pancho Villa was intent on finishing his nightly meal—carne asada, enchiladas, rice and beans, with a cerveza chaser—when a cry went up from lookouts on the camp's perimeter. "*¡Un jinete entra!*"

A rider's coming in.

The call put Villa's men in motion, rushing toward the compound's eastern side, drawing and cocking weapons as they went. Pancho himself sat still, a solid rock of seeming calm in the confusion, though his right hand moved a fraction closer to the pistol on his hip.

A wise man never let himself be taken unawares.

The new arrival had to pass through ranks of armed *villistas*, offering his name to several before he finally dismounted, ringed by pointed guns, and walked his weary horse toward Villa's place beside a separate campfire. Before arriving there, he took off his sombrero, sleeved a sheen of perspiration from his brow despite the high desert's nocturnal chill, and let the men surrounding him direct him to his goal.

"Señor Villa?" the stranger asked, ducking his head as if he were a salesman come to foist unwanted goods upon the gathering.

Villa nodded. Inquired, "Who are you?"

"*Con tu permiso*, jefe. Rafael Rayón."

"You don't need my permission," Villa said. "I did not name you."

Rayón seemed unsure whether that was a joke at his expense. He flicked a smile toward Villa, bobbed his head again, worried the brim of his sombrero with a pair of nervous hands.

"Well?" Villa snapped at him. "What brings you here?"

"Señor Zapata's order, jefe."

"Ah. Emiliano." Villa's smile was genuine. "And how much longer must I wait to have the pleasure of his company?"

Rayón swallowed a lump that had appeared from nowhere in his throat. "*Perdóname*, Señor Villa," he replied. His soft voice fell somewhere between a gasp and a whisper.

"Speak up, *hijo*," Villa ordered. "Why should you require my pardon?"

"Señor Zapata sends the message that he cannot meet you as arranged. He has encountered various obstructions on the way and is returning to Morelos. "*Con sincero arrepentimiento, jefe.*"

Villa laid his supper plate aside, forgotten, rising to his feet as anger surged inside him. "His sincere regrets, indeed! What do they mean to me, when I have fourteen hundred horses he agreed to purchase? Eh? What do you say to that?"

"*Nada, señor,*" Rayón answered. "He sends apologies and understands that you must be *trastornado.*"

"Upset!" Villa was nearly shouting now. "He makes a promise, then reneges on it and robs me of *mucho dinero.* 'Upset' won't begin to cover it, *muchacho.*"

If he had not understood before, Rayón saw now that his commander had selected him for sacrifice, surrounded by a ring of firearms that were cocking, aiming at him, all as one. To make things worse, Villa had drawn his own six-gun and held it leveled at his unexpected caller's face.

"What should I do with a *gusano* sent here by a liar to insult me, Rafael?"

"*No lo sé, señor,*" Rayón said, in a hopeless tone.

"You don't know?" Villa echoed, while his men began to laugh. "Should I accept your life as payment for Zapata's debt?"

No answer from the young vaquero as he stood before Villa, trembling.

Drawing the torment out, Villa informed Rayón, "Your life means nothing to me, *niño.* You are less than muck under my boots. You carry no *dinero* with you, I assume?"

"A few pesos, *señor.*"

"In other words, nothing," Pancho retorted. "You

come here, insult me to my face, before my men who counted on this sale, and lack the wherewithal to pay your master's debt."

Rayón apparently could think of no response to that. His trembling turned into a hopeless shrug.

After another tense protracted moment, Villa put his gun away. "I will not take your worthless life," he told Rayón. "Instead, you will perform a service for me as the cost of living to behold another sunrise."

"Anything, jefe! You have only to ask."

"I *ask* for nothing, boy. I *order* you to turn around and ride back to your master. Tell Zapata his so-called apology is worthless. I will not forget this insult or the profit he has cost me. In due time, I shall repay him in another form of currency. You understand me?"

"*¡Sí, señor!* It will be done, just as you say."

"And use my words exactly, *hijo*. Do not sugarcoat them for Emiliano's pleasure, or I'll hear of it and hunt you down before I deal with him."

"You have my word, jefe."

"Now rest your animal," said Villa. "Feed and water him. He bears no fault in this. I give you half an hour, then be on your way back to Morelos or wherever your *cobarde* of a leader goes to hide himself. From this day forward he is marked. There shall be no forgiveness."

"*Gracias, señor. ¡Mil gracias!*"

"Now get out of my sight," Villa commanded. "I sicken of looking at your face."

His gunmen jostled Rayón out of Villa's presence, prodding him with gun muzzles as he went off to tend his horse. Villa picked up his metal plate once more but found that he had lost his appetite and dumped the remnants of his supper in the campfire.

Suddenly appearing at his side, Javier Jurado asked, "What now, jefe?"

"Now, nothing," Villa answered. "In the morning we shall move the horses. Find a safer place to keep the herd."

Nodding, Jurado moved away to spread the word.

A GAINST ALL ODDS, Jesús Zarita had retrieved the cutthroat razor from his boot and palmed it, pausing to relax his aching muscles as he lay concealed beneath his saddle blanket, weary from the straining effort.

When his quaking fingers closed around the would-be instrument of freedom from his bonds, Jesús barely restrained himself from sobbing with relief. The razor bore his body's heat from nestling in his sock all day, since exiting his playmate's unkempt bedroom in Ascensión, and it was slippery with sweat. Zarita dreaded losing hold of it, then having to recover it from underneath his blankets' rumpled folds, but concentration helped him hold it fast.

Now, once he'd opened it, how should he liberate his hands without slashing his wrists and bleeding out, an unintended suicide?

"*Con mucho cuidado*," Jesús whispered to himself. Most carefully.

The nail on his right thumb had not been trimmed of late, and now Zarita took advantage of that negligence, prying the blade free of its slotted handle, trusting that its edge—while not stropped recently—should still be sharp enough to cut through rawhide. Slippage in his sweaty grasp would be a danger, working in proximity to arteries and veins, tendons and nerves, beneath the thin skin of his wrists. An accidental gash would not be fatal under normal circumstances, but Zarita could not call for help if that happened to him. Whoever might respond would immediately see his weapon, work out what he had in mind, and likely finish him instead of bandaging his wound.

"*Fácil lo hace*," Jesús muttered.

Easy does it.

The first stroke was awkward, working blind and backward, with his manual mobility reduced to nearly zero. Numbness from his hands had spread into his forearms, but within a few more seconds he could feel the razor's edge rasping on dried leather, its concave sides sliding across the balls of flesh between his thumbs and pinioned wrists. It did not break the skin, however, and Zarita used more force, trying to moderate the rocking of his body underneath the saddle blanket before someone noticed him.

Too late!

A crunch of footsteps treading sand and gravel warned Jesús of someone closing on him from behind. He left off sawing at the rawhide thongs, lay still, and closed his eyes as if he were asleep. With any luck the passing enemy would move on by and he could—

Even as the thought took form, a hand closed on the brim of his sombrero, tugged it from his head, and tossed it to one side. Before Zarita could react, the same hand closed upon his rumpled blanket, whipped it free, and let it drop onto the ground beside his boots. His adversary saw the razor, snarled, and barked something to others in the group.

Not Spanish. Not English.

One of the cursed Mescaleros, then.

Zarita looked up at him, cringing, recognized one of the red men who had guarded him throughout the long ride from Ascensión to the arroyo where his life was now about to end.

Jesús opened his mouth to plead for mercy, but the tomahawk was already descending toward his face.

* * *

CLINT PARNELL STOOD over the dead *villista*, focused not upon the ruin of Jesús Zarita's skull but on the razor that Kuruk had lifted from their captive's lifeless hand.

Chalk up another body to their tally in Chihuahua, and their night was barely getting underway.

The twin Aguirre sisters suddenly arrived on either side of him, Dolores wincing at the sight before her, asking Clint, "What happened?"

Clint showed her the razor. Said, "Whoever searched him after he surrendered missed this. Kuruk found him trying to escape."

"And had to kill him?" Sonya asked, not quite a challenge.

"He was warned," Clint said. "If he had gotten loose, he would have tried to grab a horse and maybe hurt or killed some of our people in the process."

"I understand, but—"

"We're down three men as it stands," said Clint. "And if he got away, there was a fifty-fifty chance he'd ride straight back to Villa, squeal on us, and get us all killed."

"Can we bury him at least?" Sonya inquired.

"No time," Clint answered her. "The night shift covering your father's herd should be on duty by this time. We need to get a move on."

Parnell gave the razor back to Kuruk, thanked him for stopping Zarita's getaway, and moved off toward his waiting dapple gray. The sisters trailed him by a few yards, neither speaking, and he hardly dared to face Sonya after their brief conversation earlier, afraid of what he might see in her eyes.

Well, if he came off seeming cold and hard to her, so be it. There was bloody work remaining to be done this night, a confrontation they might not survive, and it would all have been for nothing if they failed to transport Alejandro's herd back home.

One problem at a time, Clint thought. *Worry about the rest if we're alive to see the sunrise.*

Their guide, Itza-chu, was already mounted on his skewbald pony, seeming eager to be off. From what Clint saw, the prospect of more bloodshed worried Great Hawk not at all. The Mescaleros did not laugh at death, exactly, but they did not seem to fear it either, being certain of ascension to an afterlife if they were brave and did their duty in this one.

Parnell envied the stoicism of Apaches, keeping how they really felt about daily calamities hidden from eyes outside their tribe, presenting stony faces to the world at large. It was a quality ingrained over their years of sacrifice, resistance to the seizure of their homeland by invaders, that kept the braves from showing any sign of weakness, even to their families and friends at home.

Not the best way to live, Clint thought, but on the other hand, the Mescaleros did not wear emotion on their sleeves like the majority of white folks he had known, their moods as plain to read as any newspaper. Apaches saved displays of tenderness—or weakness, as it seemed to them—for people whom they loved.

Clint wondered now whether Sonya might fill that role in his own life, but he did not dare to think about that any further yet. If they survived the night, retrieved her father's herd, and ultimately got it home to Alejandro's rancho, there would be more time to think about what might be, once the memories of mayhem faded and life settled back to some approximation of the norm.

Their line of march formed up as Parnell's hunting party took their leave of the arroyo. Kuruk and Nantan

Lupan rode point with Itza-chu. Clint followed them, flanked by the two Aguirre sisters, while Ignacio Fuentes and Arturo Lagüera trailed along behind, Fuentes leading their packhorse and Jesús Zarita's horse, its saddle still in place. If that one missed its former rider, it gave no sign of distress that he was gone.

Great Hawk had told them it would take another hour, more or less, to reach the canyon where Aguirre's herd was penned up under guard. What happened once they got there, once the battle had been joined, was anybody's guess.

And if they never saw another day, Clint realized no one in Mexico would care, much less report the news to Alejandro as he waited for them to return.

Clint put that out of mind, remembering something his mother used to read aloud on Sundays, quoting from the Sermon on the Mount, allegedly transcribed two thousand years ago.

Sufficient unto the day is the evil thereof.

And this day still had hours left to run.

CHAPTER FIFTEEN

T HE UNOFFICIAL POSSE took its time crossing the desert between their arroyo hideout and the box canyon where Villa had concealed Don Alejandro's stolen herd.

Although Clint Parnell felt a sense of urgency, he also understood the risks involved with galloping a stretch of unfamiliar ground at night. Horses could break their legs stepping in burrows where small mammals made their homes, or tread upon one of the many rattlesnakes that came out after dark to hunt the burrowers. They might even mistake a gully for a shadow cast by moonlight, plummeting headfirst to crippling injury or snap a rider's neck.

There was no burning rush now if the guards had changed on time. The next replacements would not reach the canyon until dawn or sometime after, by which point—with any luck—Clint's people would have made their getaway.

And if they had not . . . well, that meant they'd never leave Old Mexico at all.

Itza-chu, on returning to their camp, had drawn a map in sand, using his hunting knife to sketch the trail. No road was visible to human eyes, but he approximated it, and Clint could only trust his scout. The canyon was portrayed as wedge-shaped. Wavy lines depicted rising hills between the gully where they'd lingered and their final destination, ragged slashes indicating trees along the rising ground's southeastern slope.

They were already climbing, which Parnell took for a sign that they were on the right track. Up ahead, the Mescaleros did not waver from their course, proceeding without pause toward the location Great Hawk had described. All three had their rifles in hand and ready if they met with opposition on the way, but none seemed tense or agitated from what Clint could see of them by moonlight, from behind.

He wondered what was going through their minds just then, two of the warriors they had started out with dead and buried now, nothing but small mementos from their bodies waiting for delivery to relatives in Doña Ana County. Were Kuruk and his friends oppressed by pondering the prospect of their own deaths far from home? If so, he'd glimpsed no sign of it behind their staid façades.

As for the twins and three hands from the hacienda, Clint surmised their feelings must be much the same as his: considerable tension, tempered by determination to succeed against what felt like overwhelming odds. If they retrieved the stolen herd and managed to escape from Villa's guards, they still had to negotiate one hundred fifty miles of hostile desert crawling with *bandidos*, *federales*, and informers who would happily betray them for a few pesos.

And if, despite all that, they made it home at last,

the U.S. Army and the State Department might have punishment in mind for flouting orders sent from Washington.

Well, Uncle Sam would have to get in line. He was the least of Parnell's problems until Clint was back across the Rio Grande.

Ahead of their procession, dark hills rose across the path now, slopes furred with creosote bushes and viscid acacias, merging with fire-barrel cactus and yuccas, ceding ground to silver maples, scattered Arizona cypress, and scrub oak as they climbed farther. Ten minutes into their ascent, Kuruk signaled a halt, then waved the others forward to confer with them.

They huddled, spoke in whispers, starting with Itzachu, who had been over this ground before. He told them that the canyon's entrance lay about two hundred yards ahead, invisible from where they sat astride their mounts. A lip of granite overhung it, where a rifleman was stationed during daylight, possibly with others after nightfall. Anyone approaching it on horseback made an easy target, but afoot, employing stealth, they should be able to outflank the guards and bring them under fire from higher slopes. Some climbing was required, but once they gained the high ground, there should be no problem taking out the guards.

Unless one of us trips and falls while climbing, Parnell thought, *or squeezes off an accidental shot.*

It could depend, as well, on how many defenders Pancho Villa had in place following sunset. Their late captive had surmised there could be four to six, but if a livestock sale was pending, Villa might have hiked that number up as a precautionary measure.

The bottom line: they would not know what they were up against until they made the climb and counted hostile heads.

One other thing occurred to Clint as well. They

needed someone covering their horses, keeping them at ease and quiet while the others made their stealthy climb to launch the raid. Clint chose Joaquín Cantú to stay behind, although his wound was healing well enough so far, and Joaquín swore it would not slow him down. He clearly meant well, but Parnell could not afford to take the risk that he might fall, exacerbate his injury, or altogether ruin their surprise.

With that settled, over Cantú's protest, the others checked their weapons one last time, confirmed that all were fully loaded, and secured their holsters if they wore any, to stop leather from slapping at their trousers as they scaled the hillside. Mescaleros leading in their silent buckskin moccasins, the posse started moving gingerly uphill through slanting shadows toward their next appointed killing ground.

DOLORES WORE A pair of denim blue jeans over sturdy riding boots. She had removed her warm serape, draping it across her saddle, and was climbing unimpeded now, with both hands free. Across her back, a makeshift sling of rope secured her Winchester. A holster on her right hip held the Colt .38-caliber revolver, while a twelve-inch bowie knife rode on a scabbard to her left. A bandolier of .30-06 ammunition for the rifle looped from her right shoulder down to her left hip, its weight pressing between her breasts.

Whatever lay ahead of her, Dolores reckoned that she was prepared.

She did not glance back at her sister, sixth in line to scale the slope, but she heard Sonya breathing as her fingers clutched at stones and bushes, helping her ascend. Dolores thought about Joaquín Cantú, left with the horses down below, imagining how he must feel at being left out of the fight.

He might be fortunate at that. If anything went wrong, at least he had the option of escape, returning to her father's hacienda as the bearer of bad news. Or would *machismo* force his hand if things went badly, forcing him to join the fight and die among his friends?

At that point, she considered, who would even care?

Her father, certainly, but if *villistas* wiped them out entirely, it might take him months to learn their fate, assuming that he ever did. And in the meantime, he could only watch his hacienda fail, the hard work of a lifetime gone for naught.

Distracted by her private thoughts, Dolores almost missed it when the Mescaleros ceased climbing and waved Clint forward. Following him cautiously, Dolores heard her sister coming after them, glanced back and saw their two vaqueros waiting for someone to signal their approach.

Once they were all together on the upper slope, above the overhanging granite ledge Great Hawk had sketched for them in camp, they fanned out, lying prone, surveying where their enemies were ranged below.

Lying beside Clint on his left, Dolores counted two *villistas* seated on the stony ledge, accessed by crude steps cut into the canyon wall. Four more were hunched around a small campfire a few yards from the canyon's narrow entrance, while the bulk of it was filled with horses stolen from her father's hacienda previously.

Whispering, Clint said, "We need to take them by surprise and drop as many as we can before they start returning fire. I know it sounds cold-blooded, but we've got no choice. The longer they fight back and drag it out, the greater chance we stand of being cut off by the rest of Villa's gang before we get the herd cleared out. Questions?"

None were forthcoming, so he issued their assignments. They had eight long guns and six live targets. If they nailed all six with their initial fusillade, killing or seriously wounding them, only a single clap of gunfire should result. Whether it carried back to Pancho Villa's base camp would depend in large part on the desert breeze and the direction it was blowing when they fired. Assuming that it *was* heard, then their team would have to race against the clock.

They had not glimpsed the base camp riding in. Itzachu's briefing had described it as three quarters of a mile due east from the box canyon, tents standing along the west rim of a gully where *villista* cook fires would be hidden from a rider passing on the open desert flats. There had been no chance for a head count of the men billeted there, which left them with an estimate from their late prisoner of thirty-five to forty men in all.

Dolores worked on the arithmetic in silence. Six from thirty-five left twenty-nine men still encamped with Villa, with perhaps another half a dozen if Jesús Zarita had been wrong. Assuming three or four of those were mounted, keeping watch over the camp by night in shifts, the rest would wait for Villa's orders when they heard gunfire and then would have to saddle up their horses in a fumbling rush. Once they were organized and riding at a hard gallop, their point men ought to reach the canyon and the stolen herd inside of thirty minutes, more or less.

That gave Clint's team a half hour to rout her father's herd from the box canyon—fourteen hundred eighty-seven head in all, if none were lost along the way between their rancho and Chihuahua—and escape before *villista* reinforcements reached the site. Her spirits fell, Dolores realizing that their task would likely prove impossible.

Instead of brooding over that, she pushed it out of mind and concentrated on the task at hand. They had six men to silence first, no chance to get in close and use their knives. Dolores sighted down the barrel of her Winchester, pinning one of the four *bandidos* seated near the campfire down below, and slipped her index finger through the rifle's trigger guard.

I TELL YOU, *ESE*," Saturnino Kahlo said, grinning, "this *chica mala* was no more than fourteen, maybe fifteen, but the body on her, *no lo creerías*."

Facing Kahlo from across the campfire, Rufino Azuela snorted laughter and a spray of coffee. "You are right for once," he said. "I *don't* believe you."

That brought snickers from their two companions, Geraldo Izquierdo and Miguel Siqueiros, seated one on either side of Kahlo. "What *I* don't believe," Siqueiros said, "is that this woman-child would give a second look to Saturnino."

"Not for love or money," Izquierdo added.

"Ah, you're fools, the lot of you," Kahlo replied. "If you could just have seen her . . ."

"Then we'd all be in a lunatic asylum," said Miguel, evoking yet another bray of laughter.

Scowling, Kahlo said, "I need tequila."

"Bring us each a bottle, eh?" Azuela goaded him. "Then we can all see this delicious beauty you've imagined."

"*¡Idiotas!*" Saturnino answered, rising on stiff legs from his place beside the fire. "You doubt my word? Next time that we are in Durango, I will show her to you in the flesh."

Geraldo Izquierdo doubled over laughing at his friend now. Said, "Three hundred pounds of flesh, I'll wager."

Muttering a string of curses, Kahlo turned away and started moving slowly toward the spot where they had left their horses hobbled, near a trickling stream with grassy banks. He had proceeded only three steps when a lightning bolt struck him below the brim of his sombrero, shattering his face and pitching Saturnino over backward. Falling, he tripped over one of Miguel's boots and sprawled across the campfire, stone-cold dead before the flames bit into him.

The other three *villistas* scrambled to their feet, gaping at Kahlo as his hat and clothes caught fire. He did not scream, and all of them could readily see why. Before the sharp crack of a rifle reached their ears, they recognized the crushing damage of a bullet that had caved in Saturnino's face, spilling his blood to sizzle on the campfire's coals.

"*¿Quién disparó?*" Rufino Azuela blurted out, but none of his companions had a clue who'd fired the fatal shot. Their first impulse turned anxious glances toward the granite ledge over the canyon's entrance, where Ricardo López and Emilio Vicario presently were stationed. While it seemed impossible, there was an outside chance that one of them had triggered off a gunshot accidentally and slain Kahlo, but when three pairs of frightened eyes picked out their comrades on the high ground, both were turned away and staring farther up the canyon's wall.

Then who . . .

The second shot plucked López from his perch and hurled him, screaming, to the ground some sixty feet below. The canyon's mass of horses had begun to seethe as the *villistas* grouped around the campfire saw a muzzle flash high up, immediately followed by three more in unison.

Miguel Siqueiros had his mouth open to shout a warning when a bullet struck him in the chest and dropped him on his backside, bootheels drumming on the ground in his death throes. Rufino Azuela managed to draw his Colt and fire a shot up range before the wet slap of a rifle slug drilling his abdomen produced a gargling scream and he in turn went down. He was not dead yet, but Geraldo Izquierdo knew he could not help his wounded friend. A bullet through the guts meant slow and agonizing death unless a hemorrhage sped up the process and relieved the victim of his pain.

Geraldo panicked, leapt across the fire, and sprinted toward the hobbled horses. He could free his own, mount up, and ride as if the devil were pursuing him— which, he now imagined, just might be the case. Who else but Satan in the flesh would dare to pick a fight with Pancho Villa's men this night, at their secluded lair?

Perhaps the *federales*, he decided, but they were as bad as demons in their own right, and he did not plan to wait around, facing them on his own.

As if to make his nightmare worse, Geraldo heard another rifle shot, immediately followed by a scream, and saw Emilo Vicario diving headfirst into the canyon from his outpost on the granite ledge above. The body landed like a sack of laundry toppled from an upstairs window, pancaked on the stony ground, and settled into dusty death.

Geraldo Izquierdo reached his horse and ripped its hobbles free, swung up into the saddle, snatching at the reins. His spurs were poised to gouge the creature's ribs, propel it to a headlong gallop, when a hammer stroke from heaven slammed into the right side of his neck and nearly tore his numb skull from his shoulders.

Dead before he hit the ground, Geraldo had no chance to ask Jesucristo for absolution from his countless sins. A black pit seemed to open up below him and he knew no more.

SONYA AGUIRRE HAD her target lined up near the campfire when Kuruk picked off one of the two *villistas* stationed on the ledge above the canyon's mouth.

Her mark was rising, turning from his fellows down below and moving toward their horses when she fired.

In darkness, with the firelight at his back, she could not see her bullet strike its target, and the crack of her Winchester covered any sound that might have reached her ears on impact. Nonetheless, the net result was obvious. Her man lurched backward, nearly airborne from the aught-six bullet's force on entry, landing in the midst of the campfire. His fallen body scattered red-hot embers toward his three companions, all in motion at the ghastly sight before them, even if they did not understand its import.

Any doubt was soon eliminated as the rest of Parnell's snipers blazed away. Sonya was busy tracking toward another target, but she missed her chance as seven weapons thundered from the wooded slope. The echo of their unified barrage reverberated through the canyon, riling Papa Alejandro's horses, but the herd had been confined too long to risk a mad rush toward the fire still blazing at the valley's entrance, corpses scattered all around and nothing but the desert night beyond.

Parnell was on his feet by then, telling the rest of them, "Come on. Quick as you can but watch your footing on the way down. We don't need a broken leg now." Leading by example, he called back over his shoulder while descending, "Fuentes, make sure Joaquín is bringing up the horses, *¿comprendes?*"

"*Sí, señor,*" Ignacio replied.

Dolores knew his job should be an easy one. Cantú was under orders to advance, leading their mounts as soon as he heard gunfire from the canyon. If he found the camp's defenders still alive and in control, he was supposed to cut and run, return to Papa Alejandro's hacienda any way he could carry word that they had failed.

Hearing Clint issue those instructions to Joaquín, Dolores had been pleased that if their fallback plan came into play she would no longer be alive to see her father's heart break one more time.

Reaching the mouth of the box canyon, Sonya at her side, Dolores heard Cantú before she saw him, galloping to join them on his brindle gelding, leading the remainder of their animals behind him on a tether line. Clint barely waited until Joaquín had reined in, mounting his dapple gray, telling the rest of them, "We've got no time to waste now. Round the others up and start them moving. Once we clear the canyon, turn the herd northwest toward home."

If we can find it, thought Dolores, but she kept the grim thought to herself.

They all knew where her father's rancho lay, of course, but it was still one hundred fifty miles away, across the Rio Grande, and for the next few hours they would have to ride through darkness, nine vaqueros herding close to fifteen hundred horses through the desert waste by moonlight, hoping that they would not lose their way or meet a troop of *federales* on the prowl.

Their greatest danger, though, was that the echoes of their gunfire would be heard in Pancho Villa's base camp, drawing him and his *bandidos* to the scene before Clint's group could bring the herd under control.

Dolores did not want to think about what would befall them if they wound up trapped inside the canyon with her father's stolen herd. Badly outnumbered and outgunned, without stockpiles of ammunition for protracted battle, they would likely be annihilated. Villa would retain the horses, sell them for a profit at his soonest opportunity, and Papa Alejandro would be left to brood over their unknown fate.

Despite his pain and grief, Dolores guessed—or hoped, at least—that he would not pursue the matter any further, wasting more lives in pursuit of justice that could never be attained. Childless, his fortune dwindling daily as he tried to build another herd and renegotiate his contract with the U.S. Army, he would be a broken man, no future worth imagining.

As for Dolores and her twin, she had already made her mind up that they would not fall alive into the hands of Villa's men. Dolores knew what would become of them in that case, had discussed it in advance with Sonya, and they'd both agreed. Before they let themselves be captured and abused, they would choose death over dishonor, even if the Holy Mother Church declared that was a mortal sin.

Before taking that last, irrevocable step, though, they would do their best to carry out their promise to Don Alejandro. And if foiled at bringing home the herd, then they would fight, taking as many of their adversaries with them as they could, each twin reserving one shot for herself.

The situation was not hopeless yet, but if compelled to wager on its outcome, she would not have bet five pesos on herself.

Pancho Villa's Base Camp

Villa was snoring, caught up in a dream of two *mujeres muy hermosas* tending to his every need, one feeding him strawberries from her luscious lips while her companion sat astride his loins, riding him like a Thoroughbred, urging Villa across the finish line.

Before he reached it, someone gripped his shoulder, shook him roughly, calling to him, "*¡Despierta, jefe!*"

"I'm awake!" snarled Villa, tacking on a curse for emphasis. "Who is that?"

By the time he asked the question, though, Villa

already knew the answer. Bending over him, Javier Jurado wore a stark expression of alarm verging on fear.

Before his *teniente* had a chance to speak, Villa demanded of him, "What is wrong?"

"Gunshots, jefe."

"In camp?" Now Villa was confused. Even the sweetest dream would have been shattered by gunfire.

"No, jefe," Javier responded. "From the canyon where—"

"The horses are!" Villa finished the sentence for his aide, threw back his blanket, lunging for his gun belt hanging from a chair beside his cot. Cursing a blue streak as he rose, he pinned Alfonso with a glare. "How many?" he demanded. "When?"

"Just now, jefe. Not many, but to count them, with the echoes . . ."

"Never mind that," Villa snapped. "Rally the men. Prepare to ride at once."

"They're getting ready now, jefe," Jurado said.

"Make them move faster!" Striding from his small adobe hut, Villa asked Soberon, "This shooting, did it sound like fighting?"

"It's impossible to say, Pancho. Perhaps, or . . ."

"If I find out they've taken liquor with them, getting drunk and raising hell," Villa declared, "I'll flay all six of them alive!"

"I doubt that they would be so foolish, jefe."

"All the same."

But even as he threatened, Villa knew the situation might be even worse. If someone had discovered where the herd was hidden, if they'd come by night to rob him, Pancho Villa, of the animals he'd stolen fair and square . . .

"My horse!" he bellowed to the night and no one in particular. "Fetch me my horse!"

"It's being saddled now, jefe," Jurado promised him.

Jogging toward his black stallion, Villa turned his thoughts toward who might dare try robbing him. At once, his mind offered Zapata as a prime suspect. Suppose the rider he had sent to Villa's camp, to cancel their arrangement, was a decoy to distract Villa while sly Emiliano made his way around to steal the horses for himself and save the price of sale they had agreed upon?

How would Zapata know where Villa had the herd concealed? Perhaps a traitor in Villa's own ranks had betrayed the location for money—his own Judas Iscariot, and not the first by any means. If that turned out to be the case, and Villa could identify the wretch, his punishment would be severe, prolonged, and ultimately terminal.

But solving that riddle could wait.

First, Villa must discover if his stolen herd was being threatened and prevent whoever was engaged in robbing him from doing so. He saw no irony in that, believed in fact that once he laid his hands on anything, that thing rightfully belonged to him, because he had the strength and nerve to take it from a prior owner who could not defend himself. If there was any honor among thieves— a proposition Villa personally doubted—it should certainly extend to professional courtesy among bandits.

But, then again, they would not be *bandidos* if they could be trusted.

"*¡Basta!*" he muttered to himself as he mounted his stallion. Enough! He was a man of action, and while known for cunning strategy at times, it also pained his head when Villa thought too much.

Most of his men were mounted now, with guns in hand or ready in their saddle scabbards. Villa shouted at the stragglers, "*¡Dense prisa, muchachos!* Hurry, boys! We have no time to waste!"

Before the last of them had clambered into saddles, Villa wheeled his mount and spurred it, racing out of camp and off to the northwest. Even at top speed, he knew that it would take the better part of half an hour to reach their destination, and a mad rush through the desert night could easily leave men and horses injured, maybe even dead.

No matter.

Villa paid his men to follow where he led and to obey his orders without question. All of them were seasoned thieves, most of them killers, who would ride into the mouth of hell itself at his command.

Tonight they would be tested to the limit, and if Villa learned that it was all a false alarm caused by his lookouts on the night shift swilling down tequila at their posts, he would have thirty volunteers to form a firing squad.

The herd was all that mattered to him now, and anyone who threatened Villa's profit from it should prepare to drown in blood.

N OW THAT KURUK saw Aguirre's stolen herd for the first time, he wondered whether it was possible to drive them from the canyon, much less guide them on a three- or four-day journey back across the Rio Grande into New Mexico. With only seven men and two women on hand to even try it, he began to think their task might be a fool's errand.

Not that he doubted Clint Parnell's commitment to the scheme, or his vaqueros' skill at wrangling horses. Even the Aguirre sisters, young as they might be, had proven themselves fighters who, if born as Mescaleros, would have made their parents proud. Bear simply questioned whether any nine individuals could manage to succeed under the given circumstances, much less when pursued across one hundred fifty miles by bloodthirsty *villistas* and amoral *federales*.

Even if they had the dozen riders they had originally started with from Aguirre's hacienda, it would be a challenge, guaranteeing sleepless nights along the trail for all concerned and caballeros who arrived at last—should they arrive at all—close to the point of falling from their horses in exhaustion.

Still, despite those thoughts, he urged Nantan Lupan and Itza-Chu to hurry at their task of moving in among the stolen animals, calming them down as much as possible, working in concert with their gringo leader and his *mexicanos* to begin shifting the herd out of its hiding place and onto open ground. Once that was done, and if they were not interrupted, waning moonlight ought to guide them on the first leg of their long trek northward.

If they were not interrupted.

Kuruk personally did not like their chances of succeeding even with that first stage of their task.

He reckoned that their gunfire, taking out six lazy, inattentive guards, must have been audible across the desert flats at Pancho Villa's base camp. True, most of the outlaw's men had likely been asleep or busy swilling down liquor, both circumstances that would slow reaction time, but there were bound to be a few guards on alert to rouse the others and their leaders in a sudden panic.

That would help Parnell's team, inasmuch as drowsy, startled men were clumsy and disorganized. Saddling horses would take fractionally longer than in daylight, when the *villistas* had been awake for hours. On the other hand, if Pancho Villa was the strategist of local legend, he would have rehearsed his men in preparation for emergencies.

At best, Kuruk supposed that getting thirty-odd *bandidos* saddled up and mounted might consume ten minutes, possibly fifteen. Hard riding toward the canyon where their nighttime guards lay dead would take another thirty minutes more or less, and Bear hoped Villa might lose horsemen on the way, to accidents.

In any case, Bear reckoned that they had less than an hour to evacuate a herd of mustangs from the box canyon where they were presently confined and turn them back toward home.

Unlikely, Kuruk thought. *Maybe impossible.* But he kept that opinion to himself.

Their journey had begun as an adventure that would benefit Bear's village—and himself if he should manage to survive. He'd undertaken it as any young brave might, to test himself and out of honor for his chieftain, Nantan. If he'd thought about his chances for survival at the outset, Kuruk would have called it even money in the white world's terms.

But now, with Bimisi and Gothalay both slain, Kuruk himself recovering from a flesh wound, those odds had been reduced. That thought did not intimidate him, as it doubtless would have done to most white men, but neither was Kuruk immune to doubt.

Not in his own abilities per se, but in full knowledge that he was not superhuman and the spirits of his ancestors could not protect him on the earthly plane. Whatever lay in store for him was destiny. Kuruk could not avoid it by sheer force of his determination or by trickery.

Come what may, Kuruk would fight on to the end without pleading for mercy from his enemies. The people of his village would expect no less from him, and if his ancestors could see him now, they would congratulate him on an ending that exemplified personal honor and commitment to his tribe.

He joined Itza-chu and Nantan Lupan in urging
Don Alejandro's horses from the canyon, starting at
the rear end of the herd, clucking at the animals without alarming them unduly, using his blood bay to nudge
them in the general direction that he wished for them
to follow, toward the dying campfire at the canyon's
mouth.

If trouble met them there, or found them later on
the northbound trail, Bear had his rifle loaded, knew
his hunting knife and tomahawk were sharp enough
for battling at close quarters.

Only death could stop him now, and if that happened, should the afterlife turn out to be an empty
myth, Kuruk would melt into oblivion without another
thought.

And anything was better, he believed, than letting
the *villistas* capture him alive.

D OLORES STAYED AS near to Clint Parnell as she
deemed feasible, at the same time keeping an eye
upon her twin. Calming her father's herd after their
ordeal was no easy task, but they were making head-
way, urging skittish horses into serried ranks as space
allowed, heading them all in one direction with a minimum of jostling.

How much time had passed so far?

Dolores did not wear a pocket watch and thought it
inadvisable to pester Clint with questions when he obviously had his hands full, giving orders to the other
caballeros while he joined in channeling the horses
toward their prison's only exit. Clint had sheathed
his Browning Auto-5, kept both hands on his gelding's
reins, using a boot from time to time when nervous
mustangs crowded in upon him from one or the other
side.

Guessing, Dolores speculated that they had used up approximately half the time allotted for hostile *villistas* to arrive and head them off, assuming that their gunfire had been heard at Villa's base camp. There was still an outside chance the shots had failed to register three quarters of a mile across the desert flats—a trick of wind, perhaps, or if most of the rustlers were asleep, even intoxicated—but Dolores knew they could not count on luck alone to let them clear the scene and ride off unmolested.

More likely was the prospect that Villa's *bandidos* would arrive before they managed to depart. And for Dolores, the worst-case scenario involved a violent interruption of their efforts when only a portion of her father's herd had cleared the canyon. In that case, she had no doubt the horses that had managed to escape would scatter far and wide, beyond recall, while the remainder and her party would be trapped inside, cut off and under fire.

There was no need to check her Winchester, which she'd reloaded after joining in the massacre of Pancho Villa's guards. She had not used her Colt so far tonight, so it had six rounds nestled in its cylinder, prepared to fire as quickly as Dolores could discharge them using double-action fire. Eleven rounds in all before she had to stop, reloading either gun.

And if she made each bullet count, Dolores realized, her party still would be outnumbered.

Never mind, she thought. Beyond the best that she could do lay only speculation and surmise. Dolores would not let herself succumb to pessimism, which to her mind was another label for defeat.

A snorting mare brushed close against her snowflake Appaloosa, and Dolores used a hand to fend it off. She felt herself about to topple from her seat and barely caught herself in time, grabbing the saddle horn with her free hand. A curse rose to her lips, but she swallowed it back, afraid to blaspheme in what might turn out to be the final moments of her life.

Ahead of her, Clint was nearing the box canyon's exit, trying to lead the mustangs now rather then goading them forward. The animals seemed nervous, passing by the burned-out campfire and the corpses sprawled around it, but they forged along with heads down, scenting freedom on the outside of their rocky holding pen.

The trick, Dolores knew, would be to stop them from stampeding once the leaders of the herd discovered they were free and clear. That impulse would be well-nigh irresistible, and once the leaders started running, it would be nearly impossible to stop them in their flight.

"*Un problema a la vez*," Dolores muttered to herself. One problem at a time.

Before they made it back to Papa Alejandro's hacienda—*if* they made it back at all—there would be ample difficulties to preoccupy them over every mile.

As if in answer to her thoughts, Dolores heard a crack of gunfire from somewhere beyond the canyon's mouth, echoing through the darkness. Trying to decide how far away the gunman must have been, she guessed a mile or more across the desert flats. It could be anyone, of course, firing for any one of countless reasons, but she saw Clint rein up short ahead of her, the other riders doing likewise.

Turning toward her twin, Dolores found Sonya was watching her, a grim frown on her face, already reaching for the Springfield Model 1903 rifle in her saddle boot. She did not draw it yet but kept her right hand resting on its stock, prepared to snatch it from the leather sheath and at need.

Within three seconds, maybe less, a second shot

rang out from somewhere to the canyon's east. No other gunfire followed, but Dolores calculated that two blasts ruled out an accident and probably a solitary rider firing to defend himself against some desert predator. She saw her sister's lips move silently and caught the warning in her eyes.

A signal.

Which could only mean *villistas* on their way and likely riding hard.

THE PISTOL SHOT behind him, somewhere in the midst of his advancing riders, startled Pancho Villa. He immediately reined his jet-black stallion to a halt and wheeled around to face the caballeros trailing him.

"*¿Quién disparó?*" he demanded, eyes scanning their ranks. When no one answered instantly, he cursed them all as one, repeating it. "Who fired?"

At last, reluctantly, a young man raised his hand, fingers still wrapped around the handle of his smoking Colt. Villa knew him as César Armendáriz, though it might have been an alias. False names were common among *bandoleros*, and Villa was not concerned with what a man had done before he joined the gang, as long as he was loyal, brought no trouble with him to their family, and followed Villa's orders to the letter.

César Armendáriz, or whatever his name was, had failed the final test.

Advancing on the young man, heedless of the pistol in his hand, Villa demanded, "What were you thinking? Do you think at all?"

"*¡Perdóname, jefe!* In the excitement—"

Villa did not wait to hear the rest of the young fool's halting apology. Instead, he drew his sidearm, aimed and fired it in one fluid motion, saw the bullet punch through César's forehead. Masked in spurting blood, his straw sombrero airborne, Armendáriz toppled from his mount and landed facedown in the desert sand.

Villa surveyed his other troops, all watching him, waiting to see what happened next. A moment later, he demanded of them all, "Is anybody else *excited*? Who else wants to warn our enemies that we are coming?"

The illogic of his own statement did not faze Villa. When none of his other riders raised a hand, he picked one nearest to the horse without a rider, barking out, "Jiménez! Bring that *idiota*'s animal. We ride, and quietly!"

Javier Jurado fell in place beside Villa, keeping his voice pitched low as he advised, "You should have cut his throat, jefe."

"I know that now," Villa replied, grinning by moonlight. "But I got excited!"

And in doing so, he realized, had replicated César's critical mistake. Villa was not blind to the flaws in his own character, but sometimes they still got the better of him. Sudden anger was a case in point, provoking him to sudden violence when he should take a moment to reflect and weigh his options, maybe choose a better course of action.

Oh, well. It was too late now. The best that he could manage was to reach the canyon where his six watchmen should have the horses from New Mexico well guarded and secure. But if those men were dead, as Villa now suspected, there was no course open to him but avenging them—and, more importantly, securing the herd that meant a fortune in his pocket and the pockets of his men.

Whoever had the gall to steal from Pancho Villa, whether that was his false friend Zapata or some other brigand he had never met, that person had a painful lesson coming to him. Although raised Catholic, like virtually everyone in Mexico, Villa had never grasped the concept of forgiveness, in this world or in the next, whatever that might be. Men earned their punishment by word or deed and there was no escaping it.

Some punishment was trivial—a slap across the face for kissing a *mujer* who was not in the mood, for instance—but in Villa's world, most penalties were more severe. A prison sentence, possibly the gallows or a military firing squad. Caught in an act of banditry, death was the probable outcome, whether it claimed the thief or one who tried arresting him.

And if Zapata, the alleged "reformer," tried to steal from Villa after lying to him, his reward for treachery would be apocalyptic.

In another moment, Pancho Villa saw the dark hills rise in front of him and marked a dark notch that must be the tight box canyon's entryway. If he was wrong about his watchmen being murdered, one of them should soon call out a warning to the body of advancing horsemen. And if they did not . . .

Forgetting caution, Villa half turned in his saddle, shouting to his men, "¡Estén listos, muchachos! Boys, be ready! Spare the horses but kill anyone you do not recognize!"

He was excited now, and no mistake. The lifelong thrill of mortal combat gripped him, urged him on to greater speed, his stallion feeling it and racing forward without any goad from Villa's silver spurs.

The next few minutes could decide the course of Pancho Villa's life or end it suddenly, in blinding pain and blood. Whatever happened, he could not turn back, dared not allow his men to see him run away.

And as always in the heat of battle, Villa scarcely

cared what happened, either to himself or any of his followers. They had been challenged, and no real man ever scuttled from a fight.

Not if he cared to live another day with anything resembling self-respect.

"*¡Adelante!*" Villa bellowed as he closed the final hundred yards. "Forward!"

The answer came from rifles, more than half a dozen of them, muzzle flashes winking at him in the night.

CHAPTER SIXTEEN

"FALL BACK!" CLINT Parnell ordered as the swarm of horsemen closed in on his people in the small box canyon. "Get the horses under cover if you can, and someone take the high ground. Fuentes and Lagüera, how about you two?"

An answer came back from Arturo, "*Sí, jefe*," as he started climbing toward the granite lookout post over the canyon's mouth, Ignacio close on his heels.

That left Parnell and the Aguirre sisters with three Mescaleros to defend the herd at ground level from Villa's raiders. They had to be *villistas*, Clint reasoned, since no one else was likely to be prowling near the scene in force, coincidentally responding to the shots that had eliminated Villa's guards.

There was no time for counting heads among his enemies, and a final tally made no difference in any case. All of the new arrivals carried guns and were presumably proficient in their use. Whether Villa himself was leading them or even present for the confrontation never crossed Clint's mind. The photos he had seen of Villa, printed next to newspaper accounts of his exploits below the border, had been out of date and blurry. Killing the mounted mob's leader might prompt some members to retreat, but they were not members of Native tribes that feared to fight past sundown and who quailed if bullets found their war chief on the battlefield.

Eliminating Pancho Villa with a lucky shot—assuming he was even on the scene—might just as easily inspire his men to greater violence, make this a replay of the Alamo minus a crumbling mission and a troop of *federales* to complete the massacre.

When their enemies had closed the gap to fifty yards, Clint called out to his team, "Conserve your ammunition if you can. Make every bullet count."

In his case, that meant deer slugs loaded in the Browning Auto-5, with buckshot in reserve for close-in fighting. Once he burned through that stockpile, Clint had his Colt Peacemaker and a hunting knife suspended from his pistol belt in case the showdown wound up hand to hand.

He glanced at the Aguirre twins, crouched side by side with rifles shouldered, aiming toward the first rank of their adversaries, wishing they were anywhere on earth away from what promised to be a slaughter. That hardly mattered now, since their father had reluctantly permitted them to come along, and if he couldn't keep the girls at home, Clint knew it was beyond his power to restrain them.

Still, the moment that Sonya met his gaze, then turned back to her rifle's sights, a stab of guilt pierced Parnell's chest. In other circumstances, minus all the hectic bloodletting, life could have been so sweet.

Now, all he saw on the horizon was a chance to finish it in smoke and fire.

At forty yards Clint chose his target, sighting down the shotgun's twenty-eight-inch barrel, braced himself, and stroked the Browning's trigger without jerking it. The twelve gauge bucked against his shoulder, and he saw the man he'd chosen vault backward, thrown from his saddle as if he had ridden underneath a taut clothesline that snagged him underneath his chin and let his mount race on without him. By the time Clint's human target hit the ground, the pistolero's animal had hesitated, wheeling back around to seek its lost rider, but the *villista* was in no shape to rebound.

As soon as Clint triggered his blast, the other members of his team cut loose in unison, their long guns echoing and smoking all across the canyon's mouth and from the granite ledge above, where Fuentes and Lagüera held the high ground, punching bullets through sombreros. Riders toppled, horses reared, and Clint saw one go down, legs thrashing through a spray of blood. He hated that but knew a spray of lead aimed at mounted *bandidos* had to strike some of their animals as well.

Precision sighting instantly went out the window, even while the other members of his team kept Clint's order in mind.

Make each shot count.

Each time a bullet missed its human target, drilling into horseflesh, it still helped to slow the hostile riders down. Where one horse fell, others were forced to veer around or else leap over it, and more of them could fall that way, unseating gunmen, fracturing their skulls, necks, arms, or legs. Clint glimpsed a slim *villista* trampled under hooves and flattened on the ground to never rise again.

And that was one he would not have to waste a deer slug on.

PANCHO VILLA FELT the hot breath of a bullet scorch his cheek in passing, ducked his head too late, but still avoided being slammed into eternity. A rider to his left, not Soberon, cried out in sudden pain, pitched from his saddle, and immediately vanished into roiling dust.

Villa fired his Colt in the direction of the muzzle flashes winking at him from the dark canyon. Between the bullets zipping past him and his stallion's headlong galloping, he could not aim precisely, but it felt important that he make some noise at least, to goad his pistoleros in their rush toward sudden death.

If Villa's .45 slug found one of his adversaries, it would be a happy accident, but he would not depend upon it. Every loping yard that he advanced improved his chances for a hit, but at the same time helped the odds that one of his opponents would get lucky, bring him down, and either cripple him or end his life.

For once he had no strategy in mind besides attacking, maybe leaping from his horse when he was close enough to fight on foot, hoping that one of his own gunmen did not shoot him by mistake. Or might one of them target him deliberately?

If Zapata was behind the raid, it meant someone had tipped him to the stolen herd's location, and that information had to come from a *villista* who accepted cash or else harbored a grudge against the leader to whom he had pledged loyalty. In that case, Villa could trust no one in his own ranks, might expect a sneak attack from nearly anyone aside from Javier Jurado.

On the other hand, he had begun to doubt Zapata's role in the attack as soon as their opponents opened fire. Emiliano would not venture from his stronghold in Morelos with a mere handful of men to drive the stolen herd back home. That notion was irrational, even bizarre.

But in that case, who *was* responsible?

Not *federales*, clearly, since they also would have come in force, intent on crushing Villa's company before they took the horses for themselves or for Porfirio Díaz. But if he could not blame Zapata or the army, who remained?

Before he had a chance to ponder that further, his aide-de-camp pulled up beside Villa's stampeding stallion, hunched over the neck of his grulla. He turned to flash a grin at Pancho by moonlight, just as a bullet from the canyon slapped into his mare's neck and the animal went down as if its spine were severed, legs splayed out in all directions. Impact sent Jurado vaulting forward, tumbling like a circus acrobat, obscured by rising dust, and Villa had no choice but to abandon him, race on into the maelstrom as he raised and fired his Colt again.

Another wasted shot, he realized, and jammed the smoking pistol back into its holster, using both hands on his stallion's reins. Although it had not saved Jurado, Villa bent forward across his saddle horn, one cheek almost against the stallion's mane. At least he made a slightly smaller target that way, and if someone shot his horse from under him, there was a chance he would survive the fall, perhaps even rise up and hobble toward the canyon in pursuit of his attacking *bandoleros* as they closed to killing distance with their unknown enemies.

If nothing else, he had to find out who the interlopers were before they shot him down. That was imperative to satisfy his curiosity, and if he had a chance to take out even one or two of them, at least he would derive some satisfaction from it as he died.

Small recompense, but Villa was accustomed to surviving on a razor's edge between calamity and tri-
umph. He had spent most of his life gambling against
long odds, and if it ended here, at least no one could
say that he had walked away without making a final bet
on victory.

The canyon's mouth was less than twenty yards in
front of Villa when it happened, as he feared it might.
He heard a bullet strike his charger's skull, a dull
sound like a gourd dropped from a height to stony
ground, and then his world turned upside down and he
was airborne. Anyone who witnessed it, if they were
not deafened by gunfire, would have been amazed.

Incredibly, Villa was laughing as he plunged toward
impact with the desert sand.

D OLORES AGUIRRE FIRED the last round from her
Model 1895 Winchester and at once began reloading its internal magazine. So far, she had dropped
two of Pancho Villa's riders but could not have sworn
that either one was dead, given the darkness, charging
adversaries, and the cloud of dust they'd raised.

Still, two down was not bad, wounded or slain, and
she had seen more falling as her sister, Clint Parnell,
the Mescaleros, and the caballeros from her father's
hacienda fired from various positions of defense. Behind her, where she crouched against the north side of
the canyon's entryway, Dolores heard her father's stolen horses neighing frantically, milling about in something close to panic as the battle raged.

She hoped none of them had been hit so far, but
could not spare the time to check—and frankly, could
not hope to see if any members of the herd were
wounded as they paced around the rocky confines of
their prison, some rearing from time to time, none

finding any egress from the trap. How many might be lamed or injured by their scuffling was a question no one could address with the gunfire continuing.

Beside Dolores, sister Sonya dropped a galloping *villista* with an aught-six round from her bolt-action Springfield, rapidly ejecting the spent cartridge while she lined up on another charging target. This time, while she only grazed the horseman, she still managed to disarm him, forcing him to drop his six-gun as a spurt of blood gushed from his wounded arm. Still, he remained mounted and rushing toward them, whooping high-pitched rebel yells until a blast from Parnell's shotgun took him down and let his horse run on alone.

Villa's *bandidos* had been whittled down, perhaps one out of five unhorsed during their headlong charge, but some of those were doubtless still alive. In fact, Dolores saw a couple of them moving toward the canyon's mouth on foot, arms raised to shield their eyes from roiling dust as they advanced. One held a carbine, while the other clutched a pistol in his fist.

Dolores lined her sights up on one of the *bandoleros* jogging in. Drew in a breath, released half of it, and then held the rest pent up inside her lungs. A horse rushed past her chosen target, and its passing cleared the dust enough to let her see the adversary's face, a mustache and goatee below a hooked nose, sunken cheeks, and tangled hair above dark eyes, with a sombrero bouncing on his back, its thong around the gunman's throat.

Enough.

She stroked her rifle's trigger, watched the young man lurch one final step, then drop. She pumped the weapon's lever action while she waited to discover whether he rose again, but he lay still, a final tremor passing through his prostrate form.

How many did that make? How many total strangers had she killed or wounded since the raid upon her father's hacienda killed Eduardo and cast all their futures into doubt? Dolores had lost count but did not let that trouble her. Right now, her one and only job was to keep firing, killing, until no more threats impeded their return of Papa Alejandro's stolen horses to New Mexico.

And failing that, she had already made a private promise to herself that she would die in the attempt. Dolores would not be the one to let her father down, disgrace their family.

She shifted her position slightly, framed the second horseless pistolero in her rifle's sights. That one had seen his *compañero* drop and hesitated for a heartbeat afterward, then forged ahead in the direction that his other friends were riding, clearly more afraid of trying to retreat than facing guns in hostile strangers' hands.

Dolores understood his choice, saw it as one that she had made herself. In truth, she felt a kind of grudging admiration for her nameless enemy's determination.

Not that turning back and running for his life would have averted her determination.

In that case, Dolores would have shot him just as quickly in the back.

This time, she sighted on the target's face, midway between the drooping brim of his sombrero and a colorful serape draped around his shoulders. She could see his thin lips moving, wondered for a second whether he was praying, cursing, or just talking to himself as in a nightmare, but it made no difference.

Her bullet struck the bridge of the *villista*'s nose, his brow and cheeks imploding as the aught-six hollow point hammered through cartilage and sinus cavities at 2,500 feet per second, striking with 3,036 foot-pounds of destructive energy. It did not blow the target's head clean off but left the upper portion of his cranium flopping against his shoulder blades in back, while his blood-soaked sombrero sailed away.

Another kill, and now, scanning the field in front of her, Dolores asked herself, *How many more to go?*

JAVIER JURADO BROKE no bones while falling from the saddle of his grulla mare but landed with sufficient force to badly sprain his left shoulder. Cursing the pain, he struggled to his feet, regained his bearing as the rest of Pancho Villa's riders galloped past them, and slogged after them, grimacing with each step as he advanced.

At least, being right-handed, he was able to withdraw his sidearm from its holster and continue on to join the fight.

His pistol was a rare LeMat revolver, manufactured in the 1860s, carried by some Confederate soldiers during America's Civil War, and later in the Franco-Prussian War between the Second French Empire and Germany. It weighed four pounds and measured thirteen inches overall, its cylinder containing nine .40-caliber rounds, while a separate barrel held a single twenty-gauge shotgun shell, discharged by flipping a lever on the end of the pistol's hammer. Loaded with birdshot, that cartridge killed only at close range, but it could wound or even blind an enemy at forty yards, perhaps inflicting injury on more than one.

For now, without Jurado's horse or rifle, still inside its saddle boot, the ten-shooter would have to be enough.

Advancing, Javier was pleased to let the mounted riders go in front of him, although the dust raised by their horses nearly choked and blinded him. Despite the throbbing pain in his left shoulder, he kept that

hand raised before his face to shield his eyes and nose
somewhat, while drawing shallow breaths in through
his mouth. Ahead of him, the sounds of gunfire multi-
plied, seemed louder to his ears, although the muzzle
flashes from the canyon's mouth told him his enemies
had no more reinforcements to commit.

Two of their shooters, maybe three, were stationed
on the granite ledge above the canyon's entrance,
where a pair of Villa's guards were normally assigned.
Their vantage point allowed them to fire down upon
the galloping *villista* band while staying out of pistol
range from enemies below. A few of Villa's riders tried
to bring them down with rifle shots in passing, but the
jolting motion of advancing horses spoiled their aim.

A sudden flash of inspiration came to Javier. If he
could scale that slope and take the snipers by surprise,
he might dispose of both before they saw him coming.
That in turn would aid his fellow raiders in their bid to
breach the canyon and eliminate the rest, whoever
they might be.

The climb was grueling, doubly difficult since Javier
was forced to work one-handed, with his pistol holstered, but he slowly gained on his objective yard by
yard. As he drew closer to his enemies, Jurado verified
that there were only two of them in place. If he got
close enough to fire a shotgun blast from his LeMat,
then follow with the nine rounds in its cylinder, he
could eliminate both men and still survive.

Unless they saw or heard him coming first.

When he had nearly reached his destination, thankful that the ground beneath his feet had leveled out a
bit, Jurado took a breath, muttered a prayer to long-
forgotten saints, and then unholstered his LeMat. He
cocked its hammer, pressed the lever to fire his shotgun shell initially, and then began to creep across the
final gap that separated him from his intended targets.

At the final instant, Javier wondered why both their guns had suddenly fallen silent.

No matter. Possibly they had run out of ammunition, were reloading, or else waiting for the dust below to clear and let them spot more targets. Whatever the case, he must move *now* or miss his only chance.

Charging the last few yards, with his LeMat held out in front of him, Jurado found both snipers facing him, their rifles shouldered, aiming straight at him. He could have sworn that they were smiling when they fired as one, their bullets ripping into Javier, propelling him back down the hillside in a clumsy somersault through darkness into everlasting black.

Sonya Aguirre fired the last shot from her Springfield rifle's five-round magazine and saw that she had no time to retrieve another stripper clip to feed it from her bandolier. Instead, she dropped the empty weapon, drew one of her Smith & Wesson Model 1899 revolvers from its holster on her right hip, while she left its twin jammed underneath her belt buckle.

The pistol had a four-inch barrel and weighed just over two pounds with a full load in its six-shot cylinder. Despite the close proximity of Villa's men—those who were still alive and mounted—she did not unload the piece in rapid double-action fire, but rather cocked it manually, braced its butt in a two-handed grip, and took the extra time required to aim.

Her nearest adversary had a pistol in his hand and could have dropped her if his horse had not reared up unbidden, its front hooves pawing the air in front of Sonya. She stood fast and tracked the horseman's unexpected rise, firing her six-gun as he reached its apogee. Her .38 slug smacked him underneath his chin, hurtling one thousand feet per second, punching through his soft palate and scrambling his brains before his lifeless body tumbled from the saddle, landing in a limp heap on the ground.

Another rider swept around the first one's fleeing horse and tried to trample Sonya where she stood. Unyielding, she squeezed off another shot that drilled the stout *villista* through his chest, an inch or so above the heart, and saw him jerk with the impact. Instead of falling, though, the nearly dead man somehow swung his animal about and galloped out of range while slumping down over his saddle horn.

Call that another kill, even if he required a few more moments to bleed out internally.

The action all became a blur for Sonya after that, more horses charging toward her out of darkness while she triggered .38 rounds toward their riders, emptying one pistol, sheathing it, and pulling out the second from her belt. Beside her, on her right, she heard Dolores firing with her Winchester, then switching to the Colt she favored. Off to Sonya's left, Parnell was emptying his shotgun, following its loud blasts with the echoes of his Peacemaker. Farther along the firing line, their Mescalero volunteers blazed into the *villista* mob with long guns, Great Hawk switching to a six-gun of his own, while Bear and Gray Wolf whooped and drew their tomahawks for fighting hand to hand.

Somewhere amid the frenzied killing, horses rearing, riders toppling, bullets humming around Sonya like a swarm of angry yellow jackets, the mayhem began to slacken, then died off entirely. Silence settled on the battlefield, except for hoofbeats in retreat across the desert and the panicked sounds from Papa Alejandro's herd inside the canyon at her back.

Could it be over? Had she been cut down during the melee, dying without knowledge of her end? Was she a shade scanning the bloody plain through ghost's eyes that would quickly fade away?

The smell of dust and cordite brought Sonya around, back to reality. She stood between her twin and Clint Parnell, both still alive, as were the Mescaleros farther to her left. The three Apache braves were smeared with blood, but in another moment Sonya realized that most of it, at least, was not their own. Before them lay the corpses of a half-dozen *villistas* they had hacked and stabbed to death during the battle's last convulsion.

"Have we won, then?" asked Dolores in a small voice, as if waking from a dream.

"I think so," Sonya answered.

"Hold on a second," Clint advised them, staring toward the field of combat while reloading his shotgun.

Sonya followed his gaze and saw a lone figure advancing on them, slowly pacing off the yards. He held a pistol in his right hand with its muzzle pointing toward the ground. Sonya surmised it must be empty, or the lone survivor hoped to close the gap and try a point-blank shot before they cut him down.

Sonya raised her second Smith & Wesson, sighting down its barrel toward the lone *villista*. Said to no one in particular, "I have him."

"Wait on that," Clint answered. "Let's hear if he has something to say."

IT SEEMED IMPOSSIBLE to Pancho Villa that his men could be defeated by a smaller force, but he could see the proof before his bleary eyes, bodies lying in twisted attitudes of death, their blood leaching into the desert sand. Some of their horses, also shot during the fruitless charge, lay wheezing now, breathing their last. Villa wished he could put them all out of their misery

but knew he must preserve the cartridges in his revolver for whatever happened next.

It crossed his mind that he should simply turn and
run. Perhaps the gunmen who had slain his *bandoleros*
would take pity on a sole survivor and allow him to
escape. More likely, though, he guessed that they would
make a clean sweep of their victory, with one or more
preferring bullets fired into his back as he retreated.

No.

Whatever lay in store for him, despite the grim hu-
miliation of defeat, Villa was determined to confront
his final moments like a real man should, no groveling
or whining, only sheer contempt for those whom he
had tried and failed to kill.

As for the herd he'd stolen from New Mexico days
earlier, it now belonged to others, who had proved that
they were big and strong enough to wrest it from his
grasp. Hope of a profit from the raid in Doña Ana
County had evaporated in a swirl of gun smoke, like
Zapata's worthless vow to take the horses off Villa's
hands.

As he approached the firing squad before him, he
forced a smile of false assurance in his own survival.
He could think of no good reason why the strangers
should not gun him down immediately, yet they waited,
weapons leveled at him, while he closed the gap between them with determined strides.

As Villa neared his likely executioners, dismay
washed over him. Not only were they few in number,
but he saw that three of them were Mescalero tribesmen, one a gringo, and the others *mexicano*. More surprising yet, he realized that two of them were women,
clearly twins, and quite attractive if he looked beyond
their grim rifles, grim expressions, and the layer of desert dust that covered them.

In other circumstances—a cantina, say, or even on a sidewalk in Ascensión—he would have found them quite delectable, drawn to the challenge of seducing both together. In his present circumstance, however, Villa guessed it was more likely that the twins would drop him in his tracks as readily as any of their male associates.

At thirty feet he stopped and asked, "Which one of you intends to kill me, then? Or will you share that honor equally?"

"Honor?" the gringo answered back. "You must think highly of yourself."

"The sin of pride," said Villa. "I confess it is among my various transgressions."

"I believe it's him," one of the sisters said, sounding surprised.

"Him, who?" the gringo asked.

"I recognize him from his photographs," the other twin replied. "I think so, anyway."

Their seeming leader frowned. Said, "Someone want to clue me in?"

The first woman who'd spoken said, "He looks like Pancho Villa."

For the first time since his stallion had collapsed beneath him, Villa thought survival might turn out to be an option after all. The stark alternative, if one or all of those confronting him harbored some private grudge or simply knew about the bounty that Porfirio Díaz had placed on Villa's head, they might as easily cut loose and riddle him with bullets where he stood.

With nothing left to lose, Villa broadened his smile, bowed slightly from the waist, and told the killers ranged before him, "In the flesh. You have me at a disadvantage now. May I be privileged to know your names and why you've massacred my men?"

* * *

FIVE MINUTES LATER, Clint Parnell sat facing Pancho from across the campfire that Kuruk had managed to rekindle, once the bodies strewn about it were removed. On either side of Clint sat Sonya and Dolores, rifles close at hand. The other members of their posse moved among the restless horses still confined to the box canyon, trying to relax them with soft words and gentle touches.

"Why we're here is simple," Clint advised their prisoner. "You stole these horses in a raid on the Aguirre ranch. We've come to take them back."

"The nine of you came all this way?" Villa's surprise was evident.

"We lost a few between times," Clint replied. "All friends of ours."

Sonya chimed in at that, her voice bitter. "You also killed our brother and more friends the night you struck our hacienda. Someone from your gang of rats wounded our father at the same time."

"Ah, then this is personal for you," Villa replied.

"A blood debt that we must repay," Dolores said.

Villa nodded his understanding. "I could easily apologize," he said. "But having been in your position many times myself, I know that it would fall upon deaf ears. You are obliged to kill me and you may as well get on with it."

Clint saw the bandit's answer take the sisters by surprise. They glanced at one another, hesitating, while hands tightened on their rifles. Finally, Dolores asked Villa, "You wish to die?"

"¡Por supuesto no!" said Villa, laughing as he spoke, the sound shocking all of them. "Of course not! Only old men who have nothing left to live for wish to die, and half of them are lying even as they say it. But

I understand the debt you owe your *padre* and *hermano*. While I did not injure either of them personally, it is clearly my responsibility. Do what you must."

Clint half expected one twin or the other, maybe both, to fire on Villa then, at point-blank range, but neither did. Instead, both looked to Clint as if he had the answer to a riddle that confounded them. Feeling their eyes upon him, waiting, he replied to their unspoken question, saying, "I suppose it's up to you-all."

As he finished speaking, Sonya raised her Springfield, aiming it at Villa's face across the fire, then hesitated with her finger on the rifle's trigger, frozen there. After a long moment she shook her head, lowered the weapon. Said, "I cannot do it in cold blood."

"Nor I," Dolores said. "But if he lives and goes unpunished . . ."

Villa saw an opening. He said, "If I may say, perhaps you might consider that the man or men who shot your relatives and friends have already been punished." With one hand, he waved in the direction of his scattered dead. "I led the raid, it's true, but always hope that no one may be slain unnecessarily. Responsibility is mine, of course. As for the triggermen, you have already dealt with them. Whatever waits for them beyond death's door, they have discovered it."

"How would you pay your debt in that case?" Sonya asked their prisoner.

Villa considered that. "For one thing, I am willing to accompany you and assist in returning your fine horses to New Mexico."

"One extra hand won't make much difference," Clint said.

"You're right, of course," Villa confirmed. "And I am not the best vaquero, what you in *el norte* call a wrangler, *¿sí?*"

"In that case," Parnell said, "you might want to explain yourself."

"If I ride with you, it would be as Pancho Villa." The *bandido* emphasized his statement with a fist thump to his chest. "I can persuade my people to assist you when we near their villages and warn them against speaking to the *federales*, eh?"

"Without your gang behind you?" Parnell challenged him.

"They will not know the difference," Villa replied. "Whoever rides with me becomes *mi pandilla*—my gang, if you prefer that term."

"And if we make it to the border?" Clint inquired.

Villa responded with a shrug. "Then you may kill me if the need compels you, or we may part company and never meet again."

"About that," said Dolores. "How can we believe that you will never cross the Rio Grande to trouble us again?"

"You have my solemn word," Villa replied.

Sonya snorted at that. "Your word?"

"It's all I have to offer, *señorita*. As you know, I am an outlaw, thief, and murderer. That said, I only lie when there is profit to be made from it."

"In this case," Sonya answered, "that would be your miserable life."

"From which you may feel free to liberate me if and when we reach the Rio Grande," Villa replied.

"Step off and let us have a minute to discuss this," Clint advised. Villa immediately nodded, rose, and moved away to find a saddled horse, escorted by Kuruk and his two Mescalero tribesmen.

When they were alone, Clint told the twins, "I know why you're dead set against it, and I don't trust Villa anywhere outside of pistol range, but there's a chance that he *could* help us get your horses back across the border."

"And what then?" Sonya demanded.

"Then, I leave it up to you," he said. "You want to spare him, I'm okay with that. Decide to put him down regardless, and I'll help you dig a hole, or you can leave him for the buzzards."

The sisters huddled for another thirty seconds, then agreed with obvious reluctance to accept the bandit leader's aid. Clint whistled Villa back, surrounded by the Mescaleros, leading a roan mare with bloodstains on its saddle from its last, late rider.

"All right," Clint told Villa. "We accept your offer with the understanding that the first time you step out of line, you're dead."

"*Por supuesto,*" Villa said at once. "Of course."

Clint fudged some on the other part of it, omitting that he'd left the twins to settle Villa's fate between themselves once they had reached the Rio Grande. Instead, he told the outlaw, "If you show up on Aguirre land again, you're done. Make no mistake about it. Anyone who spots you, by yourself or with another gang, has leave to shoot you down on sight."

"*De acuerdo, mis amigos,*" Villa answered. "I agree."

"Just so we're crystal clear," Clint said.

"And now," Villa replied, "may I suggest that we make haste and leave this place behind?"

CHAPTER SEVENTEEN

The Rio Grande

DESPITE A BROODING sense of apprehension, aggravated by two nights when no one in the rescue party slept, they reached the border without any major incidents at sundown of the third day since they had retrieved Don Alejandro's herd. Of fourteen hundred eighty-seven horses, nine had suffered fatal wounds during the canyon fight and two more died during the final trek toward home—one from a rattler's bite, the other seemingly from sheer exhaustion.

All things considered, Clint Parnell supposed they had been spared a major tragedy.

The occupants of one small village, Rocas Rojas—christened for the red cliff in whose shadow it existed—had turned out in force, all forty-two of them, to watch the herd pass by. Clint saw a couple of them packing ancient rifles, worried that they might cause trouble, but they'd backed off after Pancho Villa rode among them, warning them against unworthy thoughts of theft or scheming to alert the *federales*. Joaquín Cantú listened in, reporting back to Clint once Villa spoke his piece, and three old women acting on the village headman's orders brought them food to carry with them on the trail.

Now, as they overlooked the Rio Grande, facing toward New Mexico, Clint thought about the problems that they might find waiting for them on the other side. There was a fifty-fifty chance, he realized, that someone, somewhere, had reported their incursion into Mexico. By this time, soldiers from Fort Whipple might be on the lookout for them, but he saw no bluecoats on the north side of the river, and the desert flatlands there offered no handy hiding place.

Another possibility: if troops had been dispatched, they might be bivouacked close to Don Alejandro's spread, waiting to see if anyone returned alive from their illicit foray to Chihuahua. There was no way of resolving that until they'd crossed the Rio Grande, passing back from Mexico to the United States. The nine survivors of their quest would simply have to wait and see what happened next.

And now, before they made that crossing, Pancho Villa's fate remained to be decided by Dolores and her twin.

Clint had not raised that subject with the sisters while they traveled north, giving them time to think about it through long days and nights. Whatever they decided, Parnell meant to keep his word. If it were death for Villa, neither he nor any of his men would intervene. The Mescaleros clearly did not care and would be happy to dispatch the bandit leader on their own, taking his scalp back to their village as a trophy of their hunt.

Settled astride his dapple gray, flanked by the sisters, Pancho Villa facing them aboard his weary roan, Clint waited for the verdict to be handed down. When

Sonya spoke at last, he realized the twins had made their choice somewhere along the homeward trail without consulting him.

"You've kept your word so far," she said. "For that, we grant you mercy undeserved. But if your thoughts turn toward our hacienda in the future, rest assured that day will be your last."

"*Muchas gracias, señoritas,*" Villa said. "You may believe me when I say I wish our paths had never crossed."

"Then let them never cross again," Dolores warned. "For there is no more mercy in our hearts."

"*Eso es justo,*" Villa answered. "That is fair. *Vaya con Dios.*"

Even with their good-byes said, it took another hour and a quarter for the herd to cross the sluggish river and emerge on the far side. When all of them had safely crossed, Clint paused and looked back toward Old Mexico, where Pancho Villa still sat watching them. In parting, the *bandido* flourished his sombrero overhead, then turned away and spurred his roan mare southward, trailing dust.

"I'm having second thoughts now," Sonya said.

"Never mind, *hermana,*" said Dolores. "He is nothing to us now."

Rancho Aguirre, Doña Ana County, New Mexico Territory

Seated in a rocker on his front porch, sipping coffee flavored with a dash of rum, Don Alejandro watched another sunset creep across his land, trailing familiar purple shadows as it passed. He had grown tired of counting days since his twin daughters and the rest rode off to find his stolen herd. With each sunrise and nightfall, marking wasted time, his shoulders slumped a little more. The hair around his temples turned a lighter shade of gray, and there were new lines on his face.

Hope fluttered weakly, like a dying sparrow, in the void around his heart.

Each day at noon he visited Eduardo's grave and knelt to pray, feeling that no one heard him or that God, perhaps, had simply ceased to care. Each night he lay awake for hours, until pure fatigue drew him into a nightmare realm where bullets ripped into his son and left him dying in convulsions on the blood-drenched ground. Each dawn found Alejandro more exhausted, craving rest that lay beyond his grasp.

With a sigh, Aguirre drained his coffee mug and felt the rum burning its course down his esophagus to settle in his stomach. While he knew he might regret that later, he decided that another hefty tot of rum might be in order, this time without coffee to dilute its impact.

Maybe he would sleep better tonight if he put a few more away.

Unlikely, but it could not hurt to try—that is, until another daybreak woke him to the bleak discomforts of a headache and a sour stomach.

Then again, what did he have to lose?

He rose, turned from the vista of his property where caballeros made a show of busywork, preoccupied with petty tasks since Pancho Villa's raid had stripped them of their livelihood, as well as murdering some of their friends.

Aguirre cleared the porch, was moving through his parlor toward the lounge where he maintained a stock of liquor, when his houseman, Manuelito Obregón, barged in behind him, saying, "*¡Jefe, ven y mira!*"

Alejandro turned to face his eldest servant. "Come and see what, Manuelito?"

"You would not believe me, *señor*. You must see it for yourself."

Aguirre swallowed back a curse. Said, "*Bien entonces.* All right, then. Show me."

The houseman, jumpy and excited as a child at
Christmas, led his master back onto the broad front
porch and pointed to the southwest, where a dust cloud
was approaching slowly. Scowling now, Aguirre said,
"A dust storm? Do we treat that as a marvel now?
What's next? A passing cloud?"

"Look closer, jefe," Manuelito urged him. "That is
not *una tormenta de arena.* It is the dust from many
horses heading this way."

Alejandro did curse then. His first thought was a
band of U.S. Cavalry approaching, likely to chastise
him for allowing his employees and his own offspring
to violate the sanctity of Mexico. Well, he would simply lie to them—deny that he knew anything about it,
and could not have stopped them had he known, a
single man and wounded as he was. If God saw fit to
punish him for that in time, so be it.

What more did Aguirre have to lose except the bat-
tered remnant of his soul?

"Rally the men," he ordered Obregón. "The army
would not help us when we needed them. If they wish
to attack us now, they have a lesson coming in the
rights of private property."

"*¿El ejército, jefe?*" Obregon first looked bewildered, then a smile broke out across his face. "That is
not the army. It's a dream come true!"

"*¡No tiene sentido!*" Alejandro snapped. "That makes
no sense, you old—"

Aguirre's voice caught in his throat then. One hand
raised to shade his eyes, he squinted at the riders he
could not see in the distance, trailing dust behind
them. Reconsidering, he saw that most of the horses in
the long advancing column bore no saddles and no riders. Scattered caballeros drove them forward, gaining

speed now that the hacienda was within their line of sight.

Making for home.

Relief washed over Alejandro, weakening his knees. He gripped the rocker for support and searched the riders for beloved faces he might recognize.

There! He saw Sonya, then Dolores riding close behind her twin sister. And off some fifty feet away from them, he spotted Clint Parnell. The rest came into focus as they neared Aguirre's *casa grande*. He saw Joaquín Cantú, with Ignacio Fuentes and Arturo Lagüera. Riding farther back, he recognized the Mescaleros Bear, Great Hawk, and Gray Wolf.

Nine riders, of the dozen who had set out for Chihuahua to retrieve Aguirre's stolen herd. That meant three lost somewhere along their trek, and cause for further mourning still ahead.

Descending his porch steps, Aguirre almost lost his footing, might have fallen if his houseman had not caught one arm and offered him support. Don Alejandro moved to greet the drovers and their herd—*his* herd, shared with Eduardo's spirit and the daughters who had saved their livelihood from ruin.

Sonya and Dolores vaulted from their mounts as one and ran to meet their father, throwing arms around him, one to either side. Aguirre's foreman rode on past them, tipped his hat, and left them to their private moment of reunion while he shouted orders to the mixed force of vaqueros and Apache braves.

For the first time since the raid upon his hacienda, Alejandro felt he had a reason to survive. And the next time he went to visit his beloved wife and son in their respective graves, he would enthrall them with an epic tale of family and sacrifice.

EPILOGUE

PANCHO VILLA KEPT his word to the Aguirre family, ensuring that guerrillas never ventured onto their *estancia* again. That, however, did not end his story nor abate the interest of the Aguirre sisters in the man who'd nearly bankrupted their clan. In fact, they closely followed Villa's subsequent career through newspaper reports, by word of mouth, and later on the motion picture screen.

The revolution Villa had anticipated finally erupted five days prior to Thanksgiving 1910, continuing for nine years, six months, and one day. Villa was thirty-two years old when it began, and since much of the fighting raged through northern Mexico, daily reports of action from the battle front were inescapable in the American Southwest, with worried eyes searching for trouble on the Rio Grande.

The civil war began when Francisco Madero challenged incumbent president Porfirio Díaz in November 1910. Díaz had Madero arrested while his troops stuffed ballot boxes, but Madero's broad-based opposition responded with the Plan of San Luis Potosí on November 20, calling for revolt against Díaz and declaring Madero Mexico's provisional president. In Chihuahua, Madero ally Abraham González invited Villa to join the uprising, whereupon they captured a large hacienda, a train of Federal Army soldiers, and the town of San Andrés. He rolled on from there to defeat Díaz's *federales* at Naica, Camargo, and Pilar de Conchos before suffering his first defeat at Tecolote. He personally met with Madero in March, while revolutionary forces gathered to besiege Ciudad Juárez, across the Tex-Mex border from El Paso.

Worried about U.S. intervention, Madero sought to call off the siege, but Villa and ally Pascual Orozco Vázquez ignored that order, attacking on April 7, 1911, capturing the city's international bridges, and severing telegraph service and electrical power. Surrounded, the *federales* surrendered on May 10, and President Díaz resigned two weeks later, retiring to exile in France. That did not end the revolution, though, as combat raged on, killing an estimated 10 percent of Mexico's fifteen million people, while two hundred thousand refugees fled their homeland, mostly resettling in America's Southwest. Díaz appointed Villa as a colonel in his revolutionary army and went on to win election as president in November 1911. Villa, in turn, soon tired of military discipline and went home to Chihuahua.

Despite his status as a revolutionary firebrand, Madero proved an inept president, soon dismissing his former allies and relaxing into collaboration with Mexico's wealthy elite. Worse yet, from Pancho Villa's point of view, Madero snubbed Pascual Orozco and appointed former Díaz crony Venustiano Carranza as his minister of war. Orozco rebelled in March 1912, while Chihuahua governor Abraham González convinced

Villa to oppose his former comrade. Leading four hundred cavalrymen, Villa soon captured Parral from Orozco's defenders, then teamed with Federal Army general Victoriano Huerta to seize Torreón in Coahuila. In August 1911, Carranza secured election as Coahuila's governor—a post denied him by Díaz two years earlier—instituting widespread popular reforms.

All this, the Aguirre sisters watched with mounting interest from Doña Ana County, distracted by mourning for their father when pneumonia claimed his life in August 1912. Alejandro Aguirre lived to see his daughter Sonya marry Clint Parnell, and any disappointment at her wedding to an Anglo vanished with the birth of their first child in time to draw his final breath, ceding the ranch to his twin daughters equally.

Dolores, for her part, still mourned Paco Yáñez, but she appeared to be recovering with ministrations from Eduardo Calderon, a wealthy Luna County rancher's only son, whose love cracked her façade of ice, yet happiness eluded them. One week before their nuptials, during a celebration with his friends, Eduardo drank too much tequila before wagering that he could break the toughest bronco on his father's ranch. The horse broke him instead—his neck at least—and he expired before Dolores reached his bedside.

That time, her resumption of black widow's weeds was permanent.

Across the border, meanwhile, General Victoriano Huerta, military commander of Mexico City, schemed to replace President Madero, encouraged by U.S. ambassador Henry Lane Wilson, acting on orders from President William Howard Taft. Pancho Villa learned of the plot, and Huerta staged a preemptive strike, framing Villa for theft of a high-priced stallion. Villa punched Huerta and received a death sentence. Last-minute intervention by Generals Emilio Madero and

Raul Madero—brothers of president Francisco—spared
Villa's life en route to face a firing squad, but Huerta
still dispatched him to Mexico City's Belem Prison, then
transferred him to Santiago Tlatelolco prison in June
1912. Pancho used his time inside to study history and
civics, then escaped on Christmas Day and crossed the
Tex-Mex border near Nogales eight days later.

From El Paso, Villa sought to warn Francisco
Madero of Huerta's impending coup d'état, but in vain.
Huerta made his move in February 1913, executing
President Madero with Vice President José María
Pino Suárez on the twenty-second. Assassins killed
Chihuahua Governor Abraham Gonzáles two weeks
later, climaxing Mexico's *Decena Trágica*—"Ten Tragic
Days"—which claimed 5,500 lives and set the stage for
even worse to come.

Installed as president three days before Madero's
execution, Huerta faced immediate rebellion by Venustiano Carranza and Emiliano Zapata—forgiven in
the interim by Villa, after all—but he acted swiftly to
defeat it, driving Carranza from Coahuila to Sonora
by August. Watching the events from Texas, Villa returned to join the fight in April 1913, backed initially
by only seven men, and pack mules bearing sparse supplies.

Despite his disappointing presidential tenure, from
the grave Madero regained a measure of his reputation
as a homegrown revolutionary, murdered by the traitor
Huerta and gringo interlopers from *los Estados Unidos*. Overnight, he became a posthumous rallying
point for revolutionaries led by Governor Carranza,
forging a constitutionalist army led by seasoned fighters, including Pancho Villa, Álvaro Obregón, Felipe
Ángeles, Francisco Múgica, Jacinto Treviño, Lucio
Blanco, Pablo González Garza, and Emiliano Zapata.
Although not a military veteran himself, Carranza

served the force as *primer jefe*—"first chief"—while deferring to more experienced men on tactics.

In essence, the new army sought restoration of Mexico's 1857 constitution, minus vows of reform from the 1910 Plan of San Luis Potosí, which Carranza now deemed "unrealistic." That compromise would create rifts within the Constitutional Army over time, but for the moment, revolutionary leaders focused on deposing Huerta, whether he survived the coup and fled or joined Madero underground.

Rallying supporters to his newborn Army of the North—*villistas* in the popular vernacular—Villa returned to battle with a will. They inflicted a crucial defeat on Huerta's *federales* at Zacatecas City on June 23 and pushed on from there toward Mexico's capital, seizing Torreón, Coahuila, on October 1. One who marched beside him, making headlines in the States, was Ambrose Bierce, a septuagenarian author best known for *The Devil's Dictionary* and his short story "An Occurrence at Owl Creek Bridge." Bierce was present at the Battle of Tierra Blanca on November 23–24, 1913, then vanished in Chihuahua after penning a letter north on December 26, his fate unknown to this day. That same Christmas season, *villistas* captured Mexico City with aid from Carranza's and Zapata's soldiers, but were repulsed the following spring, whereupon Villa resumed life as a bandit warlord.

Another of Villa's American traveling companions, Harvard-educated journalist John Reed, played up Francisco's role as a rural Robin Hood, reporting that his guerrillas and female *soldaderas* frequently seized crops and gold, distributing them to the poor. Reed further wrote to U.S. president Woodrow Wilson that Villa "even at one time kept a butcher's shop for the purpose of distributing to the poor the proceeds of his innumerable cattle raids."

From personal experience with Villa, the Aguirre sisters took those rave reviews with a substantial grain of salt. President Wilson also questioned Villa's good intentions after he arrested nine U.S. Navy sailors at Tampico in April 1914, dispatching two thousand three hundred American troops to occupy Veracruz for six months, resulting in death for twenty-two U.S. servicemen and some three hundred Mexican soldiers.

Villa, for his part, briefly supplanted Carranza as governor of Chihuahua but seemed more interested in tapping Hollywood to fatten his personal war chest. On May 9, 1914, the Aguirre sisters drove to Albuquerque for the premiere of a Mutual Film Corporation (MFC) production, *The Life of General Villa*, starring Villa as himself, mixing staged scenes with authentic battlefield footage. The movie was a radical departure from MFC's normal fare of Charlie Chaplin comedies, produced by D. W. Griffith a year before he embarked on his epic production *The Birth of a Nation*. Cinematographer Raoul Walsh doubled by portraying Villa as a young man, rejoining Griffith the following year to portray John Wilkes Booth. Villa received a $25,000 advance—$651,000 today—plus 50 percent of the movie's profits.

While foreign audiences cheered that cinematic effort, Villa's war continued on the home front. Following his capture of Torreón, *primer jefe* Carranza diverted Villa's forces to Saltillo, perhaps seeking to rob Francisco of the chance to seize Mexico City. Villa complied under protest, then submitted his resignation, but withdrew it prior to capturing Zacatecas City, source for much of Mexico's silver, on June 23, 1914. That battle cost Villa one thousand soldiers, while slaying seven thousand *federales*, and when coupled with the U.S. occupation of Veracruz, it finally drove President Huerta from power, who fled into foreign exile on July 15. Huerta's Federal Army dissolved in August, while tensions mounted between rival revolutionary leaders.

To the Aguirre sisters watching events in Mexico from Doña Ana County, it initially appeared that peace would be restored below the Rio Grande. On August 15, one month after Huerta's disappearing act, Álvaro Obregón signed treaties at Teoloyucan whereby the Federal Army surrendered and recognized a constitutional government. Five days later, Carranza entered Mexico City with great fanfare and assumed command of the new government as "head of the executive power." October 1 witnessed calls for a new constitutional convention, initially convened in Mexico City, soon shifted to Aguascalientes, three hundred miles north of the capital. Hailed as a "great convention of commanding military chiefs and state governors," it was in fact the last attempt to forge a united revolutionary front, concluding without great success on November 9. Prominent warlords were barred from government positions, while Eulalio Gutiérrez Ortiz won election as provisional president.

Villa and Zapata met privately, agreeing on a mutual mistrust of Carranza and Álvaro Obregón. The latter soon withdrew to Veracruz, leaving Villa and Zapata in command of Mexico City. Carranza launched a newspaper campaign portraying Villa as a lawless bandit, and the situation rapidly degenerated into civil war.

In April 1915, while Sonya Parnell-Aguirre bore her second child, Villa met Obregón in battle at Celaya, Guanajuato, suffering a serious defeat with four thousand *villistas* slain and six thousand captured over the span of nine days. At the follow-up Battle of Trinidad, waged between April 29 and June 5, Villa suffered another grim defeat with three thousand casualties. Crossing into Sonora for another try, Villa met *carrancista* general Plutarco Elías Calles at Agua Prieta on November 1, losing many of his fifteen thousand men, while 10 percent of the survivors accepted Carranza's amnesty offer. Before that month's end, *carrancistas* captured Villa's key advisers Calixto Contreras and Orestes Pereyra, executing them together with Pereyra's son. Secretary Pérez Rul also deserted Villa, leaving a mere two hundred *villistas* for their retreat into Chihuahua's mountains.

Finally, with nowhere left to turn, Villa began to plot his next invasion of New Mexico.

Much had changed in the American Southwest since Villa's raid on the Aguirre ranch. New Mexico was granted statehood on January 6, 1912, followed by Arizona five weeks and four days later. New Mexico's population had increased by 5 percent, although most of its people still clustered in Albuquerque, Santa Fe, and Las Cruces. Columbus, founded in 1891, claimed only seven hundred inhabitants, but it lay only three miles north of the Mexican border, an irresistible target.

Striking at four fifteen a.m. on March 9, 1916, Villa and five hundred guerrillas wreaked havoc on the sleeping town, waging a ninety-minute firefight that killed nine members of the U.S. Army's 13th Cavalry Regiment and wounded seven more, slaying fourteen civilians and injuring two others. Against those casualties, one hundred eighty-three *villistas* were killed or wounded, with seven captured unharmed. Of those, six were hanged for murder, while one's death sentence was commuted to life imprisonment. Meanwhile, Columbus lay in smoking ruins, shops and homes looted and torched, while Villa and the rest of his guerrillas fled back into Mexico.

Tension ran high along the border after the Columbus raid, and Villa was not finished with his border crossings yet. He struck again at Glenn Springs, Texas, on May 15 (killing three soldiers, one white civilian, and losing two guerrillas); at San Ygnacio, Texas, on June 15 (four soldiers and six *villistas* killed, four more soldiers wounded); and at Hancock, Texas, on July 31 (killing two soldiers and a U.S. Customs inspector, losing three guerrillas). Through it all, while residents of the Aguirre ranch remained on guard, Sonya and Dolores trusted Villa's promise to avoid incursion on their land, and he did not return to trouble them.

In Washington, President Wilson abandoned any former thoughts of Pancho Villa as a modern Robin Hood. Before the ashes of Columbus cooled on March 9, Wilson appointed Newton Diehl Baker to fill a vacant cabinet office as secretary of war, mobilizing five thousand troops under Major General Frederick "Fearless Freddie" Funston to punish Villa's invaders. Funston, in turn, assigned subordinate John "Black Jack" Pershing to lead a "Pancho Villa Expedition" launched on March 14, 1916, continuing through February 7, 1917—by which time the United States was gearing up to join the First World War. Over the course of those eleven months, American invaders killed an estimated 170 *villistas*, including senior aides such as second-in-command Julio Cárdenas, General Francisco Beltrán, and Colonel Candelario Cervantes.

While that mostly futile chase went on, Mexico approved a new constitution on February 5, 1917, including a foundation for land reform and contentious terms for curbing powers of the Catholic Church. Still, peace at home remained elusive during global conflict, while Villa welcomed German arms shipments and President Carranza's paranoia mounted daily. On April 10, 1919, Carranza allies lured Emiliano Zapata to "peace talks" at Chinameca, Morelos, and shot him in an ambush. Villa fought on until May 21, 1920, when

forces under Álvaro Obregón assassinated President
Carranza at Tlaxcalantongo in the Sierra Norte de
Puebla. Adolfo de la Huerta Marcor served as interim
president until November 30, when Obregón succeeded him.

Between those events, Villa sought and secured
amnesty in July 1920, rewarded with a twenty-five-
thousand-acre hacienda at Canutillo, near Hidalgo del
Parral, Chihuahua. Two hundred surviving *villistas*
joined him there, enticed by a pension totaling 500,000
gold pesos as bodyguards for what American reporters
called a "military colony."

From Doña Ana County, it appeared to be all settled then, but such was not the case. Álvaro Obregón
heard rumors that Francisco would oppose him in the
next presidential campaign and opted for a preemptive
strike. On June 20, 1923, while visiting Hidalgo del
Parral on business, Villa drove into an ambush by
seven riflemen, their fusillade killing Villa, chauffeur
Miguel Trillo, personal secretary Daniel Tamayo, and
two bodyguards, Claro Huertado and Rafael Ma-
dreno. A third bodyguard, although wounded, shot and
killed one of the fleeing assassins.

The Aguirre sisters mourned Francisco's passing,
despite all he had inflicted on their family almost a
quarter century before. From a safe distance, they observed as Villa's name was purged from books and
monuments throughout his native land. Neither twin
was living in 1975, when a mixed delegation of Mexican and U.S. officials exhumed Villa's body, finding
that someone had severed and stolen his head long ago.
The following year, his partial remains were reburied
in Mexico City's Monument to the Revolution, belatedly accorded full military honors.